A new city, a new job  ing up for Oliver Fo ing on a successful ca..... the pain of a broken heart and broken trust behind him. The last thing he *need*s is another ill-advised romantic entanglement. But despite his best intentions, Oliver can't help his growing fascination with Nym Brown, the mysterious owner of Lakeside Lodge.

When Oliver rents an apartment in an old Victorian house overlooking Baltimore's Druid Lake, he expects it to be quaint and shabbily charming. But as Halloween draws near and all things spooky come out to play, Oliver becomes convinced there is more going on at Lakeside Lodge than meets the eye, aside from the faulty plumbing. His neighbors are a whole new definition of quirky, and his enigmatic, gruff landlord is both intimidating and dangerously attractive.

Dark and sinister secrets lurk behind the house on Druid Lake's crumbling façade. Unearthing them might yet put Oliver's future—and his heart—on the line.

THE HOUSE ON DRUID LAKE

Isabelle Adler

A NineStar Press Publication

www.ninestarpress.com

The House on Druid Lake

© 2021 Isabelle Adler

Cover Art © 2021 Jaycee DeLorenzo

Edited by Elizabetta McKay

This is a work of fiction. Names, characters, places, and incidents are either the product of the author's imagination or are used fictitiously. Any resemblance to actual persons living or dead, business establishments, events, or locales is entirely coincidental.

All rights reserved. No part of this publication may be reproduced in any material form, whether by printing, photocopying, scanning or otherwise without the written permission of the publisher. To request permission and all other inquiries, contact NineStar Press at the physical or web addresses above or at Contact@ninestarpress.com.

ISBN: 978-1-64890-389-2

First Edition, October, 2021

Also available in eBook, ISBN: 978-1-64890-388-5

CONTENT WARNING:

This book contains sexually explicit content, which may only be suitable for mature readers. References to past domestic abuse and assault (off page), references to a toxic relationship, past trauma, workplace harassment, passing illness.

Chapter One

Lakeside Lodge looked more like Dracula's castle than a gingerbread house.

Oliver paused on the stone steps that cut across a long grass knoll and peered up at his new place of residence. It was difficult to get a proper look at the house from the road, obscured as it was by the tall chestnut oaks and red maples that surrounded it. But from this viewpoint, just outside the wrought-iron gate, the massive gable above the front porch was clearly visible, as was the turret on the right side of the roof.

Comparing the house to a castle was perhaps an exaggeration, at least where size was concerned. But it certainly possessed an old-world fairy-tale charm and an intangible aura of mystery. It had been evident even in the few photos that accompanied the online listing which had sold Oliver on it in the first place, making him contact the real estate agent and take it sight unseen. Well, that and the exceptionally low rent combined with the nice location right on Druid Lake and next to the park, just a few minutes' drive away from Oliver's new job in Central Baltimore.

Also, Jake would've hated it, and Oliver felt a particular satisfaction about no longer having to conform to Jake's plans and wishes.

However, now that Oliver stood in front of the house in the failing light of an early October afternoon, a heavy duffel bag slung over his shoulder, he couldn't deny there was something disquieting, even disturbing, about the jumble of architectural elements piled in a haphazard fashion. The building was three stories high, crowned with a shingled mansard roof with prominent dormer windows which must have commanded a stunning view of the lake across the road. A wide front porch boasted square tapered columns, and a fanciful pediment in the shape of a stylized owl with outspread wings adorned the gable. It was very Victorian, with touches of Gothic Revival and American Craftsman thrown into the mix. But the style skewed heavily to whimsical as if the architect (or maybe the owner) couldn't stop themselves from adding all their favorite design elements to the project. Like a magpie decorating its nest with every manner of shiny, without sparing a thought to the harmony of it all. The end result, though imposing, was more reminiscent of a cheesy B-movie haunted mansion than an actual apartment building, old as it might be. The wilted lawn and unkempt tree garden that stretched into the backyard didn't help the impression, though the grounds, as befitting a mansion, were much more expansive than those of any of the neighboring properties.

By the time Oliver climbed the stairs to the porch, he'd begun to suspect the reason for the low rent. Up close, everything exhibited signs of mild, to even prominent, disrepair. The wooden handrails were chipped, with some of the spindles broken or missing, and the shallow steps creaked dangerously under Oliver's weight, whose physique had once been described by his best friend, Pam, as "waifish." For the first time since he'd boarded the plane to Baltimore, equipped with a healthy supply of hopeful enthusiasm and a single bag containing his most prized belongings, doubt stirred at the back of his mind.

Oliver tried the handle, but the front door was locked. There also wasn't any sign of an intercom, which left either the grimy doorbell button or the heavy brass knocker. Oliver chose to knock and then listened as the sound echoed dully within until everything was still again. He shielded his eyes and stood on his toes, trying to peek through the stained-glass transom window when the door was suddenly yanked open, and he came face-to-face with a wall of plaid.

"What do you want?" a gruff voice boomed.

Oliver risked lifting his gaze. The voice belonged to a tall, broad-shouldered man blocking the doorway. Oliver resisted the urge to take a step back under his annoyed glare.

"Hi," he offered. "I'm Oliver Foster. I'm here about the apartment I rented."

That last sentence came out more as a question than a statement, his voice rising in pitch, and Oliver winced internally.

He pushed his glasses up the bridge of his nose while the man regarded him in sullen silence. Finally, he opened the door wider and stepped back, granting Oliver access with a wave of his hand.

A single overhead light illuminated the hallway. A threadbare patterned rug spanned the length of it, leading toward a dark mahogany staircase at the back. Tiny brass plaques, tarnished with age, marked the apartment numbers on slotted mailboxes hanging on the wall to his right. Below them stood an empty black lacquered umbrella bucket. A faint smell of dust and mildew permeated the air, and Oliver's earlier premonition about the state of his chosen accommodations intensified.

"What an unusual place," he ventured, still determined not to give in to negativity. "Must have a lot of history."

The man grunted, studying him from under drawn eyebrows. His eyes, the color of light amber, glinted in the low light. Together with his pale skin, overgrown dark hair, and menacing stance, they created an unnerving effect. Oliver shifted uncomfortably under his scrutiny, wondering whether the scowl was directed at him, or if it was simply a part of the man's natural disposition.

"Where's your luggage?" the man asked.

Oliver blinked.

"It's only this." He indicated his bag. "I'm having the rest of my stuff shipped over. I gathered the apartment came fully furnished?"

"Yeah." The man turned and walked toward the staircase, forcing Oliver to trail after him. "My name's Brown. I'm the landlord and building super. My apartment is across the hall from yours."

They passed what appeared to be a large sitting parlor on one side of the hallway and a closed door on the other, but Brown stopped at neither. They climbed one flight of stairs to the first-floor landing, ancient floorboards groaning with their every step. Oliver clutched the banister, but Brown seemed unconcerned about the possibility of the staircase crumbling under his powerful frame.

"Why don't you leave the front door open?" Oliver asked. "What about mail and delivery people?"

"They know to leave stuff on the porch," Brown said without turning. "Usually whoever comes home first brings the mail in."

This was…a curious arrangement. Oliver wasn't sure he liked the idea of his landlord or his neighbors sifting through his mail.

"Aren't you afraid someone might steal your packages?" he ventured. "It's a rather busy street."

Brown did turn to him then, pausing for a moment on the top stair and looking down at him.

"All the more reason to keep the door locked. Besides, no one is stupid enough to steal from here," he said and continued on, leaving Oliver gaping at the inconsistency of those two statements.

There were only two apartment doors on the landing, facing each other across a narrow stretch of hall. Another small door, perhaps a utility closet, was tucked under the stairs. Brown produced a key from the front pocket of his flannel shirt, unlocked the door marked 1B, and gestured for Oliver to follow inside.

Oliver would be lying if he said he didn't cross the threshold with some trepidation, given the overall shabbiness, but as Brown flicked on the lights, he could see nothing out of the ordinary. If anything, the apartment was much sparser than he'd imagined. The living room, with its high windows, ornate cornices, and a fireplace tucked in a corner, opened into a small kitchen outfitted with decades-old appliances and laminate flooring. A long couch faced the windows and the wall between them, but as far as Oliver could see, there was no TV.

This looked much closer to the pictures in the posting than the dilapidated exterior, at least. And everything was clean. Worn out, certainly, but not dirty. Someone must have put in the work of scrubbing the hardwood floors and giving the walls a fresh lick of paint as the whole place smelled of pine-scented cleaner rather than mildew. Oliver lowered his duffel bag onto the floor, next to the narrow side table by the entrance, and took a cautious step inside, taking in his surroundings.

"There are some towels and bedding in the linen closet next to the bathroom," Brown said, pausing by the breakfast counter that separated the living room from the kitchen. "If you want hot water, I suggest showering in the mornings. It can run out quickly this time of year, especially in the evenings."

An image of Brown standing in the shower, a stream of steaming water gliding over his skin and plastering his dark hair to his forehead popped unbidden into Oliver's mind. It was as sudden as it was surprising, considering the man's complete lack of geniality. Oliver cleared his throat and turned to the windows to conceal his blush, shivering with the draft that made the heavy curtains flutter. He was simply tired from his flight, letting his thoughts wander in silly directions.

"Okay. Is there anything else I should know, Mr. Brown?" It didn't help matters that he could still see the man's faint reflection in the windowpane, set against the gathering gloom outside.

"Rent is due on the first of every month. I'll send you the link for the pay app for this month's fee and deposit."

"Or I can just slide the envelope with the cash under your door."

Brown's reflection frowned.

"You know," Oliver said, "because it's all so old-fashioned around here?" He paused for effect. There was only silence. "Forget it; it was a bad joke."

"I don't care either way, as long as you pay on time," Brown said gruffly. "Takes a lot to keep this place up and running."

Oliver supposed it was true. Old buildings were notorious money pits where maintenance was concerned, and from what he'd seen so far, the "up and running" part was a bit of a stretch. What the house needed was nothing short of a complete overhaul, but he judged it better not to say so to the landlord.

"Here are your keys." They jingled as Brown put them on the entrance side table. "One for the apartment and one for the front door. I'm right across the hall if you need anything."

He somehow managed to make it sound like a warning rather than an invitation.

"Um, sure," Oliver said, turning back to him. He hoped he'd composed himself enough not to betray his earlier embarrassment. "Wait. Can you recommend a place where I can order takeout? After that airplane food, I'm kinda starving."

He'd have to do some grocery shopping tomorrow after work, but he had absolutely nothing planned for dinner tonight. As if to emphasize his words, his stomach rumbled, too loud in the quiet of the room, and he flushed again, the heat creeping up to his hairline.

Brown's gaze traveled from Oliver's feet to his face as if taking his measure.

"There's a decent pizza joint nearby," he said. "I can get you their menu flier."

"That'd be great!" Oliver said, sounding fake cheerful to his own ears. The conversation, mundane as it was, had made him more and more flustered. Or was it the other man's looming presence? Either way, Oliver couldn't wait to be alone and get settled, preferably after a nice, hot meal.

Brown nodded and turned to leave without sparing another word. The door closed softly behind him, leaving Oliver alone, with only the ticking of the mantle clock to fill the silence.

Oliver took a quick tour of the place, exploring the bathroom and single bedroom.

If the ground-floor hallway had looked like the set of an Edwardian-era period movie, apartment 1B was lifted from a 70s sitcom. The furniture in the bedroom was in keeping with what he'd seen in the living room and the kitchen, reminding him of his grandad's holiday cabin in Vermont—yellowish pine, shaggy carpet, and an overabundance of plaid. A white sheet covered the queen-sized bed against the dust, which gave it a funereal appearance. The wardrobe closet and dresser were empty save for some hangers, but he did find the towels. As with the rest of the apartment, they smelled clean, but he decided to spring for some new ones as soon as he could.

After taking a few minutes to freshen up, Oliver settled on the couch in the living room. By that time, deep dusk had descended, and the room looked cozy in an old-fashioned kind of way, the rough edges of wear and tear smoothed by the warm glow of the table lamps. It was still chilly, though, the draft seeping from the windows carrying a distinctive dampness from the nearby lake. Cranking up the thermostat didn't seem to do much either.

Oliver eyed the fireplace in the corner dubiously. He supposed he could light it, but he wasn't a fan of an open fire, and the smoke would irritate his eyes.

Maybe he could talk to Mr. Brown about installing better insulation. If anything, it could knock off a sizable chunk of his heating bill. Provided, of course, the man would stop scowling at him long enough to actually listen to Oliver's suggestions.

He called his parents, assuring them that he'd had a nice flight and was settling in, and promised to check in with them again tomorrow, after his first day at work. His next call was to Pam.

"I'm at my new place in Baltimore," he informed her as soon as she picked up the phone.

"Great. Are you a Ravens fan yet?"

"Very funny."

"So when do you start at… What's that firm called again?"

"Thompson and Associates Design," Oliver said. "I'm starting tomorrow morning."

"Tomorrow? That doesn't leave a whole lot of time for sightseeing. Don't you want to enjoy being in a new city for a few days before being assigned to getting permits for garage additions?"

Oliver chuckled. She was right in that newly licensed architects were usually at the very bottom of the food chain where established design firms were concerned, consigned to the most trivial and boring tasks. But this wasn't his first job. He'd already proved his worth, having finished top three in his class and having excellent recommendations from mentors in his two-year internship in Miami. He was ready to do some serious work.

"I'm planning to stay here for a while. I might as well start as soon as I can."

"I still can't believe you've moved all the way to Maryland." She sighed. "Now who'll come with me to all the holiday parties?"

He couldn't help but grin at that. Ever since he'd met Pam during his first year at the University of Florida School of Architecture, she'd been the driving force behind his otherwise stagnant social life. She'd been the one to take him, a shy, nerdy boy, under her wing and introduce him to the college student life he would've missed out on without her, and that friendship had stayed strong even after they'd both graduated. He was definitely going to miss her the most.

"I'm sure you won't have a problem finding someone to go with. Besides, I'd only be cramping your style."

"Well, you *are* awfully uptight sometimes," Pam agreed easily. "But no, you really wouldn't. Anyway, have you met any new people there yet?"

"Just my landlord slash building super. I don't think it's the beginning of a wonderful friendship though. He's decidedly unfriendly. Cute, though," Oliver grudgingly admitted upon further reflection. "In that Alaskan lumberjack kind of way."

"Well, you do like them tall and jacked."

"I do not!" Oliver protested, the tips of his ears heating up.

"Oh yeah? Then what was Jake?"

"I couldn't help if he was tall. And...jacked."

Pam snorted. "Yeah, right. Anyway, good riddance to him."

"Yeah." Oliver pursed his lips, his mood instantly souring.

The whole mess with Jake was one of the reasons he'd decided to move to Baltimore in the first place. Not that Oliver was foolish enough to try to get back in touch, nor did he seriously believe Jake would pester him if he'd stayed in Miami. But this way, it felt like he was starting off something new with a clean slate, leaving behind any emotional baggage that would weigh him down.

There was a pause as both of them searched for a safer topic.

"Do you like the apartment?" Pam ventured at last.

Bitching about the apartment seemed better than bitching about his ex, so Oliver readily launched into a description of his new pad, not skimping on vivid imagery. He embellished the truth a little bit because, first impressions notwithstanding, the accommodations were pretty decent, but Pam didn't seem to mind his creative approach.

"Oooh, sounds delightful!" she said cheerfully when he was done. "Is it haunted, you think?"

"It's so old I imagine there's any number of dead critters inside the walls that might still harbor a grudge."

Pam made a disgusted sound.

"But was anyone ever murdered there?" she insisted. "Or mysteriously disappeared?"

"I don't know. Maybe I should read up about it."

"Or you can ask your charming new neighbor," Pam suggested playfully.

"Considering he's also the landlord, I hardly think he'd say something that might scare away a paying tenant."

"Nonsense! What can be more exciting than staying in a haunted house on Halloween?"

Oliver could imagine a lot of things that could be categorized as more exciting, starting with having a reliable supply of hot water at all hours, but refrained from curbing her enthusiasm by listing them.

"It's only the third of the month," he reminded her. "The scary things shouldn't be out and about for at least two weeks yet."

"I'm sipping my pumpkin spice latte as we speak, so as far as I'm concerned, it's almost Halloween."

Oliver rolled his eyes but couldn't hold back a smile. "Do you have your costume ready?"

"I'm still deciding between a slutty elf and a slutty zombie. What do you think I should go for?"

They chatted for a while about the relative merits of both options until a sharp knock sounded on the door. Oliver started, fumbling his phone, and huffed in annoyance at his own clumsiness.

"I'll call you back tomorrow, all right?" he told Pam before disconnecting, then hurried to open the door.

He expected to see Brown returned with the flier but, instead, found two women standing at the threshold. The first one, pale, tall, and reedy, had long blond hair held loosely by a leather band tied around her head. She wore a maxi skirt and a hand-knitted sweater the color of rotten leaves and held a chipped porcelain plate stacked with neatly sliced chocolate brownies, wrapped in pink cellophane. The other woman was short and plump, her dark brown skin offset by jet-black curls. In contrast to her companion's hippieish appearance, she rocked a distinctly Goth vibe, down to the heavy eyeliner and a pentagram chocker peeking above the collar of her military-style jacket.

"Hello!" the blond woman said brightly. "Welcome to the building! I'm Sky, and this is Aurora. We live upstairs in 2A and wanted to be the first to say hi!"

Oliver doubted any of the other neighbors were clamoring for the honor, but he was nonetheless touched by the gesture.

"It's very nice to meet you," he said. "I'm Oliver. Oliver Foster. I just moved to Baltimore."

Aurora grunted in a decidedly unimpressed manner, but Sky continued on as cheerfully as before:

"That's so wonderful! It's so nice to have a new tenant in the building. After what happened…well."

"Why? What happened to the previous tenant?" Oliver asked, both his curiosity and suspicion roused anew.

"We figured you must be hungry, so we baked you some brownies," Sky announced, ignoring his question. She proffered him the plate. "Again, welcome to Lakeside Lodge!"

Oliver took the plate.

"These aren't…" He let his voice trail off, unsure how to phrase his concern delicately enough so as not to offend his new acquaintance.

"What? Oh, no!" Sky laughed, genuinely amused. "No, just plain regular brownies. Lots of dark chocolate and walnuts. You aren't allergic."

That didn't come out like a question, but Oliver shook his head anyway. "No, I'm good. And these look delicious. Thank you."

"No problem. Enjoy!" Sky chirped. "And you can always drop by if you need anything or if you have any questions."

They both looked at him expectantly as if he were about to start asking them about the secrets of the universe at this very moment.

"Um. Okay, I will. Thanks," Oliver said, unsure as to what the proper response should be.

"Has Nym shown you the rest of the house yet? The downstairs parlor is very cozy, and there's a film projector, so we sometimes have movie nights there. Usually on Thursdays. You're welcome to join if you're a fan of the oldies."

"Nym?"

"Nym Brown. The owner," Aurora said, her voice deep and a little raspy.

The name Nym stirred vague recollections of animated mice, but Oliver was reasonably sure they had nothing to do with the taciturn landlord.

"No, he hasn't," he said. "And a movie night sounds cool."

"Great! We'll see you around, then. Good night!" Sky said. And with that, they were gone, their footsteps resounding in the dim stairwell.

"Night!" Oliver called after them. He then noticed a piece of paper on the floor. He crouched and picked it up. The pizza parlor menu, crumpled and worn around the corners. A description of a veggie Hawaiian pizza with pineapple was circled in faded blue ink, and Oliver shuddered.

Pineapple? Mr. Nym Brown was even weirder than he'd thought.

Chapter Two

The pizza (sans pineapple) was delicious. Oliver hadn't realized how hungry he was until he'd wolfed down half of the extra-large pie, standing by the kitchen counter and absent-mindedly checking his social media.

Tomorrow was his first day at Thompson and Associates Design, and now, with no immediate worry and hunger to distract him, his mind was once again abuzz with excitement. Securing a position with a well-known architectural firm hadn't been easy, much less for someone from out of state. He'd busted his tail during that last year of internship, throwing himself into work in the wake of an ugly breakup, but it wasn't as if he'd had much of a social life anyway, aside from an occasional outing with Pam and her gaggle of friends.

And in the end, it had all been worth it. He'd successfully completed the internship and gotten the job. Yes, he had to move all the way to Maryland, away from his family, but he decided to treat it as an adventure. His first real job, first time living entirely on his own—he was incredibly lucky to get to experience that. And maybe, just maybe, he'd meet someone who would...

But he'd probably have even less time to socialize now than he had before. Architectural Experience Program internships were notoriously grueling, and he'd had to prove his worth, but that was most likely doubly true for highly coveted and competitive entry-level architect positions. He couldn't afford to be derailed by a relationship.

Considering his track record, maybe this was a good thing.

Oliver sighed, put away his phone, and shoved the leftovers in the empty fridge. He briefly considered powering up his laptop or taking out his sketch pad, but he was too tired to be creative tonight, and he was planning on an early start tomorrow. He grabbed his bag and headed to the bedroom.

The room had a single window that looked out on the back garden, but it was already pitch-dark outside. Oliver unpacked his things, careful to put away everything neatly in the dresser and the closet so he wouldn't look too crumpled tomorrow. As far as he knew, there was no strict dress code he had to adhere to, but he wanted to make a good impression on his first day and had chosen a pair of black slacks and a fine-knitted gray sweater.

He followed Brown's instructions and found a set of bedsheets in the linen closet in the nook between the bedroom and the bathroom. The sheets weren't new, but the faint smell of detergent that wafted off them was encouraging. He made the bed as best he could, stripped to his briefs, shivering with cold, then grabbed his toiletry bag and stepped into the bathroom.

Like the rest of the apartment, it was spotless, but it clearly hasn't been updated in the last five decades. The white subway tile and exposed brass pipes running along the ceiling were kind of cool, if one liked that kind of unapologetically vintage aesthetic, but if the rest of the plumbing was just as old…

As if in response to his thoughts, the pipes groaned and rattled with a rush of water. The noise reverberated in the empty space, and then somebody began to sing.

Oliver started, nearly dropping his bag. The voice echoed dully along with the gurgling noises of the water running in the pipes. It appeared as if it was coming from the upstairs apartment bathroom, carried by some flaw in acoustics and amplified by the resonance of the brass pipes, but still indistinct enough so Oliver strained to make out snatches of words. The voice was in a mezzo range, with what Oliver thought a Caribbean accent, but he wasn't an expert in either singing voice types or English dialects.

"Hello?" he ventured, but there was no response.

The singing, although melodical, was beginning to grate on Oliver's nerves by the time he finished brushing his teeth. He was too tired, aching to put his head on the pillow and close his eyes. Noisy neighbors and a possible lapse in privacy added to his list of inconveniences and increased the toll on his patience.

The voice droned on as he stepped into the shower and turned on the water. The showerhead sputtered and then produced a steady stream of water which, judging by the temperature, had to have been imported directly from the melting glaciers in Greenland.

Oliver bit down on the expletives, mindful of his voice carrying with the same intensity. So Brown hadn't been exaggerating about the hot water. A quick wash would have to be enough if Oliver didn't want to turn into an icicle. So he worked the shampoo into a lather in his hair, hopping from foot to foot in a vain attempt to warm up, all to the unceasing accompaniment of his unknown neighbor singing in the bathroom above.

Just as he finished soaping himself up and stuck his head under the icy stream, the shower let out a keening wail, and the water stopped.

Oliver tugged on the shower handle, cranking it up as far as it would go, but to no avail.

"You've got to be kidding me!" he said, not bothering to lower the volume this time.

The soap was starting to crust, clinging to his skin like frost on an early winter morning. He slipped out of the shower, teeth chattering, and made a desperate attempt at toweling off the suds and removing the shampoo from his hair, wincing at the stickiness of it. Somewhere in the distance, the singing voice picked up what sounded like an old sea chantey.

Oliver gritted his teeth. Normally, he'd roll his eyes at his bad luck and go to bed, miserable as he was, but the thought of meeting his new boss and coworkers for the first time with clumped hair and an itchy scalp proved more than he could bear. He'd reconciled himself to a cold shower, but not being able to shower at all...

It was late, and most likely, the water would be back tomorrow morning, but Oliver was too angry for reason. His fingers still half-numb, he pulled on a pair of pajama bottoms and a sweatshirt and headed out.

A single overhead light bulb illuminated the first-floor landing, and the shadows gathered in the corners and under the stairs seemed even thicker and darker than before. The floorboards squeaked ominously under Oliver's feet as he shuffled over to 1A and knocked.

As weak as the heating seemed in his apartment, apparently it wasn't as bad as he thought because out here in the stairwell, it was freezing. Oliver shoved his hands under his armpits as he waited, fully expecting his breath to form little clouds of vapor and steam his glasses if he had to stand there a few moments longer.

The door opened a fraction, and Brown peeked out, outlined by the yellowish light spilling from the entryway. His hair was tousled, but he was still dressed in jeans and a flannel shirt, so at least Oliver hadn't disturbed his sleep. It made him feel marginally better about barging in on his landlord at such a late hour.

"What it is?" Brown asked curtly.

"Hi, um. Look, I'm sorry to bother you, but I'm out of water. It just stopped in the middle of my shower."

Brown's eyes, oddly bright even in the low lighting, raked over him, and Oliver shivered—this time for a very different reason. He cleared his throat to hide his awkwardness.

"Can you do something about it, please?" he asked, doing his best to sound both firm and respectful.

"It happens, sometimes, when the upstairs neighbors run a bath or take a long shower." Brown's gaze flicked to the ceiling and then back to Oliver's face. "The water should be back when they're done."

"Are you serious?" This was the most ridiculous thing Oliver had heard in his life. "I get the 'no hot water in the evening' thing, but this? You mean to tell me I have to wait for them to be done every time I need to turn on the faucet?"

"It's an old house," Brown said, crossing his arms over his massive chest. "Things don't always work as they should."

"Well, why don't you fix them, then?" Frustration bubbled to the surface again, emboldening him to the point of rudeness. "You're the super, aren't you?"

Brown's eyes narrowed, and Oliver had to stop himself from taking a step back. Instead, he glared defiantly at the other man, his head high, hands on his hips. He wasn't at all comfortable with confrontation, but he wasn't a pushover, either, even if Brown looked like he could snap him in half.

"If you want, I can take a look at your plumbing tomorrow," Brown said finally.

"But what do I do in the meantime?"

"You can use my shower, if you want."

"I…" Oliver hesitated. It was a perfectly reasonable, even courteous suggestion, yet he was suddenly leery to accept it. Not because Oliver felt Brown could pose a potential danger to him, but because the idea of stripping in his bathroom sent a surge of warm, strange excitement through Oliver.

Get your mind of out the gutter, he told himself sternly, though he didn't let his imagining progress any further that the stripping part. *Brown's just trying to be accommodating for the sake of keeping on a paying tenant.*

"No, that's okay," he said. "It's already late and I don't want to impose. Thanks anyway. I'll just shower in the morning."

Brown grunted, whether in deprecation or in agreement, Oliver couldn't tell.

"Let me know when you get home tomorrow and I'll see what I can do about the pipes," Brown said.

"Will do." Oliver stepped back just as Brown shut the door and sighed when he heard the bolt slide in place. Now that the initial surge of annoyance faded, he was beginning to regret rushing over here to demand an immediate solution to his problem and then appearing bratty by refusing the one Brown had proposed.

Oliver turned to his own door but paused at the bottom of the flight of stairs leading to the second floor. Aside from Sky and Aurora, he hadn't met any other neighbors, so he had no idea who lived in the apartment above his own. Surely, it wouldn't be unreasonable to introduce himself, explain the situation, and inquire when they'd be done with the water so he could at least wash the traces of shampoo out of his hair?

He started up the stairs, the dark wood of the banister smooth with use and age under his palm. In the dimness and quiet of the second-floor landing, snatches of singing drifted from beyond the door of 2B. Oliver took a deep breath and knocked, gently at first and then more insistently.

The singing stopped. Oliver waited patiently, and after a few minutes, the door opened. A young woman stood on the threshold, wrapped in a bath towel. Water dripped from the ends of her long hair onto her dark skin and pooled in tiny puddles around her bare feet. After a moment of silence, she arched an eyebrow.

"Oh, um, hi," Oliver said, his face heating, instantly regretting his decision. He hadn't considered she'd be alone in the apartment and he'd be dragging her out of her bath or shower right then and there. "I'm Oliver Foster, the new neighbor in 1B. It seems there's some issue with the plumbing. I was just in the middle of a shower when the flow stopped. Mr. Brown, the super, said it was because the upstairs neighbors are using the water. He promised to fix it tomorrow, but I just wanted to check when you might be done, so I could…"

He trailed off under her steady, unblinking gaze. Her eyes reminded him of the sea—a misty mix of blue and green, almost translucent, their brightness belying dangerous depths. She just gazed at him, saying nothing.

"Sorry to have bothered you," he said and took a step back, shaking his head. "I was just…sorry."

She signed something at him and cocked her head as if expecting an answer.

"Oh! I didn't realize." Oliver spread his hands in an apologetic gesture. "I don't know ASL."

The woman raised her hand, stopping him, then stepped back and grabbed a phone from a nearby side table. She typed something on what looked like a digital note app and thrust the phone at him, the screen glaringly bright in the surrounding darkness.

I'm mute, but I can hear you.

Oliver nodded. "Okay."

Sorry about the water, she wrote. *Didn't realize the place downstairs was rented. It should be okay now.*

"Thanks. Again, I'm terribly sorry for dropping by like this. It's just that tomorrow is an important day for me, and my hair is all messy."

He stopped himself from babbling on. Most likely, she didn't really care, and he'd taken enough of her time already— not to mention making her stand almost completely naked in a freezing hallway. But there was something that still perplexed him.

"I heard singing earlier," he said hesitantly, not quite a question.

As soon as she'd answered his knock, he was sure she'd been the one carrying the tune, but he'd obviously been wrong.

And yet, her apartment seemed dark and silent, and it didn't appear as though there was someone else there with her.

I wouldn't know anything about that.

"Yes, of course. Sorry." He'd apologized close to a dozen times this evening already, but it still didn't feel like enough. "Good night!"

The woman nodded, tiny droplets of water splashing in his direction, and closed the door with a soft click.

For a long moment, Oliver remained standing on the landing, frowning. He was sure he'd heard a woman singing. It hadn't sounded like something coming out of a TV or computer speakers, even if one were to install them in their bathroom.

The whole incident had a surreal feeling, as if he'd watched it in a sitcom instead of taking an active part in it, the absurdity of the situation heightened by the ever so spooky atmosphere of Lakeside Lodge. Perhaps he was a lot more tired than he thought. All he needed was to rinse his hair, get a good night's sleep, and clear his head. Surely, tomorrow things will look up and go back to normal.

He sighed, hugged himself against the cold, and hurried back downstairs to the relative warmth of his apartment.

Oliver managed to eke out some water to rinse his hair, though by that time it had gone completely frigid. His teeth chattered as he quickly changed into well-worn pajamas and then made a round of the apartment, turning off the lights and making sure the front door was locked and bolted. The neighborhood didn't strike him as particularly seedy—if anything, the lakeside drive was beautiful this time of year, the orange and red trees lining the shore, their leaves carried across the embankment on the fresh breeze—but it made sense to heed the advice of the locals.

It was already late, the clock having chimed ten, but when Oliver went to check the latch on the living room window, a movement caught his eye. He stopped and drew the curtain wider, then pushed the window open just a sliver, and peered outside.

From this vantage point, he could see the stretch of the front garden and the short pathway that led to the porch steps. A single light shone above the entrance, but the fog swirling in deep shadows lurking between the tree trunks readily swallowed its muted glow. Two men stood on the pathway—or at least one of them did. The other one, whom Oliver recognized as Mr. Brown by his plaid shirt and bulky frame, loomed on the top step, arms folded across his chest. Oliver couldn't see his face, but his pose indicated he wasn't taking any pleasure in the conversation.

The second man, on the other hand, was fully illuminated and facing the house, so Oliver got a good look at him. He appeared to be about fifty or older, with pale skin and hair graying a flattering salt-and-pepper. The casual elegance of his clothing spoke of money, and lots of it. He looked like a high-end lawyer or, rather, like an aging movie star cast as a high-end lawyer.

Either way, Mr. Brown wasn't impressed.

"I thought I told you not to come here anymore, Cox," he said, his voice edged with distinct menace.

"Charming as ever, I see," Cox remarked, unfazed by the bluntness. "I've sent you another proposal. Have you had the chance to go over it yet?"

Their voices carried on the night air in the quiet garden, the sounds of traffic faint and distant. Oliver knew he shouldn't be eavesdropping. The decent thing would be to firmly shut the window and walk away from a conversation he had no business being a part of. Yet he stayed as he was, holding his breath in an effort to not miss a word.

"I told you already," Brown said. "I'm not interested."

Cox raised a finely shaped eyebrow.

"The terms are very generous. Much more generous than what this place is worth." Cox's gaze swept across the front of the house and snagged on Oliver's window. With only a table lamp casting a diffused light behind him, Oliver wasn't sure if the man could see more than his shadowy silhouette, but he still took a hurried step back, not wanting to be caught listening.

"You have no idea what this place is worth," Brown all but growled.

"Be that as it may, you won't get a better price anywhere else. Take it or leave it; I won't be making another offer."

"Good. I'll leave it, then. I suggest you do the same."

Oliver risked taking another quick peek since they seemed to be engrossed in their negotiations or, more accurately, in their stalemate. Brown didn't move from the porch, but even from up here, the tension in his posture was palpable.

Cox put his hands in the air in a gesture of surrender. "Very well. I'll be going now, but you know how to reach me. I'll be expecting your call once you've had a chance to think things over rationally."

"Don't. And you better not show your face here again, Cox." With that, Brown turned and disappeared into the house.

The front door slammed, and Oliver heard the soft but pointed click of the lock.

He expected the other man to leave right away, but Cox lingered on the pathway, his expression thoughtful and calculating. He looked up at Oliver's window again and then finally walked unhurriedly down the path toward the gate.

Oliver quickly shut the window, closed the drapes, and switched off the table lamp, plunging the living room in darkness. He was pretty sure Mr. Brown wouldn't appreciate him witnessing that little exchange.

It had sounded as if this Cox fellow wanted to buy Lakeside Lodge, Oliver mused as he shuffled off to bed and crept under the blankets in the gloom of his bedroom. Why anyone would want it was beyond Oliver, nor was it any of his business, really. But from what little he'd seen of the house, his wholehearted advice to Mr. Brown would be to drop it like a hot potato while the other guy was still willing to take it, and never look back.

Chapter Three

Thompson and Associates Design offices looked exactly as Oliver had imagined them.

Of course, he'd seen photos online before he'd submitted his job application, but unlike Lakeside Lodge, reality had exceeded his expectations. The impression might have had something to do with the beautiful autumn day, the sun shining cheerfully despite the crispness in the morning air. Light reflected off the tall glass windows of the building's impressive, rounded facade, making it sparkle like a diamond against the vast swath of manicured lawn, vibrant green even at this time of year.

Oliver parked his rental car in one of the empty guest spots and set his travel coffee mug in the cup holder. He coughed and winced at the slight soreness beginning to scratch the back of his throat. Apparently, running up and down freezing staircases with wet hair did have unpleasant consequences. If his mother found out, he'd never hear the end of it.

And wasn't it just his luck, starting off his new job with a cold? Better add some Tylenol and Robitussin to the ever-growing shopping list, and actually go shopping.

Oliver shook his head and got out of the car. Stalling would do his nerves no good, so he adjusted his messenger bag and strode into the brightly lit lobby.

A sweeping crescent-shaped reception desk occupied half the space, manned by a single blond woman, who barely glanced at Oliver before resuming scrolling through something on her computer screen. Oliver couldn't see the interface from this angle, but he strongly suspected it was her Facebook page. Maybe Instagram, given her age. The silver tag pin on her pink blouse read "Courtney."

"Hi," he said politely, moving to stand in front of her. The desk's surface was polished to such a high gleam he could see his reflection in it—silver-rimmed glasses, short coppery hair, a spatter of freckles across a pale, anxious face. He kept his hands on the bag strap so as not to ruin the glossy shine. "I'm Oliver Foster, the new employee? I have an appointment with Mr. Thompson."

"One moment." Courtney clicked her mouse a few times and nodded. "Yep. Go right ahead. Second floor."

"Which door?"

"It's an open-space thing. He has the corner office."

"Great, thank you," he said, but she was already glued to the screen.

Just as the receptionist had said, most of the second floor was an open-concept space. No more than a dozen people occupied it, but the noise generated by talking, the ringing of phones, and the whirring of industrial-sized printers overwhelmed him at first.

Oliver paused on the landing, allowing himself a moment to take it all in. The tall windows along one curved wall allowed plenty of morning light to stream inside. Several long desks, positioned perpendicular to the windows, spanned the length of the room. Some were divided into personal workstations, while several others displayed cardboard models interspersed with printed renderings, most likely arranged for their clients' benefit. A white marble counter along the far wall served as a kitchenette and abutted a separate glass-walled conference room where a meeting was currently taking place. On the other side of the kitchenette was another room, which Oliver guessed was the managing director's office.

The office, currently empty, offered an uninterrupted view of the immaculate front lawn and older commercial buildings across the street.

Oliver drew a few curious looks as he stepped inside, but no one seemed particularly interested. He paused in indecision, fiddling nervously with the strap of his messenger bag. His gaze fell to one of the larger models on the display table, a towering concoction of reflective panels and odd angles that somehow managed to converge into a fascinatingly pleasing shape. The card next to the model proclaimed it to be the "Tower of Light," a new exhibition center to be erected on Light Street.

"Hi there. Can I help you?"

A pretty young woman, about five years his senior, approached him. She wore skinny jeans and one of those horrendous crosses between a shirt and a jacket in a deep navy color. It looked cool on her though—edgy and sophisticated. Her dark curly hair was pulled up in a tight ponytail and held in place with rhinestone-studded silver pins, framing a lightly tanned oval face spattered with freckles.

"I'm the new guy," Oliver said. "Supposed to start today."

"You need to see Colin, then. Mr. Thompson, that is." She smiled at him encouragingly. "He's in a meeting right now, but he'll be out soon. Want some coffee in the meantime?"

"Sure, that'd be nice."

She led him to the shiny white counter and pressed a few buttons on the coffee machine. Oliver had only had a cup of instant coffee in the morning, so the delicious aroma of a strong brew definitely hit the spot.

"Thank you," he said after declining the offer of sugar and creamers. "I'm Oliver, by the way. Oliver Foster."

"I'm Ela Blum." They shook hands. "Are you from around here?"

"No. Fresh out of Florida, in fact."

Ela grinned. "I'm afraid our weather isn't as nice."

"I'm kinda digging it actually. It'll be interesting to have a proper autumn for a change. I just rented a house near Druid Park, so lots of nature to enjoy."

"It's a beautiful area. Some of the neighborhoods around the park can be a little rough, but it's not worse than the rest of the city."

"The building I live in is very secure," Oliver said, recalling all the weird precautions enforced by his landlord.

"Good. The trails around the lake are great for jogging, if you're into that."

Oliver wasn't, but he agreed with her anyway.

"So you recently graduated?" Ela asked while pouring herself coffee and adding sweetener. "Forgive me for saying so, but you look awfully young."

"I get that a lot." Oliver sighed. Not that twenty-five wasn't young, but he still got carded almost every time he went out for drinks. "I graduated from UF two years ago and then did an AEP internship at Studio Garcia. I'm still learning the field, but I have some experience working on a team."

"Good." Ela nodded. "Did you work with AutoCAD?"

"Yes. And Revit too. I'm not as familiar with other software platforms though. I know a lot of architects prefer ArchiCAD."

"That's okay; we mostly use the first two anyway, and the 3D Max for presentations. But I don't think you'll be making those on your own for a while."

They chatted for a few minutes about the comparative benefits and uses of the different platforms as Oliver sipped his coffee and let himself relax. Ela was friendly and easy to talk to, and she reminded him a lot of Pam with her infectious grin. He was sorry when the door to the conference room finally opened and people started shuffling out into the open space.

"Come on; I'll introduce you," Ela said and took him by the hand, for all the world as if they were in some old-fashioned ballroom. He followed until they stopped in front of the door to the corner office, where a tall blond man in an expensive-looking gray suit was talking—or, more accurately, issuing instructions—to a young man furiously taking notes on his iPad.

"And don't forget to have that estimate on my desk by four," the older man said imperiously. "We don't want any more delays on this project, yes?"

"Yes, Mr. Thompson," the other man said meekly, color rising on his cheeks. He glanced at Ela and Oliver and scurried away, holding the iPad to his chest like a shield.

Oliver swallowed and pushed his glasses up his nose, all of his earlier nervousness returning in full force.

"Mr. Thompson," Ela said as the director turned to face them, "this is Oliver Foster, our new recruit."

"It's an honor to meet you, Mr. Thompson," Oliver said, trying his best to appear calm and confident, though he was anything but. "I'm very thankful for this amazing opportunity, and I can't wait to begin."

There. He'd practiced the little speech all morning and didn't even stutter. It had to count as a sort of victory.

Mr. Thompson didn't reach out to shake his hand. He was handsome in an overwrought way, like a TV star trying desperately to hold on to his good looks in the face of the inevitable. His teeth were very white, and his hair was tousled with what had to be extreme care.

"Oh, right," he said. "I almost forgot about you. Well, I guess it'll be nice to have someone pick up the slack for a change. God knows no one else around here does."

Oliver tittered nervously, unsure whether it was meant as a joke. Ela's carefully neutral expression indicated that it wasn't.

"I expect hard work, dedication, and none of that millennial whining," Thompson continued. "Show me all that, and we'll get along just fine."

Millennial whining?

"Of course," Oliver said for lack of a better response. "I'm looking forward to your mentoring, sir."

Thompson chuckled good-naturedly as if Oliver had said something especially funny.

"No, no, I don't have the time for that. That's why we have the best team in Baltimore. They can show you the ropes.

I'll be checking in once in a while on your progress, but coddling the rookies isn't my thing."

Was coddling rookies the thing of "the best team in Baltimore" that apparently didn't hold up to Thompson's high work standards? Oliver wisely kept his mouth shut and nodded. Pointing out all the ways in which his boss had contradicted himself wasn't a good idea in general, and certainly not on his first day on the job.

"I'm sure Oliver will do great," Ela said quickly. "I was thinking about bringing him in on the Potomac Street housing project. We could use some extra help."

"Let's get him started on that, then." Thompson glanced at his wristwatch. "As a matter of fact, your team is about to have a briefing on the client's amendments, isn't that right? I'll pop in to see what is it Cox wants changed this time."

Cox? Could it be the same man Oliver had heard arguing with Mr. Brown yesterday? It wouldn't be surprising if he were a builder or a developer.

"Shouldn't I go to HR first to get all the paperwork sorted?" he asked. "I did sign some forms online, but there has to be—"

"You can do all that later. Might as well get straight to work," Thompson said with a touch of impatience. "Ela, darling, I want to see everyone in the conference room in five minutes."

With that, Thompson strode into his office and shut the door firmly in their faces.

"Don't mind him," Ela said quietly. "Well, you should obviously mind him to some extent, but that's just the way he is, you know? He's a brilliant architect, and you can't argue with results."

Oliver supposed that was true. Thompson Designs was indisputably one of the best architectural firms in Maryland, and considering how stiff the competition was in this field, that was saying a lot.

Suppressing the urge to sneeze, he followed Ela as she rushed to assemble her team and gather all the materials before ushering everyone into the conference room. Oliver took a seat at the far end of the long table while a guy in a striped sweater hurriedly pulled presentation slides onto the huge screen and shut the blinds for better viewing.

The team consisted of five people, including Ela. They all took their seats with their folders arranged on the tabletop in front of them when Thompson entered, accompanied by the same flustered young man he'd been talking to earlier. Oliver guessed he was Thompson's executive assistant, and judging by his harried expression, he hadn't been on the job much longer than Oliver.

"Before we begin, I want to introduce the newest addition to the Thompson Design family." Thompson gestured to Oliver. "Why don't you say hello, Daniel."

"It's, um, Oliver, actually." Oliver pushed the glasses up his nose and offered an embarrassed smiled to the room. "Oliver Foster. I'm very happy to be—"

"Now they know who you are, we can leave the socializing for later," Thompson cut in. "Let's hear it, Ela."

Oliver clamped his mouth shut and dutifully diverted his attention to the project overview on the screen, which showed three adjacent buildings comprising a new housing project to be built on Potomac Street by Richard Cox Building and Development. As far as Oliver could see, these were run-of-the-mill apartment complexes for low-income families, designed with economy rather than modern convenience in mind. It struck Oliver as odd that a design firm that prided itself on its innovative approach would take on such a utilitarian project, but perhaps they handled all of Cox's developments, lavish and mundane alike.

"Mr. Cox approved the preliminary drawings," Ela said, jumping to the next few slides that presented renderings of the exterior and floor plans. "However, he asked us to eliminate this window in the living room area in all the apartment configurations." She indicated the window in question on the enlarged apartment plan.

Oliver frowned. "But that would leave the entire area with only one window," he said before he could think better of it. "That would considerably lower the amount of natural light, and the living room would feel gloomy. If anything, I'd advise adding a window on that wall, not taking one down."

A heavy silence fell on the room as everyone turned to look at him, though the dimness made it hard to make out their expressions. Was he wrong to speak out of turn? During his internship at Studio Garcia, all the team members, including the interns, were encouraged to freely offer and exchange ideas during briefings in order to arrive at the best possible solution. Perhaps here the process was different, and they weren't supposed to have a discussion until the presentation was over?

Oliver opened his mouth to apologize for interrupting, but Thompson was already shaking his head.

"Need I remind you all," he said with a pointed look at Oliver, "that this is a housing project, not a private residence.

Eliminating that one window across all the buildings would save tens of thousands of dollars in building costs, and the residents would never know the difference. After all, they won't be living there for comfort and luxury, will they? Our job is to present the developer with the most cost-effective option, especially if he specifically asks for it. Frankly, I'm rather appalled you included two windows on that wall in the first place. Whose idea was that?"

A plump woman in her thirties with a sleek dark bob raised her hand tentatively.

"Serena." Thompson's voice dripped with annoyance. "I might expect this kind of mistake from an intern, but you should know better. Our client shouldn't have to ask us to amend something that could've been done right from the start. This back-and-forth over stupid details is causing unnecessary delays—time that could be much better spent working on projects that actually make us money."

"Sorry, Mr. Thompson, it won't happen again," Serena said.

"See that it doesn't. Ela, this is your responsibility also." Thompson turned to her. "Now, if there are no more brilliant suggestions from the audience, let's continue."

Clearly, Oliver wasn't making a good first impression. He spent the rest of the briefing quietly absorbing information and trying to make himself as inconspicuous as possible, while ignoring the growing ache between his eyes. When it was over, Thompson didn't spare him a glance as he made his exit with his assistant in tow, but the expressions of the rest of the team ranged from commiserating to disapproving as they gathered their things and left the room. Serena was especially displeased and stormed out without waiting for Oliver to offer either a greeting or an apology, but he could hardly blame her.

"I'm really sorry about that," Oliver told Ela when they were alone. "I wasn't trying to get anyone in trouble."

Ela shrugged. "Colin likes to dispense with these kinds of projects as soon as possible so he can focus on other things."

"Like the Tower of Light?"

A wry smile touched her lips. "You saw that, huh?"

"It's…" Oliver searched for a word that would do justice both to the essence of the design and to his own opinion of its ostentatiousness. "…visionary."

Ela busied herself with tidying her notes.

"We handle all the architectural design for Cox Building, and that includes everything from commercial spaces to single-family homes. It's good business, but affordable apartments are low on Colin's list of priorities," she said, confirming Oliver's earlier guess. "But it's a good one to start on, even if it's boring. There are a lot of opportunities to familiarize yourself with the basics."

"I'm here to learn," Oliver assured her.

"Good." She zipped her folder and nodded at him. "I'll come with you to the HR office, and then we can get down to business. I wasn't kidding when I said we could use the help. Filing for permits might not be glamorous, but someone has to do it."

"You mean the new guy has to do it," Oliver said with a chagrined grin.

"Boy, you catch on quick." She laughed. "There's hope for you yet."

★

Deep dusk had already settled when Oliver left his car in the small parking lot at the corner of the block. He walked to the house, balancing his messenger bag and the groceries he'd picked up on the way home. The wind from the lake carried a sharp chill that slithered under his light jacket as he climbed the stone steps leading to the gate and passed the line of red maples on the way to the front porch. His eyes began to water with the wind, and the itch at the back of his throat seemed to become more pronounced with every passing minute.

Damn it. It would be just his luck if he became sick on his first day of work.

Oliver gazed up as he paused to take out his keys. His apartment windows on the second floor were dark, but light filtered from around the drawn curtains in several others. They looked like the half-lidded eyes of a giant animal watching him, quiet but alert.

He shook his head. This was ridiculous. It was just an old, silly-looking house, and he was letting his imagination and his bad mood run away with him.

He wouldn't wallow, he decided as he unlocked the front door and checked the mailbox. (Not unexpectedly, it was empty). So he'd had a dismal first day at work. Most of the time, that was par for the course for rookies. It was meant to toughen him up, see if he could carry his own weight around the office. Well, he could do that. He'd have to work extra hard, just as he'd done in college and during his internship. He'd show them he could make it, that he was talented and taking his profession seriously. It was a good thing, really, that he'd learned how to work with people of Mr. Thompson's ilk because he wasn't in any way unique in his assholishness. So, yeah, he'd chalk it up to gaining experience points. Even if the experience was a miserable one.

The stairs let out an especially dangerous-sounding wail as he reached the landing. He glanced at his feet in alarm, and then a blur of movement caught his eye. He jerked his head up and found himself staring at the most beautiful man he'd ever seen.

Chapter Four

The stranger, who paused on the last step of the next flight of stairs, was tall and slim, dressed in a silk buttoned-down shirt and dark jeans that molded to his narrow hips. His deep olive skin glowed despite the low lighting, and a lock of dark hair fell mischievously onto his forehead. The man grinned at Oliver, exposing a row of brilliantly white teeth.

"Well, hello there," he said.

No, purred. Oliver had no idea people could actually sound like that in real life, but this man, whoever he was, managed to imitate a cat with a belly full of cream, his words tinged with a heavy accent Oliver assumed to be French.

"Um… Hi," Oliver returned cautiously.

The stranger's eyes raked over him, his gaze appreciative, and Oliver's pulse quickened despite himself. Really, the man was gorgeous. Like a male model in a glossy magazine or a dashing rake in a steamy Regency novel.

"My name is Rafe. Short for Raphael. I rent a room in the eastern turret. And you are?"

"Oliver. Oliver Foster."

"Oliver." Rafe lingered on every syllable, the name more a caress than a statement, his dark eyes intense and unblinking.

Oliver shivered, imagining hot breath skimming over sensitive skin. "Nice to meet you."

"You, too, I…I guess."

"I must say, I wasn't expecting the new neighbor to be quite so fetching," Rafe said, casually leaning on the banister. "I'm kind of curious to see what you've done with the old place. May I come inside to take a better look?"

Oliver wanted to say something, but words eluded him. For a moment, he just stood there, mesmerized by the way Rafe's long dark lashes dipped when he leaned forward, so close Oliver could smell his musky cologne. Was it cologne, or was it the man's natural scent, powerful and alluring? And what was the question again?

"Tone it down, Rafe."

Oliver blinked, and the strange haze that had overcome him dissipated. He looked behind Rafe's shoulder (when had he come to stand right in front of Oliver?) to see Brown looming on the threshold of his own apartment, thick arms crossed over his chest. Brown caught Oliver's gaze and rolled his eyes at Rafe as if to say "can you believe this guy?"

Oliver chuckled awkwardly, more than a little mortified he'd been about to literally swoon over the attentions of a handsome man. The hell was wrong with him? His cold couldn't have worsened enough for him to experience time lapses. Could it?

"Hey," Rafe said easily, turning to Brown and raising his hands in mock defeat. "I was merely greeting our new neighbor. He seems nice. For, you know, what he is."

"What am I?" Oliver asked, unsure whether he should be offended.

"A charming young man," Rafe assured him, turning back to him. "*Charming.* Anyway, I must be going. Guess that tour of the apartment will have to wait for another time!"

He flashed them both a toothy smile and sauntered down the stairs, whistling a broken tune.

Brown followed him with his eyes, frowning.

"Should I...uh...be worried about him?" Oliver asked.

Now that Rafe no longer offered him that wickedly raffish grin, Oliver was once again uncomfortably anxious. A house full of quirky neighbors was all well and good, but was he safe among them? He was beginning to suspect the low rent had to be explained by more than poor upkeep, and to regret not following up on other options.

"Rafe? No, not really. He likes to..." Brown paused. "...flirt, but he means no harm by it."

Oliver raised his eyebrows. "Does he ever flirt with you?"

Brown cleared his throat, slight color rising to his cheeks. "I'm not his type."

Who is your type? Oliver almost asked, but that was way too personal, not to mention inappropriate. Really, he was too beat to think clearly. He shook his head and barely suppressed a groan when pain lanced through his temples in response to the movement.

"Are you okay? You don't look too good."

"I think I'm coming down with something, that's all. That, and I had a crappy day."

"I'm sorry to hear that."

"Yeah." Oliver finally recalled he was holding his keys in one hand, the groceries in the other, and attempting to balance the bag on his knee while he unlocked the door. A box of sugared donuts slid out of the stuffed paper bag and cluttered to the floor, and Oliver let out an exasperated curse.

Brown watched him fumble for a moment and then asked, "May I help you with that?"

Oliver nodded, the tips of his ears burning. Clearly, he wasn't making a great impression. Not that he wanted to impress Brown *at all*.

The other man bent down and scooped up the box of donuts, which thankfully hadn't burst open. He then took the grocery bag from Oliver's hand and waited while Oliver finally opened the door and switched on the lights in the hallway.

"Where do you want them?" Brown asked, coming inside after Oliver.

"On the counter is fine. Thank you."

Oliver shrugged off his messenger bag and jacket and hung them on the pegs by the door before going into the kitchen.

"That doesn't look like a healthy dinner," Brown said, nodding at the donuts.

"Said the man who likes pineapple on his pizza," Oliver countered.

Brown's hard mouth curved. "You got me there."

The smile transformed his face, softening his expression and smoothing the sharp edges into handsomeness. The change, although small, was so staggering by comparison, that for a moment, Oliver could only stare at him, so mesmerized that he missed what Brown said next.

"What?"

"I asked if you wanted me to take a look at the plumbing in the bathroom as long as I'm here," Brown repeated patiently.

"Only if it's not too much trouble."

"It's fine. Just let me get the tools."

Oliver took advantage of Brown's absence to down a couple of analgesics with a large glass of water and then splashed some from under the tap on his face. Yep, he was definitely developing a cold, if the soreness in his throat and the dull throbbing behind his eyes were anything to go by. That had to explain why he was acting like a featherbrain too.

"I'm back," Brown announced, closing the front door after him. He carried a large wooden toolbox, which had to weigh at least a dozen pounds by the look of it. "Let me see what I can do."

Oliver wiped his mouth and followed him to the chilly bathroom. Water gurgled along the copper pipes, but thankfully, no singing could be heard. He still wasn't sure where that had come from, so he decided it best not to mention it. He must have seemed foolish enough already.

He wrapped his arms around himself, watching as Brown put down the toolbox and examined the pipes that ran from the shower to the ceiling.

"Those look antique," Oliver said. "Not original to the house though. The 1940s, if I'm not mistaken?"

"That's right." Brown glanced at him, then resumed his inspection. "The place was renovated just before the war, and barely touched since then. It's all long due for an overhaul, but…" He shook his head. "How did you know about the plumbing?"

"I'm an architect. Well, I'm just starting out as an architect. Today was my first day at the firm."

"Oh, right." Brown ran his hands over the length of the largest pipe as high as he could reach. His eyebrows drew together, and he brought his face close to the pipes. His nostrils flared as if he was sniffing them. "I gather it didn't go so well?"

Oliver smiled wryly.

"Not as well as I'd have liked, no."

Brown gazed at the ceiling, his frown deepening. "There are most likely pinhole leaks in the upstairs plumbing. There's a lot of dampness there, but we seem to have caught it before any serious damage. I'll have to do some soldering, though, so I'll ask Kimona if I can drop by tomorrow to do it."

"Kimona?"

"The woman in 2B. Have you met her?"

"Only briefly." Oliver refrained from mentioning the particulars. "Can I still use the shower tonight?"

"Yeah. I don't think it'll do much harm, though you won't get much of a water pressure until the leaks are fixed." Brown fetched his toolbox and turned to Oliver. He seemed to hesitate for a moment, then said, "Look, if you need anything else, let me know, okay? I promise not to bite your head off."

"Thanks." Oliver chuckled. "It'll be just my luck if the heater dies in the middle of the night, and I have to wake you up to fix it."

"No, I meant…" Brown stopped and said in a slightly different tone of voice, "You should absolutely wake me if the heater—or anything else in the apartment—gives you trouble. I'm sorry I snapped at you about the water being cold last night.

It's somewhat of an issue around here, and I'm still trying to figure out a more permanent solution."

"I get that. I apologize for being so impatient about it."

"That's okay. The truth is, you're entitled to." Brown sighed. "I'll deal with it somehow."

He sounded bleak, and Oliver resisted the urge to reach out and pat his arm in reassurance. Brown was a grown man, and he was right in that it was his responsibility as a landlord. He certainly didn't need Oliver's help—not that he could offer much of it.

He took a breath to say something anyway and immediately doubled over in a fit of coughing.

"You weren't kidding about coming down with something," Brown remarked, not unkindly. "Let's get you something to drink."

Brown and his toolbox led the way into the kitchen, and Oliver followed, still coughing. The landlord handed him a glass of tap water, then filled the kettle while Oliver drank it, trying not to choke in the process.

"I'll make you some tea," Brown said. "In lieu of chicken soup, it's the best thing for curing a cold."

"Now you sound just like my grandma." Oliver's eyes watered, and he took off his glasses to wipe the tears. Brown's silhouette blurred, along with the edges of the cupboards and the pattern of the tiled backsplash. "But the tea sounds nice. Thank you."

Brown huffed. His figure came back into focus as Oliver pushed his glasses up his nose.

"Your grandma must be a very wise woman. I'm sure she'd say you should also eat something more substantial than those donuts. Want me to fix you something real quick?"

For a second, Oliver was sure he'd misunderstood. Was his landlord—his burly, unsociable landlord—actually offering to cook for him?

"Um," he stammered. "You really shouldn't go to all this trouble."

"It's no trouble." Brown wasn't smiling now, but his expression was solemn rather than annoyed and lacked the hostility Oliver had mistaken as inherent. "You're clearly too sick to bother with cooking, and I have nothing else better to do anyway."

The offer seemed sincere, so Oliver didn't take offense at the wording.

"That'd be great, Mr. Brown. But only if you join me for dinner."

Belatedly, he realized that perhaps he shouldn't have asked since he'd be putting Brown at risk of contracting whatever Oliver had. But he didn't seem to mind.

"Sure. And you can call me Nym."

"Right. Nym." Once again, the unusual name piqued Oliver's curiosity. "Is it short for something?"

"Yes."

Nym, however, didn't elaborate. He turned his attention to the counter and began unpacking the grocery bag.

Even not counting the donuts, it wasn't the healthiest assortment. Oliver had been wallowing in his bad mood as he'd stalked the supermarket isles, and the staggering amount of sugar and saturated fats in his selections definitely reflected that. This time, however, Brown—Nym—didn't comment on his unfortunate choices.

"How does grilled cheese and bacon sound?" he asked.

"Amazing," Oliver said with every ounce of sincerity because it did, and he was rewarded with another wry smile.

He took a seat by the counter and nursed his cup of tea while he watched Nym move about in his kitchen. Nym seemed to know what he was doing, only occasionally asking Oliver where he stored his utensils and spices (which amounted to the saltshaker he'd found in a cupboard). In a relatively short time, the kitchen filled with the delicious aroma of butter-fried bread and bacon.

"Do you like to cook?" Oliver ventured, sipping the hot tea carefully. It felt good going down, soothing both the congestion and the itchy soreness in his throat.

"I don't *dis*like it. I prep my meals when I have the time, but that's the extent of it."

"Yeah, me too. I mean, I used to cook for myself, but I'm not really good at it. Neither was my boyfriend."

He said it casually, mostly as a way to gauge Nym's reaction. Some people, especially men, got all weird when they realized Oliver was gay. Considering the awkward interlude with Rafe in the hallway earlier, it shouldn't have come as a huge surprise, but you never knew.

A slice of bacon sizzled when Nym dropped it on the hot pan. "Will your boyfriend be coming to visit?"

As far as reactions went, this one was everything Oliver could have hoped for. Well, maybe not everything, but it certainly filled him with relief, and some of the tension melted away at the easy acceptance.

"No," he said. "We broke up."

"Oh."

Was there something odd in the way Nym said that, or was it just Oliver's imagination?

"Do you, uh, often have family over?" he asked, changing the subject.

"Not often." Nym was silent for a moment, focusing his attention on flipping the sandwiches, then added, "There's not much left in terms of family. My folks live in Frederik. I moved to Baltimore after my aunt died and left me this house."

"I'm sorry." It didn't escape Oliver's attention that Nym mentioned nothing about a wife or a girlfriend—or a partner of any gender, for that matter. Not that Oliver had seen any evidence of a Mrs. Brown living across the hall, but you could never be sure. And the man could be divorced or separated.

Nym shrugged, still not looking at him.

"Were you close with your aunt?"

He probably shouldn't pry, but Oliver was genuinely curious. Despite the rough exterior, Oliver couldn't help but feel there was more to Nym than met the eye. As if the man was a puzzle he had yet to solve. Yes, he was big—six-two if he was an inch—but he was never menacing. Not in the way all the jocks who used to bully Oliver in high school had been. Not in the way Jake had been after a few drinks. Nym didn't feel like a threat, and that piqued Oliver's curiosity like nothing else.

Oliver cleared his throat, bringing that train of thought to a full stop before it could slide off the rails.

"Not very close, no," Nym said. "My parents and I only used to visit occasionally while she was alive, but she always said I was her favorite nephew. I guess that's why she left me the house, and since she had no children of her own. My other cousins either lived too far or had no interest in the property."

He scowled at the skillet as if it were somehow to blame for his wonky family relations. "They were probably smart to pass on it, but I couldn't let this place sit and rot. It didn't feel right, knowing it was so important to her."

That certainly shed some light on why Nym had been so adamant about not wanting to sell the place to Cox, though Oliver had a distinct feeling it wasn't the whole story. The memory of a beloved aunt wasn't a good enough reason to go bankrupt, but then again, Oliver had no experience with either generous aunts or owning real estate.

"It's an interesting house, for sure," he said. "So many things going on with the architecture. I was telling my friend yesterday I should try to find more information about Lakeside Lodge."

"You won't find much about it. At least, not online." Nym took out a couple of plates and stacked them with grilled cheese sandwiches and bacon. "The house was built in 1901 by my great-great-grandaunt, Despina Shaw. She was somewhat of a local celebrity in this part of Baltimore in the early 1900s, very involved in charity and conservation. Legend has it she built Lakeside Lodge as a safe house."

"A safe house? For who?"

"For folks who needed it, I guess," Nym said, his tone taking on a peculiar inflection. He set the plates on the counter and refilled Oliver's cup before pouring tea for himself, then sat down on the opposite side.

There was something sad, even wistful about his expression. It took away some of the edge in his earlier attitude, made him look younger, vulnerable even.

Oliver cleared his throat to hide that he'd been staring.

"I'm sure she was extraordinary," he said politely.

"She was," Nym agreed. "She'd done so much for…the community. Reopening the Lodge was supposed to be a way to honor her legacy, but I simply don't have the time and money to maintain it properly." He ran a hand through his shaggy hair, messing it up even further. "Not with a full-time job and the bank loans."

Oliver's thoughts shot back to the conversation he'd overheard from his living room window last night. Nym's attachment to the house was evident, but Oliver still couldn't understand why he insisted on holding on to it, let alone run what was essentially an old-fashioned boarding house. But it wasn't his place to comment, so he didn't.

Nym shook his head. "Sorry. That was probably a bit TMI. Anyway, it seems all the records were lost after Despina died. I don't think there's even a copy of the original blueprints left anywhere, and believe me, I did search for it."

"That's too bad," Oliver said, disappointed. It'd be interesting to take a look at those blueprints or early sketches, if only to try to get into the head of the designer and understand their process. "Do you know who the architect was? I'd expect something this old and locally notable would be on a preservation registry."

"No, sorry. I don't know much about the origins of the place, apart from what my aunt told me. I don't even know if the house could be considered important. Apparently, there's a difference between a historically significant building and an old house with lots of history. Unfortunately, the latter doesn't get the same kind of tax credit."

Oliver nodded in commiseration. Structure restoration was a notoriously expensive business, and Lakeside Lodge would require a lot of work.

He took a bite of the sandwich and barely suppressed a moan of pleasure. He might have enjoyed it even more if he hadn't been so congested, but even so, the food was hot, greasy, and crunchy. It hit the spot just right.

"Good?" Nym watched him, paused with his own sandwich in hand.

"It's delicious."

Nym cracked another of his rare smiles and tucked into his food. They ate in companionable silence, with Oliver occasionally leaning away to clear his throat and Nym politely ignoring it. Good thing this wasn't a date because that would've been a sure way to spoil the mood.

Not that Oliver would've opposed a date with Nym. It could've been the cold talking, though, or Oliver's unfortunate tendency to fall for the wrong men. And since nothing indicated Nym was anything but straight and grumpy, that would be a particularly wrong move.

"I'll take care of the dishes," Oliver said when they were both done with their meals. "Thank you for dinner. I really enjoyed it."

"No problem. I...um...enjoyed it too," Nym said hesitantly as if he were surprised by the sentiment. "Let me know if you need anything."

"Sure." Oliver saw Nym to the door and as he stepped into the hallway asked, "See you tomorrow?"

Nym turned to him in surprise. In truth, Oliver was also baffled at the impulse. But Nym had acted like a friend tonight, and it was nice not to feel entirely alone.

The landlord nodded slowly. "See you tomorrow, then. Good night."

"Good night," Oliver said quickly and closed the door. Recalling Rafe's oily smile, he checked the lock and threw the chain for good measure.

He paused in the kitchen, looking at the smattering of crumbs and smudges of grease on the dirty plates. His throat hurt and his head was heavy, but the warmth that spread in his stomach wasn't wholly due to the food he'd just eaten.

Tomorrow was going to be better, Oliver promised to himself as he gathered the dishes into the sink, his mood strangely buoyant despite the bone-deep weariness. Hell, it was going to be great.

Chapter Five

Tomorrow wasn't great.

Oliver woke up with congestion and a headache that reminded him of that one time when he'd been deluded enough to take Pam's bet on the number of tequila shots he could down in the course of one particularly misjudged evening. He made a valiant effort at brushing his teeth, staring at his bleary, red-eyed reflection, and even contemplated showering before dizziness and a prolonged fit of coughing forced him to admit defeat.

He shuffled back to the bedroom, wrapping a hoodie around himself like a bathrobe. The closet door stood ajar, and Oliver frowned. He didn't remember opening it, but perhaps the door didn't close very well. Shivering, he climbed into bed, put on his glasses, and picked up his phone.

Seeing as it was only his second day on the job, and considering his first had been less than stellar, calling in sick seemed like a bad move. But Oliver knew he'd be worse than useless in an office in this condition, not to mention possibly contagious, and driving was entirely out of the question.

He called the office number, anxiety lodged firmly in his throat, half-expecting to be sacked before he even began. To his vast relief, Mr. Thompson was unavailable, and Ela took the call. Upon hearing the raspiness in his voice, she agreed Oliver had made the right call by staying home and offered to send him his assignments by email when he was feeling well enough to take them on.

"Do you need anything in the meantime?" she asked. "You said you just moved in, so..."

"No, no, I'm fine," he hastened to assure her. "Thank you. I really appreciate it, and it's awesome of you to suggest it. You can go ahead and send me the assignment. And again, I'm terribly sorry about it all. I promise I won't let you down like this again."

"Just get your rest and take it easy, Oliver." He could hear the smile in her voice. "We'll be in touch."

After disconnecting, Oliver sank back onto his pillows with a deep sigh. That went much better than anticipated. He just hoped Ela wouldn't have to take flak from Mr. Thompson on his behalf. Whatever they wanted him to do, he'd have to do it well to make up for being such a dweeb.

He idly thought about getting up and making a cup of coffee, but his eyelids seemed to grow heavy and shut all on their own.

The next time he woke up, pale autumn sunlight flooded the room, and the clock on his phone informed him it was 10:10 a.m.

Oliver sat up and grimaced at the dull throbbing behind his temples. Despite being mortified at sleeping in so late, he would've gone back to sleep for a little while longer, but his bladder presented him with an ultimatum he couldn't afford to ignore. With a sigh, he scraped himself off the bed and headed for the bathroom but paused as he passed the closet door, which was tightly shut again.

Did he close it earlier? He couldn't recall, but he must have done so before going to bed. Current difficulty in breathing made it hard to focus, and his perception was a little fuzzy at the edges. It was definitely time to get properly caffeinated if he wanted to get anything at all done today.

The apartment felt chilly, but not quite as cold as the night before. After relieving himself, he grabbed a box of tissues, and padded to the kitchen.

The sight of the dishes in the sink brought back the image of Nym deftly making grilled cheese, and Oliver couldn't hold back a smile. He wouldn't have minded Nym making him some pancakes, especially if his breakfast skills were as strong as his impromptu dinner ones. But that wasn't about to happen, and Oliver praised yesterday's perspicacity in buying a box of do-nuts. They weren't fresh pancakes, but they were greasy and sugary and went incredibly well with the strong coffee. After food and a Tylenol, Oliver felt marginally better, or at least good enough to settle on the couch with his laptop and a warm blanket and try to get some work done.

It must have been the combination of the congestion, the soft light streaming through the curtains, and the incredibly te-dious paperwork Ela had forwarded as he dozed off again soon afterwards. When he finally blinked himself awake, the room was gray with the reflection of the storm clouds outside, and gentle rain rapped on the windows.

He didn't know what made him look at the large mirror hanging above the fireplace. Perhaps it was the barest hint of movement or simply that funny prickling at the back of the head when being watched. But he turned just in time to see a vague outline of a human face reflected in the depths of the mirror.

Oliver started and fumbled for his glasses, belatedly remembering he'd perched them on the top of his head before falling asleep. He shoved them on his nose and peered at the mirror again, but now it was showing only curtains and wallpaper.

He quickly scanned the room and, seeing no one hiding behind the drapes, relaxed a fraction. Still, he got up and checked behind the kitchen counter and under the table and went as far as making a round of the entire apartment, peeking into the bathroom and his bedroom. Feeling silly, he returned to the living room and stood in front of the fireplace to examine the mirror. Its surface had started to tarnish around the edges, and his own wide-eyed face stared back at him from the spotted silver glass.

Whatever he thought he'd glimpsed in the mirror, he must have dreamed it or let the dregs of a dream carry on into reality. He was stressed and sick, so no wonder he was imagining things. Oliver touched his forehead, his reflection repeating the gesture. The warmth of his skin was a relief. Who could tell what he'd hallucinate in a fever dream?

Shaking his head at himself, Oliver fetched a tissue, blew his nose, and headed to the kitchen to make a cup of tea.

Oliver was hoping he could go back to work on Wednesday, but it seemed his body had other plans and flatly refused to cooperate. His fever rose sharply in the evening, and he spent a rather miserable night huddled under every blanket he could find, waiting for the analgesics to kick in.

The next day wasn't much better. The few times he'd texted and chatted with Pam only underscored how alone he was in this new city, in this old apartment. It reminded Oliver too much of the time he'd spent in the hospital, nursing a broken rib. Thankfully, as stressed as he was now, it couldn't compare to the tumult of his mental suffering then, when the pain of broken bones echoed the anguish of a broken heart.

Telling himself sternly not to dwell on the past, Oliver dived into work. The fever-induced fatigue made him sluggish, so every task took at least twice as long as it should. But he still managed to put in a few good hours that day, fueled mostly by tea and an obscene amount of sugar.

It was a relief when he received a message that his things would arrive on Friday. In the midst of an oppressing quiet, it was something to look forward to. But when, on Friday afternoon, he discovered that the delivery person had left the shipment of boxes sitting on the front porch, the thrill of anticipation dimmed, replaced first by annoyance, and then by frustration.

By then, his temperature had returned to normal, and he was feeling much better, aside from a runny nose and a lingering cough. He didn't remember packing that much stuff, but now, standing on the porch surrounded with heavy boxes, which he'd have to haul up the stairs one by one, it seemed like an insurmountable task.

"Oh, for heaven's sake," Oliver muttered and grabbed one of the smaller boxes.

As he straightened, he saw Brown coming up the front path from the little paved patio that connected the back entrance where the landlord usually parked his pickup truck. Oliver vaguely recalled Brown—Nym—telling him he worked in construction. He must have been coming home from work, as sweat and dirt stained his plaid shirt, and sawdust peppered his shaggy hair.

"Hey." Nym nodded at Oliver as he climbed the shallow porch steps. "I see the rest of your baggage has arrived."

"Unfortunately, it didn't come all the way," Oliver said, balancing the box on his hip. "I'll have it all cleared up in a minute."

That promise was blatantly optimistic. Nym must have thought so, too, because he picked up a box with all the effort of lifting an empty paper bag.

"Here, let me help you with that."

"You really don't have to."

"It's no trouble."

Oliver wasn't so foolish as to refuse help he desperately needed, so he offered the landlord a grateful smile and led the way to his apartment. There, he lowered the box onto the floor next to the kitchen counter and quickly grabbed a tissue to blow his nose.

Nym put his box down at his feet.

"Why don't I get the rest of those in here," he said. "You stay and see if anything's missing."

"No, really, that's too much," Oliver protested, but Nym was already out the door.

Oliver knelt by the boxes and carefully opened them. The smaller one held an assortment of sketchbooks and pencils, and Oliver's fingers instantly itched to draw something. That would have to wait, though, as he had more pressing matters to busy himself with.

In a matter of minutes, Nym had all the other boxes safely inside the apartment. They didn't look quite as immovable now, neatly stacked beneath the kitchen counter, but Oliver knew it'd have taken him the better part of the afternoon to get it all inside on his own in his current condition.

"Thank you," he told Nym when the landlord had deposited the last item of Oliver's belongings. "You've been a great help."

"Don't mention it." Nym regarded the boxes as he dusted his hands on his jeans, although, given how stained the pants were, it was doubtful it'd make them any cleaner. "What's all this, if I may ask?"

Oliver shrugged. "Just clothes and household essentials, mostly. And all the equipment I couldn't take with me in one bag."

Nym glanced at the opened carton full of stationary, with a scale ruler jutting out of one corner where Oliver had carelessly stuck it as he rummaged through the contents. "I thought all architects use computers and graphic tablets these days."

Oliver chuckled. "We do. But sometimes it helps to go back to basics and draw things the old-fashioned way. Besides, sometimes I just like to doodle whatever comes to mind on a piece of paper. It's a great way to get ideas."

"If you say so. Well, if you don't need anything else…"

"No, wait." Oliver stepped forward and touched the man's arm before he could analyze the impulse. "Would you like to stay and have pizza?"

"Pizza?" Nym's eyebrows drew together as if the concept puzzled him.

"Yes. You helped me move, and I believe that's how it works. What do you say? I'll even order veggies and pineapple on your half."

Nym's lips tugged in a reluctant smile. "When you put it like that, how can I refuse?"

"Good." Oliver realized his hand still rested on Nym's plaid-clad arm and snatched it away.

"Let me just wash up, and I'll be right back."

"Sure. I'll order in the meantime."

As soon as the door closed behind Nym, Oliver called the pizza parlor (which was way too old-school to bother with an app) and began setting the round dining table.

This was not a date, he told himself sternly. Certainly not with his reticent, most likely straight landlord. It was just a friendly dinner. A neighborly dinner, really, since they didn't know each other long or well enough to consider each other friends, grilled cheese sandwiches notwithstanding. And yet, he couldn't help the thrill of anticipation as he waited for Nym to return.

Nym arrived shortly before the pizza. He'd changed his clothes to soft gray jeans and a sweater, and had apparently taken a quick shower as his hair was wet. Recalling the issues with the evening supply of hot water, it must have been a very cold shower, and Oliver found himself weirdly pleased that Nym had gone to all that trouble for his sake.

They sat down at the dinner table with the pizza and a couple of sodas. Oliver could hardly taste anything, and he took frequent breaks to clear his nose and throat, but he was surprised to discover he was hungry. That was a good sign. This bout of illness had gone on for much longer than anticipated, and he was itching to get outside.

"Do you jog?" he asked, his thoughts turning to the promise of fresh air and lush autumn foliage. "I've been told there are nice trails around the park."

"No as much as I used to, I'm afraid." Nym took a last bite of his slice and wiped his hands on a paper napkin before taking another. "But I like the park. It's beautiful this time of year, and it's as much nature as can be found in the city."

"You're an outdoorsman, then?" Oliver asked, his curiosity roused.

It had been a long time since he'd wanted to get to know someone as he did Nym, since he'd felt this pull of…maybe not attraction, as that would be both futile and pathetic, but of genuine interest. It was surprising, given Nym's initial attitude toward him, but even Oliver, whose character judgment skills were admittedly lacking, could see that Nym wasn't inherently standoffish. Reserved, perhaps, but certainly not unfriendly.

Nym nodded. "I love being outdoors. My family and I used to camp a lot when I was younger. But after I moved to Baltimore, there weren't many opportunities to go on a trip. At all." He grimaced.

"You work full-time?"

"Yes, with Mulberry Construction. They're a small firm, but there's plenty of work. Mostly single-family homes in the suburbs."

"And you never went to college?"

"I was never good with numbers and letters." Nym's smile was wry. "There was never any question of me trying for higher education."

Oliver suspected whatever difficulties Nym had had, they didn't stem from a lack of intelligence.

"You're from Florida, right?" Nym asked after taking a sip of his soda. "Why did you move to Maryland? There must be a ton of opportunities for architects in Miami."

"Oh, you know," Oliver said. "I did my internship in Miami, and after that I was ready for a little change of scenery. New city, new approach, new perspective. It's so easy to become stale in this business."

"Stale?" Nym quirked an eyebrow. "You're, what, twenty-three?"

"Twenty-five." Almost twenty-six, but saying so would sound childish enough to counterbalance the point. "And, yes, I know I look young. You don't have to say it. Again."

"Maybe I'm jealous," Nym said with fake seriousness. "I look older than I am."

Oliver scanned his face, considering. "Thirty-five?"

"Twenty-nine."

"Wow."

Nym shrugged. "Thankfully, I'm in the right line of work for not looking pretty."

Only a few days earlier, Oliver would've tended to agree about the "not pretty" part. But now, as he studied the lines of Nym's face, he couldn't help thinking that with a new haircut and a little bit of grooming, the man would be rather fetching. Maybe not classically handsome, but definitely alluring in a rugged, purely masculine way.

"Well, thanks for the pizza," Nym said, balling up his last napkin. "I should get going now."

"Got any plans tonight?" Oliver asked a little too casually and cringed internally. Of course Nym would have plans for a Friday night. What if he thought Oliver was angling for tagging along? What if he thought Oliver was coming on to him? The landlord had done the neighborly thing and helped the new tenant with the move, but that didn't mean he wouldn't be appalled at the idea of Oliver being attracted to him.

And, yes, if Oliver was being completely honest with himself, he was attracted to Nym.

Not that he'd actually do anything about it.

Nym shook his head, seemingly oblivious to Oliver's fretting. "Not unless you consider tinkering with the plumbing 'plans.'"

"Oh. Well... Good luck," Oliver said awkwardly.

Nym rose from his chair and then paused, looking down at Oliver. His expression momentarily changed into something guarded, uncertain.

"Thank you for the pizza. It's been nice," he said, his tone bemused.

Oliver inclined his head. "Yes. Yes, it was nice."

"Good night," Nym said and headed for the door. Oliver listened as it softly clicked shut in his wake.

"Good night," he murmured, but even the whisper sounded too loud in the suddenly silent room.

The Thompson and Associates office building didn't seem quite as dazzling and inviting as it had last Monday. It might have been due to the bout of particularly foul weather and the gray sky reflecting on the curved glass panes, or maybe to Oliver's own apprehension.

He wished a good morning to Courtney, the receptionist, was ignored, and proceeded to the upstairs open workspace area.

"You still look like crap," Ela said after he'd greeted her and sunk into his desk chair with a stifled groan. "Maybe you should've skipped coming into the office today as well. Though we do have a meeting with the developer, and it's kind of important for all the team to be there so we're all on the same page. Are you up to it?"

"I'm fine," Oliver assured her. "I feel a lot better now. And don't worry; I'll keep my distance just in case."

"Good. I don't need your germs to keep me company." She grinned as she said it, making it clear she was teasing him. "Anyway, you've done a good job on all those forms I sent you."

"Thanks," Oliver said, though the task had hardly been challenging, sick or otherwise. "It's good to be back."

"And not a moment too soon." Mr. Thompson came up behind Ela, frowning at Oliver.

He sported an impeccably tailored suit in a different color than what Oliver had seen the last time, his blond, elegantly graying hair perfectly coiffed by an expert hand.

"Good morning, Mr. Thompson," Oliver said politely.

"I must say, if Ela hadn't insisted on giving you a chance, I'd have sacked you already, Daniel," Thompson announced, not bothering to lower his voice in front of the other workers. "Missing a whole week of work because of some tiny cold at the risk of setting everybody back? These are not the actions of a team player."

Oliver opened his mouth to remind Thompson that his name wasn't Daniel, but Ela shot him a warning look, and he promptly closed it, striving to look properly chastened.

"It won't happen again," he assured Thompson when his boss had finally finished extolling the importance of teamwork.

"See that it doesn't." Thompson turned as a man entered the bullpen. "Ah, here's Mr. Cox. Ela, get everybody into the conference room. And let's not have any more embarrassing faux pas, shall we?"

Ela nodded, and Thompson went over to greet the new arrival—a tall man with gray-flecked hair and an expensive suit. As they both passed Oliver's desk on their way to the conference room, Cox glanced at him, and for a brief moment, their eyes locked and held. Cox's mouth curved in a ghost of a smile, and then he turned away to listen to something Thompson was saying.

Despite having witnessed the conversation between Cox and Brown at night and from a less than ideal vantage point, Oliver had no doubts it was the same man who had entreated Nym to sell him his property. Though perhaps "entreated" wasn't the right word. There had been something menacing in his insistence.

And now, as he watched the developer follow Thompson into the conference room, Oliver had an uneasy feeling the man had recognized him too.

Chapter Six

The apartment greeted him with the sleepy quiet that was quickly becoming familiar, like the feel of a threadbare blanket on a worn sofa. Which, of course, was waiting for him right there, beneath the windows, facing the empty space where a TV should be. His boxes hadn't included the old TV set with the rest of the stuff his parents had shipped over for him as he intended to buy a new one when he could afford it. He didn't miss it, having his phone and laptop with him, but it would be nice to watch Netflix on a big screen again. It would be even nicer to have someone to watch it with, cuddled together under that blanket, but that wasn't happening any time soon.

Oliver shook his head and dumped the contents of yet another bag of groceries on the counter. Nym's gentle ribbing about his unhealthful eating had echoed in his mind while he'd perused the isles, so this time, he picked up more vegetables, a box of brown rice, and some fresh salmon steaks. A splurge, for sure, but the tentative hope that Nym might drop by again for dinner had made Oliver a little carefree with his spending.

He put everything away in the fridge and cupboards. Whatever magic Nym had worked on the plumbing upstairs on Friday had worked because the water pressure had been constant, if not very strong, on the weekend. However, it did nothing for the temperature, so Oliver decided to forgo the evening ablutions in favor of an early morning shower and settled down on the couch with his laptop, a drawing tablet, a can of soda, and a box of tissues. When tasked by Ela to sift through the designs to make sure all the changes agreed upon during today's meeting still met the municipal building permits, he had a few ideas on how to better utilize lobby space. Perhaps he could pitch them to the developer tomorrow before Cox approved the final plans.

Oliver sketched for a while, alternating between sips of soda and blowing his nose, trying and discarding different configurations until he was satisfied with the layout. It wouldn't be that difficult to implement, too, and if Ela approved of the alterations…

Oliver glanced at the clock and realized with a jolt it was already past eight. He set the laptop aside and stretched with a yawn. Apparently, dinner wasn't happening tonight.

And there was no reason to feel disappointed, he told himself as he shuffled to the kitchen to fix a quick sandwich. It would be weird for his landlord to come check on him again, uninvited, and Nym must have known that.

Invite him, then, a tiny voice whispered in his ear, but Oliver ignored it. He washed down his half-hearted meal with another soda, rinsed the dishes, and picked up the trash. He planned on doing some deep cleaning over the coming weekend, but until then, he could at least keep the kitchen tidy. The last thing he needed right now was to worry about roaches and ants in his cupboards. Those things gave him the creeps.

Oliver tied the bag and stepped into the hallway. The trashcans stood by the side of the house, next to a tiny, paved patio that branched off the main pathway, so he exited the front door, leaving it ajar so as not to get locked outside.

Deep shadows lurked between the chestnut oak branches, and the rustling of leaves on the wind from the lake sounded like the whispers of ancient things lamenting ages long gone. Oliver shivered, wishing he'd grabbed a jacket instead of a sweatshirt.

As he rounded the corner of the house, he saw his neighbor, Aurora, smoking on the patio. She wore a short faux fur coat and dark jeans, her free arm wrapped tightly around herself. She nodded when she saw him and blew out a puff of smoke that dissolved in the air against the backdrop of the starry sky.

"Hey." Oliver nodded back. He went over to the large trashcan, opened it, and threw in the bag, which landed with a muffled thud.

A loud growl came from inside, and the pile of garbage bags moved, as if something big and angry was about to come bursting to the surface. Oliver jumped back with an undignified yelp, dropping the lid as if it was hot and nearly falling over in his haste to dodge whatever was about to lunge at him from the bin.

Aurora chuckled, watching him scramble, and took another drag off her cigarette.

"What the hell was that?" Oliver demanded, rounding on her. His heart still raced, further fueled by how ridiculous his reaction must have looked.

"Don't be scared. That's just Amy."

"Amy? You named the Lodge's pet raccoon?"

"A raccoon?" Aurora repeated in her deep throaty voice and laughed. "Oh, sweetie."

She didn't elaborate further. Her eyes burned like the tip of her cigarette, bright and fierce in the feeble glow cast by the front door light, just out of sight.

"Okaaaay, then." Oliver hugged himself tightly and backed off the patio, eying the trashcan nervously. "You have a nice evening."

Aurora inclined her head, and Oliver all but ran inside and shut the front door firmly behind him. Even if Aurora had been messing with him and it had been just a regular old raccoon or even an especially scrappy ally cat, he definitely didn't want it getting inside the house.

Oliver started down the dim hallway, still shivering, but stopped abruptly as a flash of movement in the parlor to his left drew his attention. He halted by the open door and peered inside.

Oliver hadn't had the chance to explore the house yet, aside from the first night's escapades with the water pressure, and so he'd forgotten all about the downstairs parlor. It was originally meant to be used similarly to an old-fashioned hotel lobby, where the guests (or the residents) would spend their evenings reading newspapers by the fire or gossiping over a cup of tea.

He took in the huge unlit fireplace in the corner and the stuffy armchairs arranged around mismatched wood coffee tables. A rolled-up canvas screen hung above the mantelpiece, no doubt used for the Thursday movie nights Sky had told him about. The grayish light of the single table lamp on a console beside the bay window was too dim to completely disperse the deep shadows lurking in the far corners. The lacy curtains rippled with an unseen draft, as if breathing in unison with the house itself.

A man stood by the window, gazing outside, his red velvet house robe worn at the elbows and around the collar. His bare feet peeked from under the hem of the robe, despite the deep cold that made Oliver's own breath come out in little white puffs. Even the hallway upstairs had felt much warmer than this.

"Hello?" Oliver ventured. In the windowpane, a faint reflection of the man's face showed his eyes, dark and unblinking against his pale wrinkled skin. "Sir?"

The man didn't answer. Oliver wasn't sure if he even heard him. Something about him felt off, but Oliver was hard-pressed to pinpoint what exactly.

Oliver stepped further into the room, shivering with the pronounced chill. "Good evening," he tried again. "I'm Oliver, the new tenant. And you are?"

The man turned to him slowly. He appeared to be about seventy or maybe older, his bushy eyebrows framing a narrow, gaunt face. His eyes fixed on Oliver, but his gaze was so vacant that Oliver wondered if he even saw him.

"Who are we, really?" the man intoned gravely. "What are we in the great scheme of things but flower petals floating aimlessly on the winds of time?"

"Uh…"

Oliver hopelessly searched for an answer, but the old man didn't seem to expect it anyway. His visage was vaguely familiar, as if Oliver had glimpsed it before somewhere, but the harder he thought about it, the more slippery the recollection became.

"I must go," the stranger announced in mournful tones. "For what can be more noble than to resign oneself to be bound by love and duty, renouncing the peace of sleeping under the wings of eternity? Farewell, young man. I hope you have a pleasant evening, the lassitude of mortal flesh notwithstanding."

With that, he shuffled past Oliver toward the door, a whiff of frosty air trailing in his wake like the train of a bridal gown.

"What?" Oliver frowned, his tired brain vainly trying to make sense of it all. His gaze fell on the window where the man had been standing, and suddenly he understood what had bothered him at the sight. It was freezing, and yet the old man's breath hadn't fogged the glass.

He stared at the window for a long moment, his heart thumping dully, and then ran out of the room.

"Hey!" he called, but the hallway was empty. There was no sign of the old man anywhere. Oliver hadn't heard the front door open and shut, or the rickety stairs creak under bare feet. There was nowhere the man could have gone to, unless…

The door across the hallway was closed, but logic dictated this was the only place anyone could have slipped off to unnoticed. Glancing nervously to the sides, Oliver crossed the hallway and gingerly tried the brass handle.

He was half expecting the door to be locked, but the door swung soundlessly inward, revealing a darkened room beyond. Oliver strained to see into the gloom, but nothing seemed to be moving. He could see the outline of a marble fireplace, a twin for the one in the drawing room, and the vague shapes of furniture. The air was stuffy, as if the room hadn't been opened in a while.

"Hello?" Oliver called, but nothing and no one stirred in response.

Where was that strange old man? He had to be hiding here somewhere, unless—

Oliver didn't finish the thought. He felt for a switch on the wall and flipped it on, flooding the room with a sickly yellow light.

The layout of the room was nearly identical to the large parlor across the hall, its tall windows overlooking the other side of the garden. The tightly drawn heavy velvet drapes on the front bay window cut off all outside illumination. However, instead of yet another drawing room, Oliver had stepped into what he could only describe as a cross between a specialty antique shop and a museum.

No, a mausoleum.

A huge, almost life-size full-body portrait hung above the fireplace, depicting an elderly woman in a forest-green gown from the turn of the previous century, her graying hair arranged in a crown of braids around her head. The brass plaque on the bottom of the frame read *Despina Alma Shaw*.

This must be the great-great grandaunt Nym had been talking about. Oliver could definitely see the familial resemblance in the curve of their eyebrows and the set of their jaws, though, of course, Despina's face was much more refined.

She smiled serenely, but the gleam in her eyes, evident even in an oil painting, belied the benevolence in her expression. The effect was further intensified by the toothy scowl of a human skull upon which she lightly rested her hand. Its empty eye sockets seemed to follow Oliver's movements as he paused in front of the mantelpiece. Half a dozen silver urns lined the marble shelf, with something that looked like a name etched on each one, though Oliver was leery of going any closer to inspect them and find out.

Instead, he took a few more steps into the room, taking everything in. Floor-to-ceiling shelves lined the rest of the walls, containing an assortment of knickknacks, books, and curios. He expected to find a thick layer of dust and cobwebs covering everything, but it seemed this room, like the rest of the house, had been subjected to regular cleaning.

Framed maps and landscape photographs, all at least a hundred years old or more by the look of them, hung in the spaces between the bookcases. Oliver didn't recognize any of the places they depicted, and characters and letters he'd never seen before marked some of the maps. In the middle of the room, several display cases held a selection of antique jewelry, glass vials, and what looked like ceremonial daggers. There were cards, sketches, figurines, seashells, and animal bones, all piled together with no apparent rhyme or reason. Oliver couldn't tell if it all had any historical or monetary value, or if it was merely a collection of junk.

He wasn't entirely surprised to discover that the old man was nowhere to be seen. The feeling of wrongness, which had been slowly building since the first moment he'd set foot in Lakeside Lodge, ratcheted to an alarming level.

He bent over one of the display cases, peering through the murky glass at a pair of porcelain miniatures that seemed to feature either dog or wolf heads with unnervingly human eyes. Were those supposed to be portraits? Why would anyone do a portrait of a wolf as if it were human? And if they weren't wolves—

"What are you doing?"

Oliver jumped a foot in the air.

At least, that was what it felt like. He wheeled round, his heart racing so fast it should have been somewhere halfway across the lake by now, and found himself staring at Nym's chest. It was a manly chest, without a doubt, but the situation was starting to grow old.

"Jesus! You scared the crap out of me," he said, not bothering to hide his annoyance. To be fair, his nerves had been more than a little frayed already, and Nym hadn't been purposefully trying to give him a heart attack, but the result was still the same. He realized he had his hand on the glass case and let it go as if burned, then crossed his arms across his chest defensively.

"Sorry," Nym said, sounding anything but apologetic, and then repeated: "What are you doing here?"

He wore a simple black T-shirt that stretched enticingly across his broad shoulders, and a tool belt around his hips. If it wasn't for the suspicious scowl etched into his features, he'd have looked like the September issue of a sexy construction workers calendar. But, sexy or not, he had no right to question Oliver in that tone. It wasn't as if he'd been warned that some areas of the building were restricted—and why would they be? It was an old townhouse in one of the largest cities in the US, not some Gothic castle in the middle of the haunted English moors. If Nym wanted to hide his potential Bluebeard-like proclivities, he shouldn't have advertised a vacancy.

Unless, of course, as a way to lure in an unsuspecting victim.

Don't be ridiculous. Just a few days ago you invited him over for pizza after he'd helped you move in your stuff, and now you're ready to believe he's a serial killer simply because he has a roomful of oddities?

"Not that it's any of your business," Oliver said, drawing himself up to his full height, "but I was following someone who came in here just a minute ago."

Nym frowned and looked around. "Who?"

"I don't know. Some old guy. I saw him in the parlor, and after I tried talking to him, he just up and left. I don't think he was entirely…" Oliver made a vague gesture. "…right. If you know what I mean. He wasn't wearing any shoes, and…"

He trailed off under Nym's inscrutable gaze. For a moment, he was sure Nym was going to mock him or, worse, call him a liar because no disoriented elder gentlemen seemed to be loitering inside at the moment.

But Nym sighed heavily. "That's Horace Livingstone. He wanders around here sometimes, but he's harmless. Don't worry about him."

The answer wasn't at all what Oliver expected, and it gave him pause.

"Does he live in Lakeside Lodge?" he asked, though it was unlikely, considering the number of apartments. He and Nym had the first floor, while Sky, Aurora, and Kimona occupied the second. Rafe apparently rented the single bedroom in the east turret. That left the parlor and the basement—which Oliver wasn't sure was actually livable—and this room, whatever it was.

"No," Nym said curtly. "He doesn't."

"Shouldn't we find him, then, and get him home? Or call someone, his family perhaps, who can come for him? He clearly needs help."

"He can take care of himself, trust me. He comes and goes on his own."

Oliver frowned, matching the landlord's expression.

"What's the point of locking the front door and making such a hassle of the mail and deliveries if you just let random people roam about the place?"

"Livingstone isn't a random person," Nym said. "He used to be a tenant here not too long ago. He's...a bit confused, that's all."

Oliver wasn't satisfied with the explanation, but he had the feeling it was all he was going to get. The old man didn't look dangerous, and yet... Should he tell Nym about the lack of condensation on the window glass or Livingstone's strange ramblings? He hesitated, but finally decided against it. Most likely, Nym would dismiss all of that as his imaginings anyway.

"All this belonged to your grandaunt?" he asked, nodding to the shelves. As far as he'd been able to see, a lot of the books were in foreign languages, but most of those in English dealt with magic, spiritualism, and the history of the occult. Considering the milieu, it was hardly surprising.

"It's all the stuff she'd collected over the years," Nym said. "Things she'd brought from her travels, things the tenants who'd lived here bequeathed her."

Bequeathed? What did that even mean? Had this Despina Shaw lady been running some sort of cult, with the members signing off their earthly possessions to her? That was how these things usually worked, wasn't it?

That would explain so much too. The strange, oppressive atmosphere of the house, the suspiciously low rent, the bizarre attitude of the tenants. Even this (for lack of a better word) shrine to the guru and founder—it all pointed to a sinister kind of purpose, meant to lure and entrap impressionable, vulnerable people with the lure of mysticism.

And yet, he had trouble reconciling Brown's image with that of either a shrewd con man or a religious zealot. If anything, he seemed more down-to-earth than most people Oliver had met. He'd never once mentioned anything remotely related to a divine purpose, or the glorious afterlife, or preparing for the apocalypse, or whatever nonsense cultists and secret society leaders used to entrap desperate people. But, wild speculation aside, it was clear there was *something* going on in Lakeside Lodge, and Oliver had to tread with caution until he found out exactly what it was.

"Well, then," he said, trying to sound as nonchalant as possible. "Since you seem to be on good terms with him, could you make sure old Mr. Livingstone gets home safely? I know you told me not to worry about him, but he seemed a little out of touch. I'd hate for something to happen to him."

"Sure. I promise to check up on him," Nym said.

"Great. Thank you. Um, good night." He made a move toward the door, but Nym didn't budge, still blocking the way.

For one awful moment, Oliver was sure Nym wasn't going to let him out. His mind short-circuited, snapping back to that feeling of fear and helplessness, of being forced to cower before someone bigger and stronger and cruel. His ribs twinged in half-forgotten pain, and he clenched his fists to stop himself from shaking. Up until this very moment, he hadn't seriously considered Nym a threat, but now... Now he couldn't help thinking he might have made a crucial error in judgment.

"Can I go now?" Oliver gritted out, hating the way his voice trembled.

They stared at each other, only inches separating them, the stale air suddenly crackling with tension.

Nym started to say something, then apparently changed his mind and simply stepped back, letting Oliver pass. Oliver dashed out of the room, making a quick, graceless escape into the hallway.

"Good night, Oliver," Nym called after him, but Oliver didn't stop until he'd slammed the door of his apartment behind him and thrown on the chain.

Chapter Seven

"I'm telling you, there's something going on around here," Oliver told Pam while pouring himself his coffee the next morning. "Like, something seriously wrong."

He was lucky Pam was a morning person through and through, otherwise he wouldn't have gotten away with acting paranoid so early in the day.

"Okay, but wrong how?" Pam was jogging with her earpiece, her breathing labored and loud. "Like, 'bodies buried in the back yard' kind of wrong, or 'the landlord is about to burn the house down with everybody in it to collect insurance' kind of wrong?"

"I don't know." Oliver went over to the window, sipping his coffee. Rain clouds were gathering over the lake, and the wind seemed to be draining the world of color. "Both, maybe. Or neither."

"On Saturday, you texted me about how this Nym guy was being all nice to you," Pam said. "Now he's Ted Bundy? What happened?"

"Ted Bundy *was* nice," Oliver pointed out. "The neighbors always say how ordinary and nonthreatening someone had seemed after the police recover human remains from their basement."

There definitely were human remains in those fancy urns on the mantelpiece in the mausoleum, albeit (he hoped) in the form of ashes. Perhaps one of those even held what was left of the famous Despina Shaw. Oliver shuddered involuntarily.

"It's a really old house," Pam said. "Turn of the century, right? It's bound to have some history, and probably not all of it is pretty. It doesn't mean there's something shady going on there now. And lots of people keep their family members' old junk like heirlooms."

"You weren't there," Oliver said, recalling the stuffy, ominous vibe of the makeshift shrine to Mrs. Shaw. "It was creepy. Maybe it'll sound like a cliché, but it was exactly what you'd imagine finding inside when you look at the house. All that was missing were bats and skeletons."

"Have you checked your closet?"

"Thanks. That'll make me sleep so much better."

"Please don't take this the wrong way," Pam said gently, "but you do tend to overreact. Especially after everything that's happened with Jake. I'm not saying you have no reason to be concerned, but you might be making more out of this than there is."

Oliver would've bristled at the remark had it came from someone else, but Pam knew him better than anyone, and she was right. He did have a tendency to spiral, his overactive imagination fueling his anxiety.

"I guess we'll see." He finished his coffee and glanced at his watch. "I have to go now, or I'll be late for work."

"How is work?" Pam asked. The dull thumping of her footsteps indicated she'd returned home and was taking the stairs up to her apartment instead of the elevator. "You were so busy telling me about your adventures in Bly Manor you barely mentioned it."

"It's okay. I guess."

"You guess?"

Oliver didn't know what to say to that. He hated to sound judgmental or ungrateful. This mentorship was an opportunity few people got to have, not to mention all the expense his parents had taken on to pay for both his education and this move. In any case, two days was too short a time to get a real sense of a workplace, especially one so dynamic. Thompson Design wouldn't be as successful if they were truly awful, would they?

"I actually have an important meeting with a client this morning," he said, though it didn't answer Pam's question in any way.

Pam whooped. "Look at Mister Bigshot there! Well, good luck. Tell me all about it afterward. That is, if you don't end up chained up in the attic with the crazy ex-wife."

"Ha. Ha. Ha," Oliver said. "Talk to you later."

"Sure will. And Oliver? Joking aside, be careful out there."

"Wow, these look great," Ela said later that morning when Oliver showed her the printouts of his alterations to the lobby design.

"You think so?"

"Yeah." Ela scanned the prints. "That's a clever storage solution, and it won't affect the overall look too much. You did a great job, Oliver."

Oliver couldn't help but preen a little at the praise. He didn't get the chance to bask in it, though, as Mr. Thompson swooped past them, inviting the team to the meeting with his usual brusqueness. Mr. Cox showed up at the office a minute later and, after a round of polite greetings, headed for the conference room.

"Owen, coffee," Thompson threw to his assistant, who trailed after him. "You remember the way Richard takes it, yes?"

Owen glanced at Mr. Cox and nodded. "Yes, sir. Right away."

He scrambled to make coffee while the others piled into the conference room. Oliver grabbed his prints and followed Ela inside, where Serena and Ethan, another junior architect, were setting everything up.

Finally, they were all seated, and Thompson took his place at the head of the table, with Cox on his right side. Owen brought in their coffee, fussing a little over the arrangement of the cups until Thompson waved him away impatiently.

"Let's go over the floor plans. We've addressed all the concerns you raised yesterday, so I think you'll be pleased with them, Richard," Thompson said.

Cox nodded. "I trust your team, Colin. Run me through it one more time, please."

At Thompson's signal, Ela launched into an overview of the design and all the alterations that had been made at Cox's request. He listened carefully, occasionally asking for clarifications.

From what he'd seen of Cox so far, Oliver got the impression of a savvy businessman. Perhaps a little too savvy when weighing the potential residents' comforts against his bottom line, but certainly practical. Short and to the point, but not self-importantly obnoxious like Thompson. He asked intelligent questions and made sensible suggestions without antagonizing the people who worked for him, which spoke of qualities Oliver could respect.

"Looks good to me," Cox said after they were done. "How are the permits coming along?"

"Oliver is handling those," Ela said, gesturing to him. "They're all underway, and we don't expect there'll be any problems so long as the infrastructure demands are met."

Cox's gaze swung to Oliver. It had a calculating, appraising quality, and once again, Oliver had the feeling that Cox knew exactly who he was.

"I'm glad to hear it." The developer inclined his head.

"Excellent, excellent," Thompson said, clasping his hands. "Now, if there's nothing else…"

Ela shot an expressive look at Oliver and nodded forcibly at Cox.

Oliver swallowed. Recalling the dressing down Serena had gotten in a similar situation, he wasn't at all sure he wanted to stick his neck out, especially as he'd already gotten on Thompson's bad side by going on sick leave. But then, if he didn't try pitching his work when he had the opportunity to do so, he would never get anywhere in this profession. If he wanted to make an impression, he'd hardly do so by spending all his time quietly filing for permits.

"Actually, there is something I wanted to suggest," he said before Thompson could adjourn the meeting. His mouth felt dry, but he made himself press on. "I've been thinking about introducing some minor changes to the layout of the communal lobby to make it more useful for families. I've noticed there's this large unused space at the back. If we add walls here and here—" Oliver tapped on the renderings. "—we could turn this into a storage room for strollers and bicycles. Maybe even add built-in stands and wall fixtures. A lot of new buildings have those, and it's something people will look for. The cost will be minimal, but it could potentially add value to the rental units."

He looked over the room. His teammates—Serena, Ethan, and AJ—examined the renderings with various degrees of interest. Ela gave him a discreet thumbs-up, and Cox studied the plan with a thoughtful expression. However, Thompson immediately shook his head.

"This is way too late in the game to introduce these kinds of changes to the design. Adding walls and whatnot—it would all require a new round of approvals with the city planning department, and this is time we cannot afford to waste. Perhaps next time, you can submit your suggestions in an orderly manner like everyone else instead of lounging at home while your teammates are actually doing something."

Oliver bit his lip. He could feel everyone's gazes on him, even as he sat down and dropped his eyes to the shiny surface of the meeting table, his face flushing.

"Mr. Thompson—" Ela began, reproach coloring her voice, but he cut her off.

"This is pointless, Ela. If Daniel here can't take valid criticism and do better, then maybe he's in the wrong place. He's not here to have his precious feelings coddled, he's here to work—which, by the way, I'm still not sure he's able to do." Thompson tapped his fingertips on the table impatiently. "We will proceed as planned. Richard?"

"I agree in that I don't want to cause any more delays to the project," Cox concurred, even though he sounded apologetic.

"Ela, darling, you're responsible for finalizing the paperwork. I want a progress report on my desk tomorrow." Thompson pushed his chair back and stood up. His assistant, Owen, tapped hastily on the iPad he was holding and all but jumped when his boss motioned for him to follow.

The rest of the team began to disperse in embarrassed silence. Even Serena threw Oliver a commiserating look before going out. Ela looked like she was going to say something, but Cox, who also stood up and finished adjusting his jacket, forestalled her.

"May I have a word with Oliver, in private?"

"Of course, Mr. Cox. I'll be outside if you have any further questions." She exited the room, leaving Oliver and Cox alone.

Oliver, about to gather the renderings still laid out on the table, inhaled surreptitiously, bracing himself. In truth, he was a little surprised Cox remembered his correct name. Would he reprimand him too? If so, he had a lot more tact than Thompson, but Oliver hardly needed another scolding, however delicately delivered.

"I wanted to let you know that I like your idea," Cox said. "If it weren't for the time constraints on this project, I'd say go for it."

"Really?" Oliver frowned.

Why didn't you say something in front of Thompson? The thought flashed through his mind, but he didn't voice the sentiment. He might be a rookie, but he knew better than to antagonize a major client by acting petulantly.

"Yes. In fact, I'd like to implement your design in my next development, if I win the tender with the city."

"Do you always work with Thompson and Associates?" Oliver asked, curious despite the earlier mortification.

"Not always, but they're my architects of choice on most of my enterprises," Cox said. "Colin can be…abrasive, but he runs a tight ship, and he knows how to deliver a product."

Oliver made a noncommittal sound he hoped resembled assent.

There was a short pause. Cox studied him with an expression Oliver couldn't decipher. He shifted uncomfortably on his feet under the scrutiny.

"You live in that old house on Druid Lake," Cox said abruptly. "Lakeside Lodge, I think it's called. Or something like that. Is that right?"

Oliver's skin prickled. Cox couldn't possibly have known that unless he'd spotted Oliver at his window that first night. And if he had, he knew Oliver had been listening in on his conversation with Nym Brown. His question was too specific and straightforward to doubt that, and it explained the spark of recognition in his eyes when he saw Oliver at the office the first time.

"I…yes." Oliver had hesitated too long before answering, and it seemed silly to hedge now.

Cox nodded with a satisfied smirk.

"How's that for a lucky coincidence?" he murmured. "Fortunately, I believe in luck."

Oliver was at a loss as to how to respond. Cox crossed his arms over his chest and casually propped his hip against the edge of the table.

"I'm sure you've already realized I'm interested in purchasing the property," he said in a conversational tone.

Oliver cleared his throat. "Um…yes. I'm not sure why though. I don't think it's worth much, to be honest."

Cox regarded him thoughtfully. "It appears the owner values it very much since he's refused all my offers—which have been extremely generous. Why do you think that is?"

Oliver's mind flashed to the mausoleum, with its exhibit cases full of dead things and maps of uncharted places.

"I'm sure he has his reasons," he said.

"Indeed." Cox watched him closely, so closely that for one uncomfortable moment, Oliver was sure he could sense the traces of the fear he'd felt last night. "But I believe you can help me."

"How?" Oliver asked.

Cox fished a business card out of the inner pocket of his jacket and handed it to Oliver, who took it gingerly.

"Here's my number. I might have a proposition for you, one that could be beneficial to both of us. A strictly real-estate related proposition," he added with an amused smile, catching Oliver's expression. "We can discuss it over dinner tonight. Say seven o'clock, at Cosima?"

Oliver hesitated, still holding the card. Would it be a smart move to accept the invitation, not knowing exactly what it was

Cox wanted to talk about? Especially considering Cox was a client? But then, what would it hurt to hear him out? So far, Cox had been nothing but polite and appreciative, which Oliver couldn't say about either Thompson or Nym. If he had an idea he wanted to discuss, Oliver could at least extend him the courtesy of a meeting.

"Yeah, okay."

"Excellent. See you there, Oliver." Cox flashed him another smile and strode out of the room, leaving Oliver staring at his drawings in puzzled silence.

Cosima looked like the sort of place Oliver's parents would have chosen to celebrate a birthday or an anniversary. Upscale in an unassuming way, the restaurant was set inside a former cotton mill, complete with an outdoor patio tastefully decorated with black-and-white streamers as a nod to the upcoming holiday. Oliver was relieved to find Cox already waiting for him inside when he arrived at the restaurant at five to seven, since the evening was too crisp to dine outside.

Despite having agreed to meet Cox, Oliver had been tempted to call him and cancel. He'd picked up the phone at least three times throughout the day but every time found some excuse to put it down.

It was just a casual meeting, he told himself as the waiter showed him to Cox's table. If he didn't like what the developer had to say to him, he could always leave.

Richard Cox waited for him at a table in the corner, right next to a tall window, sipping whiskey. He smiled at Oliver as he approached and gestured for him to be seated.

"I hope you didn't have trouble finding the place," Cox said pleasantly after the waiter placed their menus in front of them and withdrew. "I knew you're new to Baltimore."

"It was no trouble," Oliver said. "It's actually very close to where I live."

"Yes. The infamous Lakeside Lodge." Cox's smile became toothy. "How are you liking your accommodations so far, Oliver?"

"It could be worse, I suppose." Oliver picked up the menu. The food—or at least the description of it—looked good enough to make his mouth water. The smells wafting from the nearby tables only exacerbated his hunger. He had a soft spot for Italian cuisine, and he suspected this was as good an offering as he'd find in Baltimore, if the prices were anything to go by.

"My treat, of course," said Cox, watching him carefully.

"Thank you." Oliver put down the menu and met Cox's eyes. "But I still don't know to what I owe the pleasure."

"Allow me to explain, then. But it's better done over a full plate." Cox gestured to the waiter, who seemed to materialize by their side. "I'll have the *bistecca alla Fiorentina* with a glass of Pipoli."

The waiter wrote it down on his pad, complimenting Cox's choices, and gazed expectantly at Oliver.

"I, um…" Oliver hastily picked up the menu. "I'll have the swordfish with the mushroom risotto."

The waiter dutifully wrote it down. "Anything to drink, sir?"

"Monument City beer."

True to his word about discussing serious matters over food, Cox made polite chitchat until their entrees arrived, asking Oliver about his studies and qualifications and inquiring how he was liking Baltimore so far. He even looked appropriately sympathetic when Oliver told him he'd been too sick to explore the city.

The food smelled delicious and tasted equally as good. Oliver, who hadn't eaten anything since another one of his coffee-and-donut breakfasts, had to force himself to take little bites of his fish and risotto instead of wolfing them down.

"So what is it that you think I can do for you?" Oliver asked after taking a sip of his beer.

"Not wasting any time, I see." Cox's lips twitched. "Fair enough. As I've told you already, I want to buy the house from Brown. The area around Druid Lake has been undergoing a change in recent years, slowly becoming more affluent and desirable to families and young professionals who work in the city center. I'm sure you've noticed Lakeside Lodge sits on an extensive piece of property that could be appropriated for a much larger building, an entire complex of luxury apartments overlooking the lake and the park. It's a lucrative opportunity, one that would benefit a lot of people and answer a growing demand for accommodations in the neighborhood. And the Lodge itself, while charmingly offbeat... Well, let's just say it's had its day."

While Oliver had suspected the developer's intentions ran along those lines, the idea, uttered with such practical casualness, gave him a surprisingly unpleasant jolt.

"You want to tear it down completely?"

"I'm afraid it's the only choice."

"I'm not so sure about that," Oliver said.

Cox put down his cutlery, folded his arms on the table, and leaned toward Oliver.

"You've stayed at that house for over a week now," he said. "What do you think of it?"

There was a lot Oliver could say about Lakeside Lodge, but Cox wasn't Pam, and he didn't feel comfortable conveying his impressions to the man.

"It's...unique," he offered finally.

"But not in any good way," Cox said.

"What do you mean?" Oliver frowned.

Cox leaned forward even more. "You're telling me that in all the time you've lived there, you haven't felt or seen or heard anything strange? Anything out of the ordinary? Anything that would give you cause for worry, even fear?"

Oliver took a hurried swig of his beer to hide his dismay. Mysterious singing coming from nowhere and no one, wandering old men who didn't appear to be drawing breath, apparitions in mirrors—yes, one could say these were all out of the ordinary. But how could Cox possibly know all that? Even if he wasn't familiar with the specifics, how could he have guessed that Oliver had experienced things that had left him unsettled?

"It's an old house," he said, echoing Pam's sentiments on the matter. "It can be odd sometimes."

Cox shook his head. "It's more than that, and I think you know it too. There's something not right with the place. Something downright evil."

"You can't be seriously suggesting Lakeside Lodge is haunted?"

"Haunted? No, of course not. But a place doesn't have to be full of imaginary chain-rattling ghosts to be dangerous."

Oliver had the weirdest urge to disagree on the "dangerous" part. Which was silly, considering he'd had his own lapse into fanciful imaginings regarding Nym and the Lodge. But hearing Cox describe the place as evil made the notion seem that much more absurd.

He shook his head. "I still don't understand how you think I can help."

Cox smiled faintly as he absently stroked the stem of his wine glass.

"You are, in fact, in a unique position to help. You live in that house, and you're an architect. There's no other person with better qualifications to identify certain…let's say, structural deficiencies which might render the building unlivable."

"You mean code violations."

"In a nutshell, yes."

"You want me to spy for you," Oliver said slowly.

Cox steepled his fingers. "Again, in a nutshell. But 'spy' is a harsh term, don't you think? After all, I don't want to ask you to engage in subterfuge or, God forbid, sabotage. I merely want you to gather all the information you can about the condition of the property. If it is indeed in such poor upkeep as I suspect, you would be doing a good thing by helping me shut the place down."

"And if the city decides to condemn it based on your report, you'd be able to force Mr. Brown to sell—for way cheaper than it's worth," Oliver finished tersely.

"If the building is unsafe, then it's unsafe." Cox shrugged. "That's hardly on me, is it? I've been nothing but fair to Brown, and he could have made a very sweet deal. He could've had all the money he needed to open a new B and B, or whatever business he chose, somewhere else. But, unfortunately, he's not smart enough to know when to cut his losses. You, on the other hand, strike me as a very reasonable, intelligent person. Just the kind of person, in fact, whom I'd want to see as the lead architect of my next condominium."

Chapter Eight

Oliver parked his car in his usual spot in the lot on the street corner but didn't get out. Soft rain rapped on the windshield and ran down in tiny rivulets, blurring the view of the other cars and nearby buildings. He sat unmoving, his hands still on the wheel, and tried to make sense of everything.

He hadn't accepted Cox's offer to be his eyes and ears at Lakeside Lodge, but he hadn't outright rejected it either, asking instead for a few days to consider. On the face of it, it all sounded straightforward and aboveboard—keep your eyes peeled and report back everything that would prove the house wasn't fit for human habitation. And the reward Cox had promised... To be specifically asked to lead a big project by one of the firm's major clients would be a huge coup for a newbie like Oliver. This opportunity could set his entire career in motion on an upward trajectory. He could spend years waiting for a break like this, and considering Thompson's dismissive attitude toward him, it was unlikely to happen even if he worked his tail off for the foreseeable future.

Simply put, this offer was too good to refuse.

On the other hand... Yeah, it felt like a shitty thing to do. Regardless of what he thought about Brown, he'd be no better than a snitch. Oh, Cox could justify it all he wanted, but the gist of his request didn't sit well with Oliver, even though, technically, there was nothing illegal or morally reprehensible in it. It was just...yeah, shitty.

Oliver sighed and rested his forehead on the wheel for a few moments. He could talk to Pam, but this wasn't like asking for advice on his Halloween costume. This was sensitive, and Oliver had no right to place the responsibility for his ethical behavior on someone else. The main reason he'd moved to Baltimore was to prove he could make it on his own. That he was an adult, a creative professional with a well-defined plan, not about to let anything or anyone dictate his actions or control his wellbeing ever again. He couldn't fool himself into being that put-together person if he ran to his best friend or his parents for help every time life presented him with a challenging decision.

He should know. He'd made these kinds of decisions before. So why was this one so difficult?

Oliver exhaled noisily and got out of the car. He knew which way he leaned toward on the matter, but he didn't have to give his answer right away. There was still time for him to investigate, to try to understand what was going on behind Lakeside Lodge's shabby facade. And if it was as sinister as he suspected and as Cox had implied...then at least he'd know what to do.

Despite Oliver's best intentions, he didn't have time to do much in the next two days. Finalizing the plans for the Potomac Street housing complex meant his team was swamped with work, putting in a lot of overtime. On Wednesday, he returned home so late he only had the energy left to brush his teeth and crawl into bed, falling asleep immediately and waking up after what felt like only five minutes.

He finished work at a normal hour on Thursday, but the cumulative fatigue of stress and aftermath of illness had him dragging his feet and wishing for a hot greasy dinner when he came home that evening. A din of voices and laughter greeted Oliver as he entered the front door to Lakeside Lodge. Curious, he peered inside the parlor, where Sky busily arranged bowls of popcorn and plates of cookies on the side tables. The other neighbors lounged in the armchairs placed in a semicircle around the spread, facing the screen Nym was unfolding above the fireplace, where a cozy fire crackled, exuding comfortable warmth.

Right. Thursday communal movie night. Oliver had almost forgotten about that.

"Oh, hey!" Sky exclaimed when she glanced up and saw Oliver dawdling on the threshold. "Oliver, come in, join us."

With all eyes in the room suddenly fixed on him, Oliver shifted uncomfortably.

"I...I just got home, and I'm a little tired. I think I'll just turn in."

"Nonsense! It's only six o'clock, and I baked chocolate chip cookies. They're your favorite." Again, this didn't come off as a question. "Come on. As the newest addition, you can choose the movie."

"Yes, do come in," Rafe drawled. "Let us get to know you better."

He sprawled in a red velvet armchair, one leg draped over the hand rest, looking for all the world like an indolent prince in an edgy young-adult movie. He was certainly handsome enough to star in one, with his bedroom eyes and cheekbones so sharp they could probably cut glass.

The tips of Oliver's ears burned. Rafe gazed at him as if he was undressing him with his eyes and liking what he saw. Oliver had rarely been regarded with such appreciation even when he *had* been naked and intimate.

Instinctively, he glanced at Nym. The landlord had paused in the middle of adjusting the projector and was now looking between Oliver and Rafe. His frown deepened, turning into a scowl, and he lowered his eyes, pretending to tinker with the projector.

Was Nym upset by Rafe's flirting or by the possibility of Oliver intruding on their little get-together? He hadn't spoken with the landlord since that scary night in the memorial room across the hall, and now he wasn't sure where things stood between them. No more friendly visits seemed to be forthcoming, that was for sure.

Maybe he should stay, if only to observe his neighbors, perhaps even to establish a connection. If he were to discover the secrets of Lakeside Lodge (at least, where its living inhabitants were concerned), he wouldn't accomplish it by hiding in his bedroom and refusing to talk to anyone.

"Okay."

Oliver sank into an empty armchair and put his bag on the floor next to his feet. Kimona, in a chair on his left, nodded her greeting. She wore baggy jeans with a black silk button-down, her long hair pulled back into a sleek ponytail. Oliver nodded back at her, and then at Aurora, who stared at him unblinkingly across the arrangement of refreshment tables. He shifted in his seat and turned his attention to the screen.

"What are you guys watching?" he asked.

"Since it's Halloween season, we are on a classic horror roll," Sky explained.

"Last week, it was *The Masque of the Red Death*," Rafe chimed in.

"We were thinking either *The Haunted Palace* or *The Pit and the Pendulum* this time." Sky brandished a USB drive in the shape of a panda.

"Oh, I love Vincent Price!" Oliver perked up despite himself. "The Pit is one of my favorites."

"For real?" Aurora quirked an eyebrow, clearly amused at his admission.

"In case you haven't noticed, I'm kind of a nerd," Oliver said, pushing his eyeglasses up his nose.

Sky laughed, and Aurora chuckled. Even Kimona smiled. Rafe hastened to assure him he was the cutest nerd ever.

"Are we gonna watch it or not?" Nym all but growled.

Rafe rolled his eyes, and Sky plugged the drive into the projector and selected the movie. They all settled into their chairs, and Nym took a seat between Rafe and Oliver after dimming the lights.

As the opening credits rolled to ominous music, Oliver surreptitiously studied the rest of the party. Everybody seemed relaxed, their attention riveted to the screen as unsuspecting Francis arrived at his brother-in-law's forbidding castle. Even Rafe was engrossed in the movie, foregoing his earlier attempts at making eyes at Oliver, his posture as languid as a cat's. Nym, on the other hand, sat straight and rigid in his chair, his jaw set firmly.

They sat at least two feet apart, but Oliver grew increasingly aware of the other man's presence, as if the heat of Nym's body radiated enough to envelop him. Oliver felt the strangest urge to reach out in response and take Nym's hand into his.

It was ridiculous, of course. They weren't on a date, and after Oliver's escapade in the memorial room, they weren't even friends. They certainly wouldn't be on good terms if Nym ever found out Cox had asked Oliver to spy on him. But he couldn't help imagining, for one brief moment, how Nym's hands, rough and calloused, would feel sliding over his naked skin.

Appalled at himself for this unbidden flash of fantasy, Oliver shifted in his seat to hide his body's involuntary reaction and his discomfort. He really should quit lusting after men who were bad for him. Not only bad, but also, in this case, clearly disinterested.

As if in answer to Oliver's wayward thoughts, Nym turned his head in his direction. His nostrils flared, as if he were sniffing the air, and then his eyes, dark and intense, met Oliver's.

Awareness zapped between them. Oliver's breath hitched as he watched Nym's lips part. With all that dark stubble and the prominent eyebrows, he never noticed how beautiful Nym's lips were, the lower one full and entirely kissable. Despite Oliver's earlier self-admonitions, his jeans grew even tighter. He just hoped that no one paid him enough attention to notice his embarrassing condition.

Well, except Nym. He had no doubt the landlord had noticed. Hell, he acted as if he could *smell* Oliver's arousal. Their eyes were still locked, Nym's gaze pulling Oliver with irresistible force. He flushed, gripping the armrests as if to keep himself from leaning toward the other man.

"Adulterer!" Price screeched on film, wielding a red-hot poker, and Oliver started. Sky squawked in horrified delight, and Aurora took her hand, squeezing it in reassurance.

His gaze dropped to his own hand, white-knuckled, clutching the armrest, his heart pounding. When he raised his eyes, Nym had already turned away, facing the screen. The tension, so palpable before, was gone, burst like a soap bubble on the wind.

Disappointment washed over him, every bit as bitter as it was pointless. Clearly, Nym wanted nothing to do with him, and Oliver was letting his fervid imagination run unchecked yet again.

He folded his arms across his chest, sinking deeper into the plush armchair, and watched the rest of the movie in silence, his enjoyment dampened by chagrin.

"That poor woman!" Sky exclaimed when the ending credits started to roll and Nym got up again to turn on the lights. Oliver flinched at the sudden illumination, though it could hardly be called bright.

"She got what she deserved." Rafe yawned and stretched, his lean muscles rippling under his navy Henley. The casualness of the gesture was somewhat spoiled by a pointed glance in Oliver's direction, which Oliver pretended not to notice.

"How can you say that! No one deserves being buried alive," Sky chided.

Kimona signed something, and Aurora nodded in agreement. "Yes, exactly."

Oliver made a mental note to watch some YouTube videos on ASL so he could understand her with the same ease, while Sky shook her head at all of them, clearly displeased with her friends' apparent callousness.

"What do you think, Oliver?" she asked him.

Oliver shrugged. "I mostly just like how campy the acting is. Though that petrified corpse scene terrified me as a child."

Nym muttered something that sounded like "silly" as he got up to dismantle the projector and the screen.

Resentment flared, fueled in no small part by frustration. All of a sudden, Oliver was sick of people being snide and condescending to him—Mr. Thompson, Mr. Cox, Jake, and now Nym. He itched to say something cutting and storm off, but that would only look petty and childish, and he knew he'd regret it in retrospect. He wasn't a child anymore; he was a smart, capable professional, and he would act accordingly, no matter how much the landlord's dismissive attitude rankled.

He swallowed the caustic remark that hovered on the tip of his tongue and helped Sky gather the mostly empty dishes.

"We usually hang out longer on Thursdays," she said apologetically, "but Rafe has to work today."

"Yep," Rafe confirmed, though he didn't seem too cut up about it.

"Where do you work?" Oliver asked. "I haven't seen you leave in the mornings."

"I'm a nurse at Johns Hopkins."

If Oliver had been given a thousand tries, he'd never have guessed Rafe's occupation.

"You're a nurse?" he repeated, his disbelief clear in his tone.

Rafe laughed, his teeth flashing an impossible shade of white.

"Some of my patients have the same reaction," he said with a wink. "But yes. Scrubs and everything. I work night shifts, so I'm usually getting my beauty sleep during the day."

Oliver had a very hard time picturing Rafe in hospital scrubs (though the man would surely look good in anything). He didn't say anything, however.

"Well, I have to run," Rafe said. "See all you guys and gals later."

He threw Oliver one last look which couldn't be classified as anything other than sultry and sauntered into the hallway with a wiggle of his elegant fingers.

"I think he likes you," Sky said with whisper loud enough to have been heard all the way to the roof.

On the edge of Oliver's vision, Kimona rolled her eyes, took out her phone, and typed something before holding it aloft.

Rafe likes everybody, a robotic female voice of the text-to-speech app announced.

"Yeah, remember he tried to hit on me when we first moved in?" Aurora chuckled. "That was so funny."

"That doesn't mean he and Oliver couldn't have a good time together," Sky said, a bit defensively. "They'd make a beautiful couple, and Rafe can be terribly romantic."

Oliver supposed he shouldn't be surprised at his neighbors making sweeping assumptions about his sexuality without asking him first. If anything, he waited for Nym to make some kind of observation, but he remained silent, taking an exceptionally long time to roll up the screen as if using it as an excuse to listen in on their conversation. His back was turned, so Oliver couldn't tell whether it amused or vexed him.

Sure, he can be romantic. For about ten minutes. The guy has the attention span of a fly when it comes to hookups. Kimona looked at Oliver. *Unless it's your thing.*

"It's not," Oliver hastened to assure them, though it was hardly any of their business. And yet, he sensed they weren't prying to be nasty. "I'm actually not looking for any kind of relationship right now."

"In that case, you might want to make sure not to invite Rafe over to your place," Aurora said.

"Why?" Oliver hoped the pang of unease wasn't too noticeable. Then again, he had a good reason to be wary of entitled men who couldn't take no for an answer and considered the slightest rebuke as a wound to their ego.

He'd invited Nym over. He'd even hoped it wouldn't be a one-off kind of thing. But, unlike Rafe with his pointed attentions, and despite his formidable size, Nym hadn't made Oliver feel uncomfortable. Not until that run-in the mausoleum when Oliver had been sure Nym was about to… What? Throw him out? Lock him up? Murder him? And yet, he hadn't so much as laid a finger on Oliver. In fact, he hadn't so much as berated him for trespassing.

It was all too confusing.

"Rafe has a tendency to consider invitations a permanent thing." Aurora's tone was perhaps a little too careful, as if she was painstakingly choosing her words. "Ask him to come over once, and he'll just be in and out of your place whenever he likes."

Oliver quirked an eyebrow. "Yeah, okay. Thanks for the warning, I guess."

He grabbed his bag but paused at the door, struck by a sudden idea. He turned back to them.

"Do any of you know a person by the name of Horace Livingstone?"

A dead silence fell on the room as everyone stared at him. Outside, the wind howled, rattling the branches of the nearby maples. Nym turned around, glaring at him, but Oliver ignored him, focusing instead on the others.

Aurora was the first to break the silence. "Why?" she asked.

"I met him in this parlor Monday night," Oliver said. "But he slipped away before I could assist him."

Kimona's eyebrows rose, and she exchanged an uneasy glance with Aurora.

"You…saw him?" Sky sounded incredulous. "He *spoke* to you?"

"I told you already," Nym said harshly. "Livingstone used to live here, and he still wanders in and out sometimes. That's it."

"He was the previous tenant in 1B, wasn't he?" Oliver inquired. It was a long shot, fueled by a flash of inspiration, but Nym's expression told him he was right. "What happened to him?"

"He won't be bothering you again," Nym said with an air of finality, just as Sky started to answer. She immediately fell silent.

"Right." Oliver studied their faces, but no new information seemed to be forthcoming. "Well, good night then."

He left to the unsteady chorus of the women dispensing their goodbyes. He stopped midway to the stairs and then tiptoed back, halting just outside the edge of light spilling from the parlor. Plastering himself against the wallpapered wall, he leaned in, straining to hear the soft voices coming from inside.

"…think we should tell him," Sky said.

There was a pause.

"Kimona is right," Aurora said. "You can't just spring something like this on a guy who's only been living here for a few days."

"But we can trust him," Sky insisted. "You heard it. Horace himself chose to appear to him. I have a good feeling about Oliver. A premonition."

The way she uttered "premonition" suggested it was A Thing.

"No." Nym's raspy voice held a note of finality. "I don't care what Horace does. His perspective is skewed anyway. It's much too dangerous. We can't afford any more mistakes."

Sky said something too low to hear, but after that, they switched the topic to tomorrow's weather and weekend plans. Oliver listened for a few more moments and then slunk back down the hallway and up the stairs, wincing with every pop of the floorboards.

He shouldn't have been surprised that his suspicions had been confirmed, but he couldn't believe he'd been right. He was used to being doubted and to doubting his own judgment. Ignoring his instincts in the past had landed him in a bad place, and still he was quick to dismiss his own misgivings as irrelevant and inconsequential. Maybe, in this particular case, he'd wanted to be wrong.

But no. Nym was hiding something, something bad, some dark secret about Lakeside Lodge, and all the tenants were in on it. Nobody lived in a half-dilapidated haunted mansion unless they had a very compelling reason.

Well, he too lived in the same half-dilapidated haunted mansion, but for him, it was a temporary situation, just until he was secure enough in his job and future prospects to find a better place. All the rest of his neighbors seemed comfortably settled in despite the shoddy plumbing, inadequate heating, and unidentified wild fauna living in the trashcans.

Oliver shut the door firmly behind him, set his bag down, and went to the kitchen to make a cup of tea. His cold was all but gone, but he needed something hot and soothing to help him focus and think in the chilly apartment.

He grabbed a notebook and pen, and sat on the couch, his feet tucked beneath him and his tea cooling on the coffee table. If he wanted to get to the bottom of this thing and decide whether to accept Cox's offer, he needed a more concise plan of action than occasional eavesdropping.

The first thing he needed to do was talk to Sky. She seemed the most talkative and open of the bunch and was more inclined to include him in…whatever was going on. He could start by complimenting her cookies, ask for a recipe, and work his way from there. Oliver couldn't bake to save his life, but Sky didn't need to know that.

He paused at the second bullet, tapping his pen on the notebook in thought. Extensive research into the history of Lakeside Lodge seemed like a given, since his cursory Google search hadn't yielded anything other than a few mentions on lists of historic properties in Baltimore. Nym had claimed the records were lost, but there was a chance, however slim, that there might be copies in the city hall archives. And, of course, the man himself had to be looked into, as much as Oliver could manage without access to police records.

It was all mounting up to be a daunting task—and it didn't even include inspecting the house itself to make a list of all possible code violations, per Cox's request. Oliver was still debating whether to go along with the developer's scheme, but maybe he should start, just in case. With the hours he had to put into work, it'd all keep him busy round the clock.

Maybe it was a good thing he had no personal or social life to speak of, movie nights and random hard-ons notwithstanding. At least that way, he could spare some time for spying on his landlord and neighbors.

Oliver sighed, took off his glasses, and rubbed his face. What was he doing, lusting after a man who acted so cagey, who could very well prove dangerous? It wasn't the first time Oliver had asked himself what was wrong with him, and once again, he had no satisfactory answer. Clearly, something was defective in the wiring of his brain because no rational human being would keep making the same mistakes over and over again.

Sleep sounded like an excellent idea. He was tired, and his thoughts were beginning to tie themselves into knots of anxiety. Anything productive would have to wait for the weekend.

Still, even after going to bed and closing his eyes, Oliver couldn't sleep. He tossed restlessly, listening to every groan and grind of the house's bones, startling awake every time the wind knocked a branch against the window.

"Oh, for God's sake." He sat up in bed and grabbed his glasses and his phone from the nightstand. It was a little past midnight.

Oliver settled back against the pillows and scrolled through his Twitter feed, squinting owlishly at the screen. Maybe he could chat with Pam if she was awake, or pick something to read from his ever-growing book wish list—

"Oliver," someone whispered in his ear.

Chapter Nine

Oliver started and dropped his phone. The voice seemed to be coming from nowhere and everywhere at once, soft and weirdly incorporeal. For a moment, Oliver was convinced he must've imagined it, but then the whisper repeated:

"Oliver…"

"Who is it?" He grabbed his phone and turned the screen outward, illuminating the bedroom with its faint bluish beam.

"Oliver…" The voice persisted, weaker this time, but with the same otherworldly inflection.

"Okay, whoever this is, it isn't funny!" Oliver snapped and flicked on the bedside lamp. He expected it not to work, but the warm light suffused the room, revealing nothing but the old furniture and the worn rug.

Maybe it was just a trick of acoustics, like the singing he'd heard in the bathroom. Sometimes he imagined he could still hear it in the evenings, but it would stop the moment he turned on the faucet. But who would call him by his name in the middle of the night?

He snatched his hoodie from the chair by the bed and shrugged into it as he walked over to the window. The frame made a scraping sound when he opened it and peered outside.

The gust of arctic wind felt like a slap in the face, carrying with it scents of wet earth and decay. The garden below was silent and empty, as far as he could see, apart from the branches of the chestnut oak that scraped against the side of the house and the glass pane. Dead leaves blew across the ground, catching in the thick roots that rose from the fog-shrouded earth like exposed bones from a mire.

"The hell." Oliver closed the window with a thud after one last sweeping look at the ground. He turned around and froze.

The closet door stood open.

It had been closed before; he was sure of it. Could it have opened by itself? Maybe it didn't shut properly, and the draft from the window had pulled the door loose.

Or maybe he'd fallen asleep, and this was a dream. An especially creepy, wake-up-in-cold-sweat-from kind of a dream.

Oliver clenched his fists, digging his fingernails into his palm, and hissed at the sting. Okay, maybe not a dream, then.

"Hello?" he called, just in case. Though, if someone *was* hiding in his bedroom closet, they probably weren't about to offer greetings.

He cast about for something he could use as a weapon, but the bedroom was sadly lacking in options. The tarnished brass candlestick on the dresser—most likely belonging to the previous lodger, be it Horace Livingstone or somebody else— came closest to what he was looking for, so Oliver grabbed it and advanced toward the closet. He swung the door open all the way and jumped back, candlestick raised.

The single light bulb inside the closet swayed gently on its cord, but there was no other movement. Oliver's clothes hung neatly on the rail, filling barely half of the space, so it was plain to see no one crouched inside, waiting to pounce.

Oliver released a long breath and lowered the candlestick, relaxing a fraction. The door must have opened on its own, and he was so wound up he was jumping at shadows. Maybe he *had* imagined the voice whispering his name or dreamed it while dozing off.

He was about to shut the closet door when a marking on the back wall, which he'd first mistaken for a swirl in the wood-grain, caught his attention. The clothes had partially obscured it, so he pushed his things aside to take a closer look. The faint outline of an animal, something vaguely reminiscent of a running wolf, a few inches long, had been drawn on the wood with a pencil. No wonder he hadn't noticed it before in his hurry to arrange his stuff throughout the apartment.

He traced the outline with his fingertips. It seemed like the wolf was running toward a dark knot in the woodgrain. Without thinking, Oliver pressed against the knot, then sprang back with a curse when the rear panel swung open on invisible hinges.

"The fuck," he muttered, staring into the darkness lurking beyond the narrow opening.

Somehow, it seemed par for the course that a house this old and strange would have secret passageways, but he hadn't been prepared to find one in his own bedroom. Who might be using it? Who might be watching him while he slept?

The thought did nothing for his composure. If he were smart, he'd march to Nym's door right now, wake the landlord up, demand his deposit back, and move to a hotel until he found lodgings in a nice, boring high-rise. But then he'd have nothing to report to Cox, and his chance of jump-starting his career would vanish. He'd spend the next two or three years in Thompson's employ—not even that if Cox decided to bad-mouth Oliver to his boss. Oliver didn't doubt whose side Thompson would pick if it came to the choice between retaining an already troublesome new employee and preserving a business relationship with a major client. His career wouldn't only fail to take off—it would be over before it even began.

No. If he wanted to keep his options open, he had to forget about acting smart.

Okay, that didn't sound good.

Taking another deep breath, Oliver braced himself and pushed the panel all the way back, revealing a small stone landing. Scenes from today's movie flashed through his mind, and he used one of the boxes inside the closet to prop the secret door open. The last thing he needed was to get trapped in the bowels of a decrepit house with no chance of rescue.

He got his phone, tapped the flashlight app, and shone it in into the musty gloom. Narrow stairs led up and down from the landing. Which direction should he take?

Remembering the torture chamber from the movie again, Oliver decided he could only take so many revelations in one night. If the staircase indeed led to the basement as he guessed, it'd have to wait till he could explore it in the full light of day, and hopefully armed with something more substantial than a candlestick.

He started up the stairs, holding his phone in one hand and his makeshift weapon in the other. His slippers weren't warm enough to shield his feet from the deadly cold of the stone. There was no railing, so he kept as close to the wall as he could, occasionally brushing against it. The sheer amount of dust and cobwebs on the treads was reassuring since it meant the stairway hadn't been in regular use.

How could he have missed a secret passage behind the walls? He should have noticed the discrepancy in the proportions of the rooms, especially since logic dictated there had to be a twin passage on the other side of the house. But he'd been so focused on other things he'd never thought to look for something so obvious. He'd have to do better if he wanted to discover other secrets that surely lay hidden behind the Lodge's exterior.

The second-floor landing greeted him with a wooden panel door identical to the one he'd stepped through in his closet. Most likely, it opened into the bedroom closet in Kimona's apartment, but Oliver wasn't about to check. He continued upward until he came to the last landing where the stairs ended, and another door.

He paused, considering. This had to lead to the attic, which he hoped was unoccupied. Rafe lived in the turret room, and he knew of no other neighbor, not counting the roaming Mr. Livingston. Unless this was some kind of Jane Eyre-type of thing, he wouldn't be disturbing anyone.

Oliver took another deep breath, shoved the candlestick under his arm, and tried the doorknob. He was fully expecting—hoping, rather—that it would be locked, but the door opened outward with suspiciously little noise.

A strong stale smell permeated the large and spacious attic. High slanted ceilings and exposed beams supported the mansard roof. Thin shards of light, a mix of moonlight and the distant streetlamps on Lakeside Drive, filtered through the closed shutters on the dormer windows that overlooked the porch entrance. Given the size, Oliver thought the space could easily be converted into an open-plan loft.

But he wasn't here to propose renovations. Besides, shelves, furniture, and boxes took up almost every inch of the floor, including all the bits and ends that somehow always ended up stored out of sight for years instead of thrown out when they outlived their usefulness. If he had to venture a guess, this was several generations' worth of junk.

He stepped inside, maneuvering between the metal shelving units and the larger pieces of furniture, most of them covered in white sheets. Their eerie appearance reminded Oliver of a graveyard, and the chilly, dank air did nothing to dispel that impression. A thick layer of dust lay everywhere, and as soon as Oliver noticed it, he was overwhelmed by the urge to sneeze.

In doing so, he momentarily lost his balance and, to steady himself, grabbed onto the nearest covering draped over something tall and spindly. The candlestick he was holding caught on the sheet, and it slipped to the floor with a soft whoosh. All of a sudden, Oliver was staring into the gaping, empty eye sockets of a human skeleton.

He yelped and jumped backwards, hitting his leg painfully on the corner of some chest or dresser. The skeleton wobbled, and for one terrifying second, Oliver was sure it would reach out and grab him by the throat.

The skeleton regained its balance on its perch, its jaws parted in a mocking sneer. Now that Oliver wasn't scrambling away in blind panic, it was easy to see its bones were a little too white, too lightweight, its composition too intact.

Plastic. It's plastic.

"Fuck my life," Oliver muttered, wiping his forehead his phone hand, his heart still going a hundred miles a minute.

And then, as if in answer, something stirred amid the pile of boxes next to one of the windows. A shadowy figure rose slowly from the floor, looming tall and large against the needle-thin rays of moonlight.

Oliver froze. He would have screamed, but his throat seized, and all he could do was stare with growing panic at the apparition. With his last ounce of rational thought, he lifted his phone, directing its harsh light toward the figure.

Nym squinted and raised his hand to shield his eyes.

"Can you put it away?" he said gruffly.

A wave of relief swept through Oliver, so strong it nearly knocked him off his feet, only to be replaced with renewed apprehension. Continuing to point the phone at the landlord's face, he raised the candlestick, ready to defend himself. His experience had taught him not to harbor any delusions about his chances of emerging victorious from a scuffle with a man of Nym's size, but he knew (also from experience) he wouldn't go down without a fight.

"Stay back," he warned when Nym took a step forward. "Don't come near me!"

Nym halted, his hand still raised to his face. "What the hell are you talking about? You surprised *me!*"

The sheer annoyance in his voice gave Oliver pause. On second thought, it *was* highly improbable that Nym would lie in wait in the attic on the off-chance Oliver might discover the secret passage and be foolish enough to stick his head in. But there was something decidedly suspicious about the landlord skulking around the dark corners of the house at this hour.

Oliver lowered his hands. He didn't turn his phone off, directing the beam to the floor rather than blinding the other man.

"Why don't you turn on the light?" he asked—the first thing that popped into his head, though perhaps not the most pressing.

Nym lowered his hand as well. Now that the glare of the flashlight wasn't directed at his face, his amber eyes seemed to glow eerily in the gloom.

"There's plenty of light from the window," he said, though it was clearly a lie.

"What are you doing here?" Oliver demanded.

"What are *you* doing here?" Nym countered.

Oliver had to concede the point. But rather than hastening to explain or apologize, he tilted his chin up.

"I just discovered a hidden staircase behind my bedroom closet that my landlord failed to inform me about. Why do you think that is?"

Nym quirked an eyebrow, unperturbed. "Why it's there, or why I didn't tell you about it?"

"Either. Both. You did know it existed, didn't you?"

"Yes. In fact, there are several secret passageways throughout the house, but they haven't been used in years."

His assertion matched Oliver's own conclusion, but he wasn't about to let Nym off the hook so easily.

"Don't you think it's strange that there are secret doors leading to every apartment in the building?" he asked. "Secret doors that the tenants aren't aware of? That has to be a gross violation of privacy."

Oliver had the impression that Nym gritted his teeth, but when he spoke again, it was calmly enough.

"As I said, those passages are a feature of the house. I can't help them being here. All I can do is assure you nobody is using them to spy on you, if that's what you're worried about. My guess is they were intended for smuggling."

The implied condescension smarted, and Oliver's hackles rose even more.

"What kind of smuggling? This house is older than the Prohibition."

Nym shrugged. "I'm neither a historian nor an architect. All I know is this house has many secrets, and even I don't know all of them. Some things are better left to rest."

Nym hadn't moved during their entire conversation, which Oliver found reassuring. If Oliver had inadvertently stumbled on his landlord engaging in some illicit activity, surely Nym would've tried to silence him by now.

Unless, of course, he was waiting for Oliver to turn around so he could bash his head in and stash his corpse in one of those boxes.

Nym must have sensed his apprehension because he said in a much more genial tone: "I was just looking for some stuff. As you can see, it's a storage locker up here."

Oliver still hesitated.

"Did you call my name earlier?" he asked.

"I'm sorry?"

"I heard someone calling my name while I was getting ready to sleep. I went to check the window, but no one was there. Next thing I knew, the closet door was ajar, and that's when I noticed the hidden panel inside it."

On second thought, maybe he shouldn't have told Nym all this, but Oliver *had* heard something, and if the landlord knew who was pulling his leg, it'd solve the mystery.

"It wasn't me," Nym said.

"Do you have any idea who it might be?"

"No."

Once again, Oliver could have sworn Nym was lying, at least about not knowing who the prankster was. If it really had been a prank.

He was at a loss as to what to do next. Should he press Nym further on the subject? His "no" had sounded final, and Oliver had no means to pressure him into honesty.

"What are you looking for?" he asked, mainly to stall until he could gather his wits.

"Halloween decorations."

"Halloween decorations," Oliver repeated flatly.

"We have a tradition of throwing a large party at the Lodge on Halloween," Nym explained. "It's kind of a big deal. I would've started decorating last week, but I was pretty busy at work and with all the repairs around here…" He trailed off apologetically. "Anyway, it's a lot of stuff, and it needs sorting before I take it all downstairs. You're welcome to help if you want, by the way."

Curious despite himself, Oliver approached him cautiously and craned his neck to peek into the open cardboard box at Nym's feet. The beam of his phone flashlight picked out a tangle of black-and-orange tinsel, with a batwing sticking out.

Maybe Nym was telling the truth, however improbable.

"Is that what that thing is?" he asked, pointing behind his shoulder at the fake skeleton.

"A part of it, yes. There are a couple of smaller ones that go on the porch."

Oliver sighed. "Can you turn on the light? Some of us can't see in the dark, and this is getting creepy."

To be fair, "creepy" was a dot in his rear-view mirror by now, but downplaying the events of the evening seemed a better option than freaking out, at least until he could do so in the privacy of his apartment.

Which turned out to be not so private after all. Oliver shivered. Who was to say there wasn't an underground tunnel opening into his kitchen cupboard? Or a dungeon concealed behind the bathroom mirror?

Perhaps *The Pit and the Pendulum* hadn't been the best choice of entertainment today, all things considered. At least it hadn't been *Candyman*.

Nym moved aside, navigating deftly through the sea of junk, and flipped the light switch by the door that led to the main staircase. Oliver shielded his eyes, though the overhead light was just as dim as the rest of the light fixtures throughout the house. He turned off the flashlight and slipped the phone into the pocket of his hoodie.

"Wow. There's…a lot."

He meant the assortment of Halloween decor, which, upon closer inspection, took up at least four boxes, but the statement held true to all the contents of the attic. If anything, the collection of junk looked even more overwhelming now that he could see it more clearly.

Nym came back and crouched beside Oliver. He rummaged around in the box, carefully avoiding Oliver's gaze.

"So it's a big party?" Oliver asked.

"I guess. Just us, and some family and friends. We usually have it in the front parlor, so that's where most of this stuff goes. And in the entry hall, of course."

"If you cleared all this stuff, you could have the party here," Oliver said, only half joking. "Leave the spider webs and the stained wallpaper, and bam! Instant ambiance."

Nym looked around as if seriously considering the possibility but then shook his head. "Too much work."

"It's a great space," Oliver said. "It's so big, it's practically a ballroom."

"This place is old, but it has good bones," Nym agreed.

Oliver hummed noncommittally. He watched as Nym got up again and lifted a small wooden crate from one of the higher shelves, noting the way his muscles flexed, noticeable even underneath the flannel shirt. His mouth went a little dry. Meanwhile, Nym lowered the crate onto the floor next to the open box, kneeling so close his thigh was almost brushing against Oliver's, and tackled the lid.

"Can I come?" Oliver said.

Nym turned to him, his eyes flashing.

"What?"

"To the party."

Nym hesitated, and a flash of irrational disappointment sliced through Oliver.

"Never mind," he said, lowering his eyes. "Forget it."

"I thought you might have other plans," Nym said, his tone a bit too careful.

"I'm new around here, so I don't exactly drown in invitations."

"What about people from work? Don't you have friends there?"

"One or two," Oliver said. He certainly considered Ela his friend, though it hadn't occurred to him to meet up with her outside the office. Maybe Nym was right in that he should. Pam was one of the pillars of his life, but he couldn't keep calling her every time he felt lonely.

He sighed. "I'll ask what their plans are. And it's a big city. I should be able to find something to do."

"It's not that I don't want you at the party," Nym said hastily. "I just think you wouldn't enjoy it."

Oliver looked up at him. "Why wouldn't I?"

"I don't know." Nym shifted, looking away. "For one thing, Rafe might not be there. He usually has some other thing going on for All Hallows' Eve."

"Good."

Nym's gaze snapped back to Oliver's face.

"I'm not interested in Rafe," Oliver said. A blush crept up his cheeks, but he kept his voice steady.

"But I thought… Today, when we watched the movie…" Nym trailed off.

Oliver knew he should be mortified that Nym had noticed his arousal, but he was more anxious to correct him regarding the object of his excitement. Suddenly, it felt like the most important thing in the world.

"That wasn't about Rafe. It was about you."

They studied each other, Nym's odd, shiny eyes intent on Oliver's, as if trying desperately to read his every thought, his every desire. The musty air between them grew heavy as if in anticipation of a summer storm that was about to break.

Oliver couldn't tell who moved first, but the next thing he knew, they were kissing, Nym's lips pressed hard against his own, his stubble scraping the tender skin of his cheek. He opened his mouth, and the slide of Nym's tongue was like the first crack of lightning that tore the sky to release a deluge.

Chapter Ten

Oh yes. There was something deeply, horribly wrong with him. Oliver realized it even as he threw his arms around Nym's shoulders, drawing him closer.

For all he knew, Nym could be an ax murderer, or at the very least a clever conman who'd been evading the notice of the authorities. There was also a highly improbable, but not entirely nonexistent possibility that the house was actually haunted. Either of these should've been enough to send Oliver packing, but all he could think of at the moment was that Nym's mouth tasted every bit as delicious as he'd imagined.

Obviously, this wasn't what one would call sensible behavior. In fact, Oliver was pretty sure it might be the hallmark of an unhealthy emotional coping mechanism. But then Nym placed his hand on Oliver's nape and delved deeper into his mouth as if determined to explore every nook and cranny with his tongue, and every trace of rational thought evaporated.

Nym smelled faintly of sawdust and wet earth, with an undercurrent of sharp musk that could be the traces of his cologne or his own unique scent. Every whiff made Oliver's head spin and his body grow hot in a way he'd rarely felt before.

On their knees on the dusty hardwood floor, locked in an embrace, their hands roaming, they kissed until Oliver couldn't breathe. He broke off, gasping, and tore off his glasses before they could really get in the way. But before he could launch himself at Nym with renewed vigor, Nym pulled away, sitting back on his haunches and raising his hand in front of him as if to fend Oliver off.

"No," Nym said. "We can't."

"What? Why?" Oliver asked, baffled, but then an awful realization sank in. What if he'd misjudged the situation and Nym didn't want to be kissed? Maybe he didn't find Oliver attractive. Maybe he was straight after all.

Nym licked his lips, and something flashed in the depths of his eyes. But without his glasses, everything around Oliver was slightly out of focus, and he couldn't make it out. He shoved his glassed back on—flimsy armor to hide his vulnerability—now painfully aware of how wanton he must've looked.

"It wouldn't be right," Nym said. "I'm your landlord, you're a tenant. I'd be taking advantage."

"Advantage? Come on; it's not like I was going to ask for a discount on my lease in exchange for sexual favors," Oliver said sharply.

"I know you wouldn't." Nym ran a hand through his hair, which was already as unruly as it would ever be. "But still, I...I can't."

Oliver clenched his teeth against the rising argument. He wasn't so pathetic as to try to cajole someone into kissing him who didn't really want to. It was clear Nym would hold on to his excuse, whether it was the real reason for his rejection or not, and nothing Oliver could say would change his mind.

Perhaps he should appreciate Nym not taking advantage of what could well be a mutual momentary lapse of judgment, brought about (at least on Oliver's part) by a surge of adrenalin. He still wasn't sure where Nym's preferences fell on the sexuality spectrum, but he hadn't seemed disgusted by what they'd done. It would've been easy for him to press on even if Oliver had been the one to voice his reservations. But he hadn't, and Oliver had to respect that and his choice not to pursue a more intimate connection.

His hard-on, which had been raging just a few minutes ago, wilted rather uncomfortably. Oliver's only consolation came from noticing the considerable bulge in Nym's jeans as the man got on his feet. At least he hadn't been wholly unaffected by their frantic groping.

He got up, too, dusted his pajama bottoms, and then picked up one of the stuffed boxes.

"Where do you want these?" he asked.

Nym looked at him with surprise. "You don't have to do this. It's late; you must want to go back to sleep, not haul gewgaws up and down the stairs."

"I can't believe you just used 'gewgaws' in a sentence." Oliver shook his head. "Anyway, I promised I'd help."

"You didn't."

"It was implied," Oliver said impatiently. "So where do you want these?"

There was a pause as Nym regarded him silently.

"The front parlor," he said finally. "That's where most of these will be set up."

"Lead on, then," Oliver said, adjusting his grip on the box, which was heavier than he'd originally thought.

Without another word, Nym grabbed another box and headed toward the stairs. They waded through the sea of junk in awkward silence. The top landing was narrower than the rest, with another, smaller staircase leading still upward to the room in the east turret where Rafe lived.

Nothing stirred as they took the stairs down to the ground floor. Light shone from the crack under Sky and Aurora's door, but the apartment was quiet.

They deposited the boxes in the dark, silent parlor. Oliver was grateful to find it vacant as his nerves couldn't sustain any more surprises. In fact, just the thought of going back to sleep in his bedroom filled him with dread. There was no way he'd get any rest tonight while straining to hear disembodied voices calling out to him or the sound of someone traipsing the secret passages inside the walls.

It had taken three trips upstairs to bring everything down to the parlor. By then, Oliver's muscles had started to ache in protest against such uncharacteristic exercise.

"That should do it." Nym set down the plastic skeleton, which he'd cradled in his arms all the way down from the attic with the gentleness of a parent holding a sleeping baby, and dusted his hands. He studiously avoided meeting Oliver's eyes. "Thanks."

"No problem." Oliver put the last box by the fireplace and turned to leave.

"Wait." Nym made a step in his direction but stopped when Oliver faced him. "Look, I realize that some things...may seem a little weird around here."

Oliver arched an eyebrow. "You think?"

"I just want you to know you don't have to worry. There's nothing here that would harm you."

That was an odd way to phrase the sentiment, and it didn't sound as reassuring as Nym probably thought it did.

"I'd be a lot less worried if you could actually explain to me what is going on," Oliver said.

Nym regarded him solemnly with those luminescent eyes of his, and Oliver's heart picked up speed again, though he couldn't tell whether it was in alarm or in anticipation.

"Maybe someday," Nym said.

"Great." Oliver aimed for breezy sarcasm, but it came out more bitter than anything. "Now, I need to catch up on my sleep."

"Just one more thing. This party… I'd love it if you could come."

"I appreciate it, but I don't need a pity invite."

"It's not. Really." Nym took a deep breath and scratched the back of his head. "It's just… Well, it's been a while since I liked someone, and I'm a little out of my depth here. It seems everything I do and everything I say makes things worse, even when I try to do the right thing."

Oliver went very still. "You…like me?"

Nym smiled wryly. "I thought it was rather obvious by now."

"I'm confused." Oliver shook his head. He was tired, coming down from an adrenaline rush, and Nym probably wasn't saying what Oliver thought he was saying. He only knew he'd been willing to let things progress beyond a kiss, and had been flat-out rejected.

"I'm kinda confused myself, to be honest." Nym bit his full lower lip. "I meant what I said about not wanting to take advantage, but… Can we, maybe…I don't know, be friends first, and see how we go from there? That way I won't feel like I'm rushing you into anything, and you'll have the chance to figure out if that's something you want. You've barely been in Baltimore two weeks. Maybe you'll meet someone, and then…" He sighed. "I'm babbling. Sorry."

"No. No, I get it."

Maybe Oliver wasn't entirely on board with Nym's reasoning, but he could at least understand it, and the fumbling admission was like a balm to his bruised ego.

"I get it," he repeated more softly. "You want to get to know me better before anything happens. Or doesn't happen."

Nym inclined his head. "Yes. Are you okay with that?"

"I think so? I mean, yes," he amended hastily. "Of course I'd love to get to know you too."

Nym smiled broadly and extended his hand to Oliver.

"Friends?"

Oliver looked down at Nym's rough palm, calloused at the base of the fingers.

Did he really want this? And if he did, could he trust Nym not to make him regret it?

The truth was, he didn't know. And yet he wanted so badly for the answer to be "yes."

Well, he'd already established there was something wrong with him. His lips tugged in an involuntary smile at the thought as he shook Nym's hand.

"Friends."

Nym glanced at the opened boxes at his feet. "Want to help me with these tomorrow? That is, if you have time."

"Sure, I'd love to. Call me when you're ready?"

Nym nodded. "I will."

Oliver turned to the door again, but then remembered something and resisted the urge to roll his eyes.

"Do you have a master key or something?" he asked.

Nym's eyebrows drew together. "Yes. Why?"

"My door is locked from the inside. If you could open it, it'd save me the trouble of going back up to the attic and through that passageway again. Frankly, if I never see the inside of it again it'd be too soon."

Nym chuckled. "I can do that. Come on."

They shuffled up the stairs to the first floor. Nym took out a key fob from the pocket of his jeans and opened Oliver's door.

"Here you go. See you tomorrow?"

Oliver stopped with his hand on the door frame, gazing up at Nym's eyes.

"See you tomorrow."

There was the barest of pauses at they both seemed to be waiting for some kind of sign from one another until, finally, Nym took a step back, and Oliver followed suit, retreating into the cold darkness of the apartment hallway. The door swung shut, and he hastened to turn the lock. After a moment's hesitation, he threw the chain. That he hadn't done so earlier in the evening worked in his favor now, but he really had to be more cautious than that.

On an instinct, he peered through the peephole. Nym still stood in front of his door, his head bowed, and Oliver wondered what was going through his mind. At length, Nym turned and disappeared behind the door of his own apartment, which clicked quietly behind him.

Oliver exhaled and leaned his forehead against the door.

"What are you hiding?" he whispered, barely audible to his own ears. Unsurprisingly, silence was his only answer.

Sleeping in his bed, with the knowledge that the secret door was right there in the closet, had been out of the question. Immediately upon returning to his apartment, Oliver had made sure the wolf-marked back panel was firmly shut, then took out all his stuff from the closet to later distribute between the dresser and the linen cupboard. On further reflection, he'd jammed a chair under the closet doorknob. If anyone—or *anything*—was determined to get inside, it probably wouldn't stop them, but the ensuing racket would prevent them from slipping by Oliver unnoticed.

Consequently, Oliver had spent a particularly miserable night (if a couple of hours of fitful sleep could be classified as a "night") on the living room couch, wrapped in all the blankets he could get his hands on.

He stared blearily at his cup as he heated water for his morning coffee. In the bleak light of a gray, rainy morning, the events of last night felt like a particularly bizarre dream. But as tempting as it was to discard the memories, he knew it had all been too real. He *had* heard a strange voice, he *had* found a hidden staircase, and he *had* kissed his landlord. And having done all these things meant he was now embroiled in something he couldn't understand.

Once again, he contemplated calling Pam as he sipped the strong, scalding coffee at the counter. He'd run the chance of being late for work, having taken too much time to rouse himself that morning, but there was no way he'd pop behind the wheel without coffee in his system. Pam would know what to do, even if she teased him mercilessly about his misguided attraction.

But he had to figure this all out on his own, didn't he? Even if he was in over his head. He wasn't naive enough to believe Cox was being entirely sincere with him regarding his motives, or trust that the developer would keep his word about giving Oliver that job. And even if he did, there was something really underhanded in this way of doing business. But on the other hand, Nym wasn't being honest with him either. It wasn't just a matter of Oliver being unnecessarily suspicious and overly imaginative—the landlord was hiding something, something all the other tenants were in on, to the exclusion of Oliver.

How could he be sure what the right thing to do was if he couldn't trust anyone to tell him the truth?

By the time he finished his coffee, he'd reached no insight. He hurried to get dressed, gathered his things, and ran out the door. Nym's pickup wasn't in its parking spot, so he must've left for work already.

To Oliver's relief, Mr. Thompson didn't come into work that day, and the change in atmosphere was nothing short of staggering. If he'd been in better shape and his mind wasn't as addled by lack of sleep, he would've appreciated the stress-free vibe and easy chatter around the office. As it was, he eked out another cup of coffee from the sleek and intimidating machine and sat down at his desk to go over his daily project assignment list, which was already full.

"Hey," Ela said, coming over to his station. Because of the relaxed dress code, most of the coworkers sported a casual style during the weekdays, but today, her outfit was even more so— a chunky knitted cardigan thrown over a tracksuit set.

"Hey," he said, looking up at her with a smile. "You look ready for the weekend."

"Definitely looking forward to it." She winked. "Actually, a bunch of us are meeting up tonight. There's this cool little pub on 36th Street that serves awesome burgers and craft beer. Want to come?"

Oliver hesitated. He genuinely liked Ela, and the idea of spending Friday night unwinding with her and the rest of his new colleagues over food and drinks actually sounded really nice. After all, that was what he wanted, wasn't it? To meet new people, make new connections, explore everything the city had to offer. It was exactly what he was supposed to do. What he wanted to do—or at least told himself he should want.

But then, he had promised Nym he'd help him decorate. And while it sounded far less exciting than an evening out on the town, Oliver was surprised he was looking forward to spending time with the laconic landlord.

"Thanks, but I've already made some plans for tonight," he said apologetically. "I'd love to join you some other day, if that's all right?"

"Sure. I know it was a short notice." Ela tipped her head to the side and regarded him curiously. "Don't tell me you got a hot date?"

"No!" Oliver blushed. "I mean, no, it's not a date. I just promised to help a friend with something."

"Riiight." Ela's tone teased. "Anyway, I hope things go well with this friend of yours."

By lunchtime, the office had started to empty. People were eager to kick off their weekend and took the absence of their boss as an opportunity to leave early. Oliver couldn't blame them, but he opted to take advantage of the quiet and convenience of a well-lit office to get some work done, and he dove right into it, equipped with his coffee and a hastily put-together sandwich.

He'd just finished working on a short presentation when his phone rang. No one sat close to him, so he answered at his desk instead of going out into the hallway.

"Hello?"

"Oliver," Cox's deep, cultured voice said in his ear. "How are you this afternoon?"

Oliver shifted uncomfortably and leaned back in his chair, instinctively glancing to the sides to make sure no one was listening in.

"Good afternoon, Mr. Cox."

"I'd hate to put any pressure on you, but I wanted to ask if you've had time to consider my offer, and if you've made any progress with your observations."

Oliver drew a deep breath. He'd been sure he'd have a little more time to prepare before this conversation, which was going to be decidedly unpleasant—especially seeing as Cox seemed convinced his answer would be positive.

He could stall, of course, buy himself a little more time, so he'd word his refusal carefully. Unlike Nym, his position was precarious; he had a lot to lose by upsetting a man like Cox. But it wouldn't be fair to either of them.

He licked his lips and adjusted his glasses.

"I'm grateful for your proposal, Mr. Cox, and I appreciate the trust you put in me. But I'm afraid I can't be of service to you."

There was a ringing pause on the other side of the line.

"I see," Cox said finally. "May I ask why?"

Because I've grown to consider Nym Brown a friend? Because I want him to be something more? Because, in my heart, I don't believe the house and its inhabitants, however strange and quirky, harbor true evil? Because it'd be wrong for me to sell them out so you can make money off their misfortune?

Oliver couldn't say any of it out loud, especially the last part. He settled for:

"I just don't feel I'm the right person for this task."

"Perhaps you're not entirely satisfied with the terms of our agreement? Maybe a cash bonus on top of the job arrangement—"

"No, no. That's not it. I don't want any money. I'm sorry, Mr. Cox. I can't in good conscience do this."

"Well. I can't say I'm not disappointed." Cox's voice lost some of its oily smoothness, but his tone was still polite. "In that case, I'll have to explore other...avenues of action. If you ever change your mind, Oliver, you have my number."

With that, the developer disconnected, and Oliver slumped in his chair in relief.

It was done, and it had been much less awful than he'd expected. Cox could still be harboring a grudge, of course, but there was precious little Oliver could do about it now. Maybe if he thought Oliver could still be persuaded to help… But no. Relief slowly transformed into hopeful buoyancy, and Oliver knew he'd been right. It was akin to flipping a coin and examining his instinctive reaction to the outcome. Heads—satisfaction, tails—disappointment.

Heads. It was definitely heads.

Some of the anxiety that had been gnawing at him since his meeting with Cox on Tuesday finally eased. And yet, something about Cox's vague mention of "other avenues of action" prevented it from easing completely.

Chapter Eleven

When Oliver returned home, he was greeted by two small skeletons lounging on the porch steps.

Tied to the porch posts in a tangle of silvery cobwebs, their eye sockets and teeth glowed an eerie green, no doubt thanks to a coat of luminous paint. A few bats hung from the gable, swaying violently in the rain-scented wind, and a cluster of oversized, hairy-legged spiders scuttled across the front door. Instead of appearing cheesy and over-the-top, the holiday accoutrements looked disconcertingly like they belonged there. Only jack-o'-lanterns were currently missing from this natural habitat of all things spooky.

He found Nym in the parlor on a stepladder, fixing a garland of fairy lights underneath a mesh of cobwebs that hung above the fireplace.

"Hey," Oliver said, dropping his bag near the door and surveying the room. The large skeleton that had given him such a fright last night stood in the far corner, grinning at him from beneath a crown of black crepe flowers, looking like a black-and-white illustration of Poe's collected works. Oliver shuddered.

"Hey." Nym's voice held an unmistakable note of warmth. He was dressed in his usual flannel and worn jeans, which stretched rather enticingly over his powerful thighs as he reached up to adjust the last of the tiny lights. "What do you think?"

"Huh?" Oliver tore his gaze away from the impressive lines of his body. "Oh. The installation. Yeah, it looks good. Might need a few spiders to make it pop though."

"Got them right here." Nym grabbed a rubber spider the size of a small cat from the mantelpiece and wiggled it in the air. "I hope you aren't afraid of spiders?"

"Not artificial ones. I thought you weren't going to decorate until later this evening."

"They let us go early at work, so I thought I'd get a head start." His brow furrowed. "You're not upset, are you? I'm sorry I didn't wait—"

"No, that's okay." Oliver grinned. "There's plenty of work left for the two of us."

"That there is." Nym pinned the spiders in place at the epicenter of the web and leaned back to admire his work. "You want to grab something to eat and then come down here?"

"Actually, I thought we might go somewhere to eat later." Oliver managed to refrain from biting his lips nervously, though his attempt at feigning nonchalance probably fell a little flat. "Not like on a date, or anything. I'm just a little tired of takeout and sandwiches."

Nym regarded him for a moment. "Sure," he said finally. "I'd like that."

Oliver's heart leapt despite his promise to himself to act cool.

"All right," he said briskly to hide his pleasure at Nym's assent. "What do you want me to do next?"

"There are all these to go around the parlor." Nym nodded toward the boxes stuffed to the brim with decorations. "And then there are a couple more things to hang out front."

"Let's get to it, then."

They spent the next hour or so strategically placing various knickknacks around the room until it resembled a Tim Burton movie set. In Oliver's humble opinion, if Nym wanted to wow his guests with spine-chilling ambiance, all he had to do was move the party to the room across the hall under the watchful eye of the late Mrs. Shaw, but maybe that would be a touch *too* authentic.

It was also the first time Oliver had seen the parlor fully illuminated, which was why he stopped next to the bay window, holding a bunch of candles he intended to place on the windowsill, and cocked his head to the side, frowning.

"Is it me, or is the floor slanting?" he asked.

"It might." Nym didn't appear to be taken aback at the question. He didn't even glance down from where he was replacing the lacy curtains with fake-blood-drenched rags on the other window.

"That's…not good."

Nym sighed, fitting metal drapery rings that held the rags over the curtain rod. "Tell me about it."

"No, I mean it." Oliver put the candles down and crouched, trying to find the correct angle to examine the floor. "I'm not a structural engineer, but I think you might have a problem with the foundation."

Nym finally turned to him and grimaced. "I know. And it's going to cost upward of fifteen thousand bucks to repair."

He shrugged at Oliver's expression. "I may not be a structural engineer either, but I know a thing or two about construction."

Oliver bit his lip. The thought that this was exactly the kind of thing Cox would want him to report flashed through his mind. In itself, it wasn't enough to get the building condemned, but add in the leaky plumbing, the faulty heating, the ancient wiring, and the secret passages that would never pass a safety inspection—and Nym would have to shell out a huge amount of money if he wanted to keep the place. Money which, of course, he didn't have.

It was a moot point as far as Oliver was concerned, but should he tell the Nym about Cox's plans? If he did, Oliver would have to explain why he'd waited so long to speak up about it, and he wasn't about to confess to Nym that he'd seriously considered taking Cox up on his offer, however briefly. Their budding...whatever it was, wouldn't survive such an admission. And besides, it wasn't as if Nym wasn't aware of the developer's intentions to lay his hands on the property. With Oliver now out as a reliable source of information, Cox had made it plain he'd seek other ways to influence Nym. Perhaps he might even decide the Lodge was more trouble than it was worth and stop trying to get it altogether.

No, it was best not to mention any of it to Nym for now.

"Just another thing to worry about, I guess." Nym got down and folded the ladder. "Anyway, I believe we're done in here."

Oliver stood and surveyed the room. For once, its dated shabbiness worked in its favor as a backdrop for the spooky props. There was no mistaking the distinct look of a drawing room in a haunted mansion.

"It's as ready as it's going to be," he agreed. "You could charge people money for the attraction. And Rodger adds a nice touch."

"Rodger?"

Oliver nodded to the skeleton scowling menacingly in the corner. "Doesn't he look like a Rodger?"

Nym's gaze swung to the skeleton, then back to Oliver. A smile tugged at his lips. "Yes. I suppose he does."

"What now?" Oliver asked, ignoring the ridiculous surge of pleasure at the sight of that smile.

"There's still some stuff to be hung around the porch, if you're up to it."

"Sure."

Nym grabbed the last box and headed for the porch. As they passed into the entry hallway, the corner of the box he held caught on some letters and fliers sticking out of the slotted mailboxes on the wall, and they scattered on the faded carpet in a flurry of paper.

Nym muttered something under his breath and stopped.

"Let me." Oliver bent over to retrieve the mail. He began sorting it back in the designated slots when a name on an official-looking envelope caught his eye.

"Nymphus Brown," he read and then stared at the landlord in astonishment. "Your name is Nymphus?"

All the scruffy facial hair couldn't hide the blush that suffused Nym's face. It spread from his cheeks down to his neck and all the way to the tips of his ears.

"Yeah," he all but growled. "What of it?"

"Nothing. That's…" The first word that sprang to Oliver's mind was "adorable," but he had the feeling Nym wouldn't appreciate that particular adjective, so he settled for: "…unusual."

"My mother has a thing for traditional names." Nym opened the front door and strode out to the porch.

In what universe was Nymphus a "traditional name"?

"Every tenant carves their own jack-o'-lantern, and then we stack them on the steps," Nym said briskly in a clear attempt to change the subject. "I imagine they'll all be ready by next week. You're more than welcome to add one of your own."

Oliver nodded. "I will. What do you want me to do now?"

"Let's hang this on both sides of the door." Nym unrolled a bolt of gauzy fabric adorned with rusty stains and bloody handprints. "There are nails in the trimming that you can fix this on. I'll bring the ladder."

"No need. I can just climb on the railing real quick. Help me up, would you?"

"You sure?"

"Yeah." Oliver took the end of the fabric and got up on the railing with a boost from Nym. He balanced precariously on the railing cap while the landlord hovered below, frowning as Oliver stretched the ghoulish rags across the trimming.

"All done," he called and took a tiny step back on the wooden cap to check if the fabric was even.

A low groan was his only warning, and then one of the spindles beneath his feet snapped with a loud crack. The entire railing shook. Oliver tried to grab the nearest post but lost his footing and fell with an undignified yelp, crashing down on

Nym, who moved to catch him. They both hit the wooden deck, Nym sprawled on his back with his arms instinctively tightening around Oliver, and Oliver landing squarely on top of him.

For a second, all Oliver could do was stare into Nym's amber eyes, their alarm mirroring his own. Then his gaze slipped lower, to Nym's lips and the hard line of his jaw.

Nym's body was very still beneath his, but his heart thudded against Oliver's chest. How easy it would be to lean down, cross those last few inches that separated their lips, and be reminded of the taste of a summer storm.

But he'd promised Nym he wouldn't pressure him into anything he wasn't ready for. Besides, passionate kisses, spurred by adrenalin, worked on screen but could be incredibly awkward in real life. He only had to recall the faux pas in the attic to know that.

Oliver heaved himself upright gracelessly and got on his feet.

Nym followed a heartbeat later. "Are you okay?"

"Yes." Oliver gave an unsteady laugh. "Sorry."

"These are more rotten than I thought," Nym said, turning his attention to the railing spindles. He sounded sheepish, as if the poor state of the decking was his fault. Though, perhaps, to some extent it was.

"It would be easy enough to fix," Oliver said, dusting the front of his jeans. "It'll take a bit of work, but I could help with that, if you that's fine with you."

"You don't have to do that."

"No," Oliver said softly, watching Nym rattling the railing to test it. "But I want to."

★

He was running down the stairs of the secret passage hidden inside the wall. Icy wind blew in his face, threatening to fling him from the wobbly staircase into the darkened well, but he didn't stop. Something was chasing him, something large and feral. Its claws scraped on the steps; its breath heated the back of his neck.

The staircase only extended a few floors, but it seemed endless, getting narrower and damper by the second. A low, guttural growl reverberated down his spine, and he lost his footing with a strangled cry. He tumbled down the last few steps and sprawled on the hard concrete of the basement, which looked exactly like the dungeon from *The Pit and the Pendulum*. The cavernous space with its vaulted ceilings opened up in front of him, revealing hanging chains and torture devices along the walls.

He swallowed hard and tried to get up, but a hard, warm weight plopped on top of him, pinning him to the floor, knocking the wind out of him. He angled his head, trying to get a glimpse of his attacker. A huge paw, its claws extended a full couple of inches, filled his vision. Something hard and purposeful poked his thigh, and he realized with a jolt that he was stark naked. More surprisingly, his own cock swelled in response to that insistent nudging, and he writhed on the floor, unable to tell if he wanted to get away or thrust up into the friction.

"You can't run from this," Nym's voice whispered in his ear, hot and heavy with promise. "You're mine now."

Sharp teeth pierced the skin on his shoulder, and he screamed.

★

It was way too early to be awake on a Saturday morning.

Oliver stared out the window, trying to glimpse a spark on the surface of the lake through the tangle of maple branches as he sipped his third cup of coffee. It promised to be a beautiful clear day, a welcome respite from the incessant rain since the beginning of the week, but Oliver was too tired to appreciate the weather. He'd hardly slept at all, and for once it had little to do with the uncomfortable couch.

He'd woken up in the middle of the night from a dream (a nightmare, really) drenched in sweat, heart racing, and sporting a painful hard-on. For one terrifying moment, he'd been sure there was someone in the living room with him, watching him. He'd bolted upright and flicked on the table lamp, but unsurprisingly, no one was there. Even the spotty mirror above the fireplace didn't show anything but his own bleary-eyed reflection. The sensation of being watched slowly receded, along with his arousal, but it did little to sooth his jitters and embarrassment.

He'd tried to go back to sleep after that, but every little noise and creak of the floorboards jolted him awake. Finally, he'd admitted defeat and settled in a nest of blankets with a cup of tea and his sketchpad. Drawing in such poor lighting strained his eyes, already aching from lack of sleep, but it was a good distraction. Oliver let the pent-up frustration and confusion that lingered in the aftermath of the dream leak onto the page through his pencil, making a few quick sketches of Lakeside Lodge from various angles. Then, as his mind slowly switched gears, he turned a page to draw a portrait of Nym, doing his best to capture the rare and fleeting expression when the corner of his lips tugged in a reluctant smile and his eyes crinkled briefly in amusement.

Oliver glanced at the sketchpad he'd left lying on the coffee table. Why was he obsessing so much about a man who wasn't even on the same page as him where sexual attraction was concerned? And that dream... Was his subconscious trying to warn him about getting close to someone who could yet prove dangerous, or was it just a fantasy that reflected Oliver's preferences when it came to bed partners? Not that he'd had that many of them over the years, but Pam had been right. He was partial to a very particular type of man, and Nym, with his broad shoulders, towering height, and quiet strength, fit that type like a round peg to a round hole.

Thinking about pegs sliding neatly into holes really wasn't helping him any. Oliver swallowed the dregs of his coffee, checked the clock on the mantelpiece, and picked up his phone to call Pam. At 8:30 a.m., she should be back home from her usual morning run.

"What's up?" Pam asked, picking up after a few rings.

"Do you think it's possible to like someone who you don't trust?" Oliver let out in a rush.

"Wow. Good morning to you too."

"Sorry. I've been up for a while. Too much coffee."

Pam snorted. "Something has gotten your panties in a bunch. Or is it 'someone'?"

"Well, yeah. That's why I'm asking."

"Is this about this Nym guy?"

"Maybe," Oliver hedged.

"Right, maybe." The sarcasm in Pam's voice came loud and clear even from a thousand miles away. Then her tone grew thoughtful. "As to your question... Yeah, I think it's possible to like someone you don't trust. I guess it's even possible to fall in love with them. But making something last without trust... No, I don't think it'll make for a viable relationship."

Oliver let out a long sigh and plopped on the couch. "I just don't know what to do. I like Nym, but I can see he's hiding something. What if it's something I should be worried about?"

"Did he give you a reason to be worried?"

Instead of answering right away, Oliver took a moment to think it over.

It hadn't been as cut and dry as that, had it? Nym had never gotten physical with him in a bad way. Not in the way Jake had. Hell, he hadn't even gotten physical with him in a good way, despite Oliver pushing for it. All Oliver had were suspicions, founded on nothing more than some odd behavior and vague hearsay.

Was that enough to condemn someone?

"Not really," he admitted finally. "There's definitely *something* going on here, but I didn't get the impression he meant to do me harm."

"Well, why don't you confront him on it?"

"I did. Kind of. He wasn't very forthcoming." Oliver sighed.

"Then he sounds like more trouble than he's worth," Pam proclaimed with an air of finality. "Darling, you've been in Baltimore for, what, two weeks? Why hook up with the first man you meet? I don't care how buff he is; stop throwing yourself at the wrong people."

Oliver bit his lip. It was everything he'd been telling himself, so why did he feel like arguing the point? Pam was right; until Nym came clean with him, he didn't deserve Oliver defending him to anyone. And yet, despite everything, he couldn't wholeheartedly agree.

"I'm sorry," he said finally. "I don't know why I'm bothering you with all of this."

"Because you miss me and are looking for excuses to talk to me?" Pam said teasingly.

Oliver chuckled. "You're right on the money, as usual. What about that Halloween costume? Did you decide what you want to be?"

"Might go with a slutty zombie after all. What about you? Are you going to a party? There have to be quite a few happening in your corner of the woods."

Oliver thought of Nym's half-hearted invitation, or what seemed so at the time. "Not sure yet."

"Well, you better. And don't forget to send pictures! You know Halloween is my favorite holiday. Must be all the chocolate."

They talked some more, tactfully avoiding the issue that Oliver was suddenly loath to discuss, and he wasn't sure he felt better about his choices when they finally disconnected.

Bright light of a Saturday morning streamed through the windows. Oliver contemplated going back to bed, but he was too pumped on caffeine to relax.

Besides, he had to do something to get his mind off this hamster wheel of anxiety. Like maybe doing some deep cleaning and finding a more permanent solution to his sleeping arrangements. The couch was killing his back, and it seemed silly to spend the night in the drafty living room because he was scared of monsters in the closet.

Oliver began by tidying up the kitchen, rinsing the dishes that had piled up in the sink, and wiping down the counters. He cast a critical eye over the contents of his fridge and dumped anything that smelled funny. He shrugged into his jacked and collected the garbage bag from the bin to take it out. Usually, whatever lived in the trashcan outside was either dormant or absent in the early morning, so he preferred to take the garbage out during the day whenever he could. Perhaps he should've insisted on Nym calling animal control, but none of the other neighbors seemed bothered by Amy's presence, and he didn't want to antagonize them by eradicating what they all considered their shared pet. And they obviously did. One time, Oliver caught Sky placing a bowl of milk by the trashcan and Rafe leaving what looked like restaurant-packaged leftovers of a steak dinner on the lid.

In Oliver's opinion, it was a sure way to attract every wild critter in the vicinity, but then again, maybe they knew better than to try to steal Amy's grub.

He came out onto the landing just as Nym was closing the door to his own apartment. Curious, Oliver craned his head to peer inside over the man's shoulder but saw nothing but a dim stretch of hallway very similar to his own.

"Hey," Nym said, his face momentarily brightening with genuine pleasure, the sight of which made Oliver's heart skip a beat. "What are you doing up so early?"

"I just couldn't sleep," Oliver said, heat creeping up his cheeks at the memory of the dream. Steamy breath gliding over exposed skin, hard weight pinning him down, sharp claws digging into the concrete floor by the side of his head… Okay, where had that last bit come from? Clearly, Oliver was getting into the Halloween spirit a little too much.

He cleared his throat before a certain part of his anatomy could take renewed interest.

"What are you doing?" he asked.

"Gonna fix the porch railing." Nym gestured to his tool belt. "Make sure it stays up, at least."

"Let me throw out the trash, and I'll join you."

"Yeah?"

"Yeah." Oliver smiled. "If you don't mind me helping, of course."

"No, I don't mind." Nym seemed to hesitate for a second. "Listen, I've been thinking… If you don't have any plans for tomorrow, would you like to go to the park with me? We could make a picnic lunch out of it."

"Sure, I'd love to." That came out a little too quickly, and Oliver added, "I mean, if it doesn't rain tomorrow."

"No, the weather will hold," Nym said with unwavering certainty. "It's going to be a beautiful day."

Oliver could have sworn the man's shoulders sagged infinitesimally in relief at hearing his assent. Or was it just wishful thinking?

In any case, he'd never been so eager spend a Sunday at the park.

Chapter Twelve

Nym had been right.

Sunday morning rolled in, and there wasn't a cloud in sight. Oliver woke up to birdsong in the garden, feeling more energized than he'd felt in the last two weeks (having barricaded the door to the closet). The sun shone brightly in the sky as if in defiance of the fact that it was the middle of October in Maryland, and thankfully, his sleep hadn't been troubled either by nightmares or any unexpected visitors popping over from the hidden passageway.

Nym had promised he'd pick him up around noon, so Oliver spent a chill morning catching up on his social media, finishing some work assignments, and fixing some sandwiches to take with them. He didn't know what Nym had planned for them, but he figured it never hurt to be ready.

At exactly twelve, Nym knocked on his door, holding an honest-to-God picnic basket. It seemed so incongruous to his ripped jeans and bomber jacket, and yet so sweet at the same time.

"Ready?" Nym asked.

"Ready," Oliver affirmed, grabbing his own jacket and keys and following him out the door.

They opted to walk along a trail that snaked around the lake and led into Druid Hill Park. The 745-acre park had been dubbed as one of the top attractions in Baltimore, and Oliver could well understand why. It offered a variety of features, including the Maryland Zoo and an eighteen-hole golf course, and those who didn't opt to partake of the organized amenities could still enjoy the picturesque, almost wild way autumn seemed to reign here. The light breeze rippled across the endless sea of trees swathed in every shade of yellow, red, and orange, the colors bright against the pallid sky awash in sunlight. It carried the fresh scents of wet earth and rotten leaves that unmistakably reminded Oliver of Nym.

They skirted the man-made lake to the west, walking at a leisurely pace and chatting about nothing in particular, keeping the conversation on neutral topics like the weather and the plans for restoring the front porch. Yesterday, Nym had done his best to secure the railing and the posts as a temporary measure, with Oliver helping (mostly by handing him the right tools and wooden planks), but it would take a lot more to properly return the dainty spindles to all their original glory.

The wind ruffled the surface of the lake as they made their way around it on the west side. Big parts of the lake and the surrounding area were closed off for construction, yellow excavators dominating the shoreline.

"What's going on here?" Oliver nodded at the excavators.

"The city is installing new buried water tanks in the lake," Nym said. "This whole area will have a new waterfront for sports and recreation. They also plan to lay down new bike trails and renovate the roads. It's going to be busy around here for a while."

He frowned as he said it, as if he could already imagine construction teams milling on the Lodge's doorstep, but to Oliver, Cox's preoccupation with the property had suddenly become a lot clearer. Urban development projects like this would usually guarantee an influx of younger, trendier, and, more importantly, more affluent residents. By getting a head start on the action, Cox stood to make a lot of money by increasing the amount of luxury lodgings on offer.

They walked down Swann Drive, passing the Chinese Pavilion, greeted by chattering birds and joggers taking advantage of the clement weather to ramp up their weekend exercise routine.

"Wow, this is beautiful," Oliver gasped when they neared the Rawlings Conservatory.

"Yeah, I thought you might like it," Nym said with a smug smile.

The nineteenth-century structure was every bit as grand as the British Victorian greenhouses Oliver had only seen in pictures. Nestled against the backdrop of beautifully manicured gardens, it glittered like a multifaceted jewel, scattering the rays of an autumn sun off its many windows.

"Do you want a tour of the inside?" Nym asked.

Oliver was tempted, of course, if only to examine the structure's stylish architecture, but it was equally tempting to spend the lovely day outside, taking in the fresh air and enjoying the company. Besides, it would give them something else to do together on another occasion as the conservatory wasn't going anywhere for the foreseeable future, and neither was Oliver.

"I would, but we can do that later," he said. "Right now, I'm starving."

"Come on, then."

They found a secluded spot with a picnic table under the shade of an old linden tree, within view of the stately conservatory across a sweep of lawn. It was as pastoral a place as Oliver had even seen, and he imagined it would be even more beautiful, though perhaps busier, in the spring and summer months. Oliver was glad he opted to wear one of his warmer sweaters under his jacket because the air held a distinct nip despite the bright sunshine.

They spread out their food on the table. Nym's basket also included plastic plates and glasses, so it turned out they were having lunch in style. The food was good too—club sandwiches, salad, even freshly cut fruit. It made Oliver's efforts seem meager in comparison, but he didn't mind it at all.

"For someone who doesn't cook a lot, you sure know what you're doing," he said, filling up his plate as Nym produced bottles of soda and light beer.

Nym shrugged. "Doesn't seem much point to go to all the trouble when it's only me."

"Well, I wouldn't mind someone cooking for me," Oliver said and bit his tongue. Was that too suggestive? Was he being too forward again?

The wry curve to Nym's lips suggested he wasn't alarmed. "Actually, I wouldn't mind having someone to cook for," he said. "It just that the opportunity hasn't come up."

"Never?" Oliver asked before taking a bite out of his sandwich.

"Well, obviously I've been in a few relationships where I could cook for the other guy," Nym clarified, cutting right to the point with his usual bluntness. "And you already know I'm not one for casual dating. As a matter of fact, one of the reasons I came to Baltimore was to get some distance after a bad breakup."

"Really? What happened? That is, if you want to tell me. It's okay if you don't," Oliver added hastily, afraid he'd touched on a sensitive subject.

Nym stared down his plate, absently fiddling with a napkin. For a minute, Oliver was sure he wasn't going to answer, but at last Nym shook his head.

"I'd been with this guy for about a year. His name was—well, is—Max," he said, still keeping his eyes down. "I was in love with him, or at least I thought I was. And I believed he was equally in love with me. I made a decision to confide in him about something—something that is very important to me. A secret."

Oliver didn't move, afraid to breathe so as to not spoil the rare moment of candidness.

"Unfortunately, Max didn't take it well," Nym said. Tiny pieces of the shredded napkin fluttered away on the breeze like white butterflies, but he didn't seem to notice. His expression was neutral, carefully so, but his voice took on a raw edge Oliver hadn't heard before. "I suppose it shook him. Even frightened him. Which is okay. I get it. Some things aren't for everyone, and…" He fell silent and then shook his head. "Anyway, he was so upset with me he threatened to make my secret public. So when I found out about the inheritance, I figured it'd be good for me to get away, start fresh somewhere else. Have a purpose, even if it's a little one in the grand scheme of things."

Silence settled between them. Nym's words resonated heavily with Oliver, and he wished he had some time alone to process everything Nym had told him. The fact that there was some deep dark secret, something another person might find extremely upsetting, was confirmation for Oliver that he hadn't been imagining things or looking for mysteries that weren't there.

Of course his first impulse was to try to discover what the secret was. What could possibly be so dire as to make someone's boyfriend flip out like that? Was it as bad as the outrageous scenarios Oliver had been playing in his head, about Nym being a con artist or a criminal on the run?

Was it worse?

But he knew this wasn't the time or the place to ask. Nym had just admitted something that had to have given him huge trust issues with new people in his life. Oliver could understand that, because he had the same issues, and for a similar reason. Maybe, just maybe, if he showed Nym some measure of sincerity, he would eventually feel comfortable enough to open up to him in return.

"I can understand that," Oliver said hesitantly. "I came to Baltimore to have a fresh start too."

Nym raised his head, meeting his Oliver's gaze for the first time since starting the conversation. "I thought it was because you got a job with this fancy architectural firm."

Oliver gave a crooked smile. "Why do you think I applied for the position in the first place? I have no ties to Baltimore; all my family lives in Florida. But I saw an opportunity to get away, and I took it."

"What happened?" Nym asked, not bothering to tiptoe around the question the way Oliver had done.

Oliver drew a deep, shaky breath. When he realized he was bracing against the edge of the picnic table, he forced himself to release the white-knuckled grip and folded his hands in his lap instead.

It was difficult to talk about, even after all this time; to analyze what had happened. But it was even harder to face that he'd let it happen for as long as it had. He knew none of it was his fault, but that knowledge hadn't penetrated his soul quite yet.

"I was in a relationship too," Oliver said. "I met Jake in college. I was an architecture major, and he studied political science. I, too, thought I was in love. Most likely I was, at least at the beginning. When we graduated together, I wanted it to be the start of our life, with both of us getting through our internships, living together, saving money to buy a house. You know, the usual stuff. But then..."

He paused to take another deep breath. Damn it, he couldn't fall apart now, not after promising himself to look at the situation clinically, objectively. He'd dealt with it, and it was all behind him now. Still, his ribs twinged in phantom pain at the memory.

"Then?" Nym prompted. He leaned in, arms folded on the table, the remains of his sandwich forgotten. His honey-colored eyes brimmed with concern, and it was the only thing that gave Oliver enough courage to continue.

"Then Jake turned violent. I thought he was only being playful at first, you know? Like, being rough in the bedroom, things like that. It was even exciting at first, but it quickly bled into all other aspects of our lives. Every time something went wrong at his job, he'd take it out on me. And for a while, I really thought I was doing something wrong. Saying the wrong things that would piss him off, not being attentive enough, not spending all my free time with him."

"He beat you?" Nym asked. His voice was tight, but his eyes seemed to change color, going darker, the honey turning to glowing embers, and it took Oliver a moment to realize why.

Nym was angry. Angry on Oliver's behalf.

"Yeah," Oliver said, averting his eyes because he couldn't bear the intensity of Nym's gaze. "Silly, right? I mean, it went on for months. I should have ended it sooner, but I kept thinking it was just a temporary thing. That Jake was too stressed at work, or too confused because I liked it when he was being bossy in bed. I only told him it was over after I found myself in a hospital with two broken ribs and a bruised larynx."

Nym's eyebrows drew together, and he scowled.

"He broke your ribs, and you're the one who's 'silly'? Screw him," he said fiercely. "He's an abuser. You should be blaming him, not yourself. No one is allowed to hurt you like that, for whatever reason."

Oliver's heart clenched, momentarily overwhelmed by emotion. He uncapped a bottle of beer and took a long swig to steady his nerves before continuing.

"Anyway, we broke up, and that was it. He stayed away from me, and I didn't press charges. I know I should have," Oliver said at Nym's expression. "Today, I would have. But then, all I wanted was to heal and finish my internship so I could start over somewhere new, far away from Miami."

"Baltimore?"

Oliver nodded.

"Well, I suppose you could do worse," Nym said with mock gravity.

Oliver grinned. "Actually, I kinda like it here so far. It has its ups and downs, for sure, but at least here I'm not constantly reminded of everything I regret."

"I get it," Nym said, his tone turning serious again. "It'd have been nice if the bastard had gotten his comeuppance, but your well-being is equally, if not more, important. You had to do what you had to do to get your life together. And it seems to me like you're doing a good job of it."

Warmth crept up Oliver's cheeks. "Thanks. I can say the same about you."

Nym took a sip of his beer. "I don't know about that."

"It must be difficult to juggle so many things at once, especially when money is tight. But you do know you don't have to do it all alone, right?" Oliver set his beer down and put a tentative hand on Nym's arm. "I know it's not much, but I'll do whatever I can to help, and I'm sure all the other tenants will pitch in if you ask them."

Nym studied him from under his brow. "Why would you do that? I thought… Well, for a while, I was sure you didn't like me."

"It wasn't that. It's just…weird things keep happening around the house, and you haven't exactly been forthcoming. I guess it's still difficult for me to trust people, and maybe I do tend to jump to conclusions, but…"

He trailed off, unsure how to articulate the subject he so desperately wanted to bring up, and which he was so afraid of.

The gentle breeze played with the tips of Nym's shaggy hair and rippled the grass around them. There was another pause, accentuated by the singing of birds and the laughter of children coming from another picnic table where a family had sat down to have lunch.

"You're right," Nym said finally, his eyes bright. "I haven't been forthcoming, and now you know the reason."

"Because you're scared I'm going to react the way your ex-boyfriend did?"

"Yes."

"I like to think I can keep an open mind," Oliver said gently. "Whatever it is, I can see you're a good person, Nym. Maybe in time you'll feel comfortable enough to let me see the whole of you."

"Maybe." Nym continued to regard him with an unreadable expression, but he didn't move his arm from where Oliver was touching it. "I hope so."

Oliver nodded, and after a second, Nym nodded back as if sealing some unspoken agreement between them.

Looking back on those last two weeks of October, Oliver could genuinely say he'd felt happy.

Since their not-a-date in the park on Sunday, they'd gone on several more, with Nym showing him his favorite places to grab a burger or have a drink after work. Sometimes they'd spend the entire evening talking (well, mostly Oliver talking) about everything under the sun—books, movies, TV shows, traveling. Admittedly, they both didn't have a lot of free time for TV or hobbies, but that only gave them an excuse to watch their favorite shows together while sharing a pizza in Oliver's living room on those rare occasions when they could spare an entire evening hanging out.

Other times, especially lazy weekend mornings, they'd go on long walks in the park, not saying anything at all, simply enjoying the fresh air and the ever-shifting color palette of the foliage. Sometimes they'd hike around the lake, trying to spot the house turret from various vantage points.

As Halloween drew nearer, Lakeside Lodge had transformed into a veritable haunted mansion—not that it needed much in way of modifying. Pumpkins, carved by the tenants, adorned the front porch, steps, and stoop, each more elaborate than the next, luminous faces grinning mischievously from the shadows when Oliver came home in the evenings. With the decorations already in place, he and Nym decided to postpone the refurbishment until after the holiday. In the meantime, Oliver amused himself by drawing the detailed new design while Nym made new spindles to replace the broken ones in his makeshift workshop in the shed.

It all boiled down to Oliver liking to spend time with Nym. He liked talking to him, appreciated the unexpected insights Nym had to offer, his dry and often sardonic sense of humor. And he would've been comfortable continuing their non-dating for as long as Nym wanted. So it came as a surprise when Nym asked him, formally and a little stiffly, to have dinner with him at a swanky Thai restaurant on Saturday night, the day before the big Halloween party.

Oliver was surprised to see Nym forgo his usual "lumberjack chic" attire and opt for what clearly was his best dress shirt. He'd even attempted to slick back his unruly hair, but it had regained its perpetual tousled state by the time they arrived at the restaurant. It all made Oliver wish he'd put a little more effort into his own appearance.

"Do you like Thai food?" Oliver asked once they were seated and given their menus.

"Not sure." Nym glanced around the stylish interior and then at the menu. "I've never tried it before."

"Why did you choose this place then?"

Nym cleared his throat, never taking his eyes off the printed offerings. "Google reviews said it's romantic."

"Oh." Oliver's cheeks heated, and he looked away to hide an involuntary smile.

They chatted a bit until the waitress brought them their orders of papaya salad and tom yum soup.

"How's your work going?" Nym asked, picking at his salad.

"Pretty good. I have a better feel for the place now," Oliver said, though he didn't elaborate on whether that was necessarily a positive thing. "And how's yours?"

"Okay, I guess. I asked if I could put in more hours, but there are no rush jobs at the moment, which means less overtime." Nym frowned at the slice of papaya before popping it into his mouth.

Oliver thought that if Nym worked even longer hours, he'd have no time to sleep, but it wasn't his place to comment, especially knowing that extra income was a touchy issue for the landlord. So he only hummed noncommittally and sipped his soup. The spicy heat tingled pleasantly on the back of his tongue.

"Did I tell you about this new documentary on Netflix?" he asked to change the subject to something more upbeat. "It's true crime mixed with all sorts of inexplicable events and sightings, like ghosts and UFOs. I've only watched the first episode so far, but it's really interesting."

"Do you believe in them?" Nym asked, his gaze sharpening.

"UFOs?"

"Ghosts."

Oliver's memory skittered back to the night he'd met Mr. Livingstone. He couldn't deny that the thought of him being…something other than a living, flesh-and-blood human being had occurred to him at the time, but would he consider it in all seriousness? He'd probably appear foolish even discussing it.

"I don't know," he hedged. "Maybe ghosts and apparitions are just natural phenomena we don't understand yet."

"Maybe," Nym conceded. "And maybe I could watch that documentary with you. Tell me more about it?"

He reached out and covered Oliver's hand with his own, his touch oddly timid. Oliver flipped his hand, palm up, and gently squeezed Nym's fingers in encouragement.

"I would love to."

Chapter Thirteen

"I had a really great time tonight," Nym said as they crossed the entryway and climbed the stairs to the first floor after coming home from the restaurant.

"Yeah, me too," Oliver said, wondering at the sudden painstaking carefulness in Nym's voice. "You were right; it was romantic. And the food was good."

"I believe it could even be classified as a great date," Nym said.

They paused on the landing, midway between their respective doors. The circle of light cast by the single bulb pooled around them as if they were the leading couple in a black-and-white movie, caught in the spotlight.

The moment stretched, and Oliver tipped his face up, gazing into Nym's eyes expectantly, though he didn't know exactly what was it he was waiting for. His heart thudded in anticipation regardless, so loud Oliver was sure the other man must hear it echoing in his own chest.

"Yes," he agreed again, a little breathlessly. "One of my best dates to date."

Nym licked his lips, his amber eyes flickering with a strange emotion. Uncertainty? Hesitation? Apprehension?

Either way, it was an expression Oliver wasn't used to seeing on the landlord's face.

"Would you...would you like to come in?" Nym asked in a husky voice.

Oliver's already elevated heartbeat ratcheted wildly. *Yes!* he wanted to cry but instead settled for a soft: "Are you sure?"

Nym nodded gravely. "I am."

He extended his hand to Oliver, and Oliver took it before following Nym inside his apartment. Only the faint light streaming from the living room windows illuminated the entry-way, and Oliver took advantage of the darkness to boost his courage. He took off his glasses while Nym was busy locking the door behind them and shoved them in the inner pocket of his jacket. As soon as Nym turned around, Oliver grabbed him by the collar and pulled him down for a kiss.

Their lips bumped against each other almost painfully, Nym smothering a tiny gasp of surprise. But a second later, he caught on, plunging his tongue deeper into Oliver's welcoming mouth, and it was Oliver's turn to moan in startled delight. He never knew the feel of a rough beard scratching his face could be erotic, and yet it was an exciting, even thrilling, new facet of this physical connection.

Nym pushed him against the wall, deftly navigating around the console table and the coat rack. Oliver wrapped his arms around the other man's neck, holding on for dear life. Every whiff of Nym's heated skin, every slide of his tongue against his, tinged with a spicy hint of green curry, sent an electric current down to Oliver's groin, his cock hardening painfully in the confines of his jeans. He whimpered when Nym grabbed his crotch, gently squeezing him through the rough fabric.

"Oh, God," Oliver managed when Nym finally broke their sloppy, wet kisses. "God, I want you so much."

He probably wouldn't have said it to Nym's face in the light of day, but now, in the moonlight-infused darkness enveloping them like a protective cocoon, the words tumbled out on their own, and he had no desire to hold them back anymore. They were true; he wanted Nym like he hadn't wanted anyone else in his life, not even Jake when they'd first started dating.

The last thing he needed right now was to think about Jake.

Nym made a low, growling sound that reverberated through their pressed bodies and latched his mouth to the underside of Oliver's jaw, nibbling and sucking on delicate skin. Oliver tipped his head back to allow him better access and writhed under the combined pressure of his lips and fingers, thrusting into his touch.

"Then you're going to get me." Nym's voice was a hot whisper in his ear, and Oliver shuddered. "All of me."

His teeth closed on the skin beneath Oliver's ear, his hand squeezing him hard at the same time, and suddenly it was more than Oliver could bear. He screwed his eyes shut against the fireworks that blossomed in his vision and cried out, an aching, keening, inarticulate sound of complete surrender.

Oliver's knees would've buckled, but Nym held him tight, pinned safely between the wall and his hard body. His grip eased, his touch becoming gentle, soothing.

"Fuck," Oliver muttered, his shoulders sagging. Now that the haze of orgasm slowly dissipated, embarrassment—no, mortification—set in. "God, I'm so sorry. It's been a while, and…"

Here he was, finally getting the chance to get it on with Nym, and he just blew it by creaming his pants like a sixteen-year-old in the middle of his first groping session. He would never live it down.

"That's okay," Nym murmured. "Actually, it's kinda hot."

Oliver raised his eyes at him.

"It is?"

Instead of an answer, Nym undid Oliver's jeans and slid his hand right into the mess inside Oliver's underwear. Oliver held his breath as Nym brought his slick hand to his mouth and licked it.

"So good," he murmured, and Oliver's cock gave an involuntary twitch, despite being utterly spent.

Nym, however, wasn't done. He brushed his come-sticky thumb across Oliver's lips, and acting on impulse, Oliver caught it in his mouth and sucked on it hard, tasting himself on Nym's calloused skin.

"Yes," Nym breathed. "Do that."

Oliver wasn't perhaps the savviest person when it came to sex, but he knew it for the invitation that it was. And it was one he didn't mind accepting.

He dropped to his knees, his fly still gaping open, and reached for Nym's belt. The other man leaned over him, helping Oliver free his cock out of his jeans and boxers. Even in the dimness, it was impressive in its size, hard as a rock and leaking precome when Oliver took it in his mouth.

He was still weak and shaken in the aftermath of his own orgasm, otherwise he'd have prolonged the experience, or taken the time to admire Nym's assets. As it was, he did his best to get Nym off as fast and as efficiently as he could.

Nym's hand tightened in Oliver's hair and then relaxed. When Oliver risked a quick look up, he saw him biting his lower lip, his eyes half-hooded. The movements of his hips were shallow in a measured way, as if he was holding back, and, conversely, it made Oliver double his efforts.

Nym's cock began to throb on his tongue; the other man was close. Oliver bore down, gagging a little, but in that same moment, Nym pulled back and out, and came with a low, forceful grunt. Come splashed all over Oliver's face, his shirt, and his jacket.

Oliver sat back on his heels and looked up at Nym, who was breathing heavily, his hand still resting lightly on Oliver's head. His eyes smoldered as if alight from within rather than reflecting the faint glow coming from the living room.

"You look so…" Nym didn't finish the thought, his tone wondering and awed.

The word he was probably looking for was "debauched," but maybe Nym was into that. He was certainly gazing at Oliver as if he was ready to devour him, even though his touch remained featherlight.

Oliver flicked his tongue to the side to catch the drop of come gliding down his cheek, and Nym shuddered. Yep, the man definitely had a thing for come play. Again, Oliver couldn't say he minded. In fact, just the thought of it turned him on a little, even though the sensation of having come drying on his skin was a strange one.

Nym helped him up and drew him in for another kiss. Their tastes mingled in Oliver's mouth, his tongue tingling with the new flavor.

They shrugged out of their jackets and continued kissing languidly, the earlier urgency gone but the desire still simmering beneath the temporary fatigue.

"Let's get you cleaned up, shall we?" Nym suggested in between planting tiny kisses on Oliver's jaw.

"Here?"

"I have better water pressure."

Oliver barked a laugh. Well, why not? It was clear he'd be spending the night anyway, and he was already itching to get out of his soiled clothes.

He nodded assent, and Nym led him to the bathroom.

Momentarily blinded by the bright white light, Oliver halted at the threshold. Under the comforting protection of darkness, it had been easy to get carried away and let himself do things he'd never normally do, but now he felt as though his every flaw was under scrutiny. He caught a glimpse of his reflection in the bathroom mirror above the sink, and even though the details were a little fuzzy without his glasses on, he could still make out the outline of his hair standing on end, the streaks of white come on flushed skin, and the bewildered look in his eyes. Without question, this was an image of someone who'd just had sex, but he wasn't at all sure he was in any way sexy.

"Come on." Nym gently nudged him from behind, and Oliver stepped inside.

The small, tiled bathroom felt crowded with the both of them inside, and they stripped awkwardly, trying not to jostle each other. The harsh lighting that had seemed so unforgiving to Oliver was an advantage where Nym's physique was concerned. This was the first time Oliver had seen Nym completely naked, and he paused in removing his own briefs to admire his broad shoulders, flat abs, and powerful thighs covered with a dusting of dark hair. He was the very image of rugged masculinity, and Oliver drank in the sight, for a brief second forgetting his own insecurities.

Nym, for his part, seemed to regard Oliver with equal appreciation. His gaze slid down Oliver's body, almost as tangible as a caress, then snapped back to Oliver's eyes.

"So who's going in first?" Oliver asked, his cheeks heating up again.

"I think we can fit there together," Nym said.

Oliver finally disposed of his briefs, grimacing at the stickiness that met his fingers, and stepped into the shower, with Nym joining him.

The water pressure was unquestionably better, and Oliver gave himself a moment to revel in the strong stream hitting his body, washing away the traces of their fumbling releases. Nym grabbed a bar of herb-scented soap, and they took turns washing each other, their touches slowly progressing from practical to exploratory. By the time they were both clean, the fresh-smelling lather washed away, they were both aroused again, their cocks sporting a hopeful half-mast.

Nym turned around to replace the soap, and Oliver, emboldened by the gentle intimacy between them, ran his hands over the hard globes of Nym's ass.

"Mmmm. Feels nice." Instead of turning around right away, Nym leaned against the wall, pushing back into Oliver's touch.

Oliver went down on his knees and pried open Nym's buttocks with his thumbs. He craned his head and slowly, deliberately, licked inside, making sure to lavish the most attention on the tiny puckered hole of his anus.

"Jesus," Nym muttered from above, his voice uncharacteristically shaky.

Oliver licked again, breathing in the scent of herbal soap, clean skin, and an underlying hint of heavy musk.

"What do you want?" Nym asked in a low rumble that rang loud in the small space. "We can do anything you want."

That was unexpectedly generous. Or maybe it wasn't entirely unexpected. So far, there hadn't been a moment when Oliver had felt intimidated or even uncomfortable in Nym's presence. Things had happened naturally between them, and they were content to let them, gradually finding their rhythm. So when faced with such a direct question, Oliver was at a momentary loss.

Maybe it was because he'd rarely been allowed to decide on what happened in bed.

And yet, he knew exactly what he wanted. He'd wanted it ever since their first awkward kiss in the dusty attic, or maybe even before that. Maybe he'd wanted it ever since Nym had opened the front door to let him in, which seemed like ages ago but had only been four weeks.

"I want you to fuck me," Oliver whispered, his words ghosting across the skin of Nym's ass.

He knew Nym had heard him because his muscles flexed instinctively. Then Nym turned around, turned off the water, and offered Oliver his hand to help him up. As soon as they were out of the shower and toweled off, Nym scooped Oliver in his arms, ignoring his undignified squawk, and carried him to the bedroom like he weighed nothing at all.

Oliver landed on the bed with a whoosh. Nym paused to flick on the bedside lamp, but Oliver barely had time to take in the rest of the room before Nym was back on him, kissing and nibbling and licking every inch of his naked skin, lightly teasing one nipple with his teeth, then the other. Oliver spread his legs to accommodate Nym's powerful body, his hands roaming freely across the expanse of the man's broad back and shoulders.

"So we both agree this is a date, right?" he asked, a little breathlessly.

Nym raised his head from Oliver's chest, his lips swollen and glistening.

"Guess so," he said. "Why?"

"Because you're about to have sex on a first date, Nymphus."

There was a moment of stunned silence, and then Nym snorted, eyes crinkling with laughter.

"Oh, shut up."

Oliver wiggled under him suggestively. "Make me."

Nym made another one of those low, rumbling sounds that seemed to originate at the base of his throat and proceeded to do just that.

"You have condoms and lube, right?" Oliver asked when they broke off again.

Nym nodded and paused to rummage in his nightstand drawer. It took him a good minute, but finally, he produced a tiny tube and a silver wrapper.

"Sorry. It's been a while for me too," he said apologetically.

Oliver didn't want to examine the reason why this confession made his heart skip a beat, but it had. It wasn't as if he didn't already know Nym wasn't seeing anyone, or that for him, the desire for sex had to spring from a deeper emotion. But that meant Nym had to have some feelings for him, that he wanted Oliver because he genuinely cared for him. And that was kind of a big deal for both of them.

"How do you want it?" Nym asked, giving Oliver's cock an encouraging tug before unscrewing the lube.

Images of Nym fucking him face-to-face with his legs thrown over Nym's shoulders flashed through Oliver's mind. But as tempting as that option was, he really was a little out of practice, and doing it the other way would perhaps be a little easier on him. Besides, being taken from behind came with its own unique set of perks.

He flipped around on the bed and shoved a pillow beneath his hips without asking for permission. Nym hummed appreciatively and squeezed Oliver's buttock with one hand, making him squirm and open up his legs even wider.

A lube-slicked finger brushed against his hole, and Oliver closed his eyes, holding his breath in anticipation. Being breached in the most intimate of places was always strange at first, and it was strange now as Nym's blunt finger pushed inside. Instead of focusing on the vague promise of the pain to come, Oliver conjured a mental picture of how they must look, Nym's bulky body covering his slender one, pinning him down with nothing but his finger. He whimpered and writhed against the sheets, the sound turning into a broken moan when Nym added another finger, stretching him to the edge of his limits.

"Easy," Nym murmured, slowly twisting and turning his fingers.

"I don't want easy," Oliver panted. "Make it hard."

His forwardness was rewarded with a sharp intake of breath.

"God, Oliver." Nym's voice was low and husky with lust. "I can't believe…"

"Come on," Oliver urged. "Fuck me."

He snapped his hips, driving the point home, impaling himself further on Nym's fingers, and whimpered again when Nym withdrew them.

The sound of tearing foil, another squirt of lube—and Oliver couldn't suppress a cry when the tip of Nym's cock pushed inside the ring of loosened muscle.

Nym halted, half-buried in Oliver's ass. His tension was a palpable thing, washing over Oliver's heated skin in waves, but he stroked Oliver's hips gently, soothingly.

"Okay?"

"Yeah. Yeah, go on."

Nym rolled his hips, lodging his cock deeper with every move, taking Oliver past the burning toward tentative pleasure. He adjusted his position to a new angle that sent a flurry of sparks up Oliver's spine and then settled into a steady, slow rhythm.

Oliver closed his eyes and braced his hands on the mattress, his breath hitching with every push. The pain of intrusion receded, replaced with waves of pleasure that rocked his body with Nym's every thrust and Oliver's every exhale. It spread through his limbs, setting all his nerves alight, making them sing with pure delight.

But it was too slow. Oliver hadn't been kidding when he said he wanted it hard, and now Nym's even, measured movements weren't quite enough to bring him to the edge. He squirmed, lifting his hips to urge Nym to move faster, and grunted in frustration when the man's gentle hold tightened, pinning him to the pillow.

"Harder, please," he begged, his voice hoarse with need.

"Not yet." Hot breath raised goose bumps on Oliver's damp skin. "Trust me."

Oliver made a strangled sound. *Trust me.* Such a simple, straightforward request, and yet, in some ways, the hardest one to grant.

Did he trust Nym? With his body, his safety, his satisfaction, maybe even his heart? Oliver wasn't sure. The only thing he knew was that he wanted to, so badly.

He made himself relax, slumping into Nym's embrace, letting the other man set the pace and call the shots, falling in sync with his thrusts, taking everything Nym was giving him without question.

Behind him, Nym hummed his approval, the low sound echoing in Oliver's chest, and slid his hand beneath him, taking hold of Oliver's leaking cock and pumping it with the same deliberate, maddening slowness. Oliver quivered like a taut bowstring, riding the sensations that threatened to overwhelm him. The weight of Nym's body on his back, his big cock stretching him, filling him, pumping into him with unyielding strength, his large rough hand squeezing him with every stroke—it was as if Oliver were living out every single one of his fantasies at once.

His moans took on a dangerous edge, coming closer to broken sobs. Maybe Nym felt the change, too, because his movements took on speed and urgency, becoming faster and shallower. A knot of white-hot radiance began to tighten in Oliver's groin, Nym's insistent stroking pushing it closer and closer to the surface until it exploded behind Oliver's tightly shut eyes in a flurry of incandescent fireflies.

He cried out, and Nym grunted in his ear, his own body going rigid and his cock burrowing inside as deep as it would go. For a few moments, they floated together on a wave of pleasure before crashing down in a tangle of limbs, sweat, and bunched bedding.

Oliver collapsed onto the pillows, breathing hard. Nym shifted so as not to crush him but didn't let go entirely. Instead, he snuggled against Oliver's back.

Oliver turned around, wanting to say something, but words and thoughts and emotions jarred together, refusing to assemble into anything coherent as sweet lassitude spread to the tips of his toes.

Nym must have read something unspoken in Oliver's eyes because he smiled faintly and whispered: "Shhh. It's okay. I got you."

Oliver wanted to smile in return, but his eyelids grew heavy, and he allowed himself to sink into Nym's embrace yet again.

Oliver woke up with a jolt, and it took him a few seconds to remember where he was. Darkness hung around him like a thick, warm blanket, so he knew it was still the middle of the night. The curtains fluttered with the fresh breeze coming from the half-opened window, the patches of moonlight shifting on the floor with their every move.

Nym lay next to him, his arm wrapped casually around Oliver's middle, but the unsteady rise and fall of his chest suggested he wasn't asleep.

Oliver turned to look at him, catching the eerie glint in Nym's eyes.

"Why aren't you sleeping?" he asked softly.

"Just thinking," Nym replied, equally quietly.

"What about?"

"You. Us. This. Everything."

"Wow. That's some heavy stuff."

He felt more than saw Nym's smile.

"I guess," Nym said. "But it's a good kind of heavy."

"Yeah?"

Nym found his hand in the tangle of sheets and slowly stroked his palm with his thumb. "Yeah. Will you be at the Halloween party tomorrow?"

"Of course. I wouldn't dream of missing it after putting in all that hard work with the decorations."

"Good." Nym continued to stroke his hand, his touch more soothing than suggestive. "What's your costume?"

"It's a surprise."

"Is it something naughty?" Nym teased.

"You'll just have to see for yourself, won't you?"

Nym chuckled. Oliver expected him to pull him closer, maybe hug him to his chest, but it looked as though Nym was deliberately giving Oliver his space while still keeping contact, and Oliver appreciated that.

"I might have a few surprises for you too," Nym said, so quietly it might have been a whisper.

"What kind of surprises?"

"If I told you, it wouldn't be a surprise," Nym chided. "But it's time we had a talk, don't you think?"

"At a party?" Oliver couldn't keep the incredulity out of his voice.

Nym didn't say anything for a moment. His strokes slowed, became almost weightless.

"I didn't think I could grow to care about anyone again like I cared for Max. The way things ended between us broke my heart, and I told myself I'd never be so foolish as to fall for someone ever again. And yet, here I am."

Oliver propped himself on one elbow, looking down into Nym's gleaming eyes.

"You…care for me?" he asked, careful not to let the emotion that swelled in his heart flood his words.

Nym nodded. "I do. More than I thought possible. And I think—I hope—the feeling is mutual."

"It is," Oliver said with a certainty that surprised him. "Mutual."

Nym brought Oliver's hand to his lips, rough beard grazing his knuckles, and kissed it.

"But that also means there can be no more secrets between us," Nym continued. "You deserve to know the truth."

"What truth?"

"Tomorrow, Oliver," Nym said, brushing his lips against the pulse in his wrist. "I promise you will learn everything tomorrow."

Chapter Fourteen

When Oliver woke up in his barricaded bedroom on Sunday, he knew something big was about to go down.

When he'd left Nym's bed that morning to return to his apartment, his body was still sore, his brain still buzzing pleasantly. It'd been a wondrous, busy night, so he opted to take a shower and another nap to get some rest. He wasn't in the habit of sleeping in, even on the weekends, but the few hours of uninterrupted, dreamless sleep went a long way to restoring his energy.

Nym had insisted that tonight's party would hold a few surprises for him, so Oliver wasn't to go down to the parlor before 7 p.m., not even to help with the spread. Thankfully, he had a hefty list of assignments Ela had emailed him on Thursday—nothing urgent or crucial, mostly technical stuff that would make the team's life easier come next week. He ate while watching the renewed rain beat steadily against the living room windows, then tidied up and called Pam, who was busy getting ready for her own party (having finally decided on the guise of a slutty elf).

He did his best to focus on all his tasks, but the truth was, he was too excited not to be distracted. This was it. Nym had promised to reveal his secret, whatever it was. Oliver ran countless scenarios of this revelation, ranging from innocuous to criminal, but couldn't decide on the most likely one.

Maybe he should've insisted on Nym telling him the whole truth before jumping to bed with him, but hindsight was always twenty-twenty. Also, he had to admit he hadn't exactly been thinking with his head last night. It wasn't as if he'd ruin his chances of having sex with the man he'd been attracted to almost from the moment he'd seen him by insisting on a full disclosure before things could progress any further.

Besides, how awful could this secret be if Nym planned to reveal it in the middle of a party?

He'd never been a Halloween enthusiast, not to the extent Pam was, anyway. Sure, he enjoyed watching scary movies and getting pumped on candy as a kid, but as an adult, he wasn't that into dress-up and cheesy decor. This Halloween, however, was different. He'd picked up his costume last week and now spent almost half an hour in front of the mirror, fussing over every little detail until it was finally time to go down.

The sounds of music, loud voices, and laughter drifted toward him as he descended the stairs, holding his hand over the pummel of his fake sword so it wouldn't bump against his legs. Soft orange light shined from the parlor, illuminating the hallway festooned in fake cobwebs and cut-paper ghosts floating across the faded wallpaper. It seemed Nym hadn't been kidding about going all-out on the Halloween celebration because none of this had been here yesterday when they'd gotten back from their date.

Well, when they'd gotten back to take their date up a notch or two. Oliver's cock gave a hopeful twitch at the memory, and he forced himself to rein in his exuberance. They would have to take this slow, because it wasn't just about the undeniable sexual attraction. Oliver had grown to genuinely like Nym and his unique blend of scruffiness and empathy. Perhaps "like" was even too weak a word for what he was feeling, but he wasn't yet ready to delve deeper into his heart. A day at a time seemed to work for them at the moment, so that was what they were going to do.

He stepped into the parlor and was immediately greeted by Sky. A midnight-blue velvet robe, hemmed with silver stars and crescent moons, accentuated her long black dress. Her blond hair cascaded in elegant curls over her shoulders and the lowered hood. An antique-looking silver pentagram hung on a leather cord around her neck.

"Wow, you look amazing," Oliver said. "Where's your pointy hat?"

"Oh, those are ridiculous. A real witch wouldn't be caught dead in one," she said breezily. "And what are you supposed to be? Zorro?"

"Dread Pirate Roberts actually." Oliver adjusted his mask self-consciously.

"Oh. Well, you do look a little like Westley."

That was far more kind than it was true, but he thanked her anyway.

"Come on, everyone is waiting for you," Sky said and stepped back with a welcoming gesture.

Oliver couldn't quite put his finger on what Nym had added to the room since they both decorated it together, but it felt different somehow. Of course, it looked as spooky as could be, with bloody rags thrown over the table lamp shades to diffuse the light, and with every single one of the several dozens of candles he'd arranged over the windowsills and the mantelpiece lit. "Natural" by Imagine Dragons played on the stereo in the background.

Rodger grinned at him from his corner as if mocking him for some blunder Oliver hadn't committed yet. The living occupants all turned to look at him simultaneously.

Oliver had expected more guests, but only the Lakeside Lodge tenants, minus Nym, were present. Their appearances made Oliver wonder if he'd missed some memo regarding a mandatory theme because they were all dressed as paranormal creatures in the true spirit of the holiday, and none of the costumes were of the "store-bought is fine" variety.

Rafe occupied his favorite armchair in his usual languid sprawl, his elegant black slacks impossibly tight and his white silk shirt hanging loosely in a tumble of laces and ruffles. His dark hair was slicked back, and he smiled in greeting, his teeth very white against his red lips. He looked like one of those Victorian poets who dedicated their life to finding meaning in decadence and dissipation, or maybe a faineant pirate who had just crawled out of someone else's bed.

Sky went to join Aurora, who stood near the fireplace. She'd exchanged her leather jacket for what looked to be a dress or a tunic made of overlapping layers of sheer iridescent fabric that shimmered and changed colors with her every move. A matching cape with a shredded hem, thicker and made of some stiffer material, hung over her back. A gold circlet encrusted with green and purple gems was nestled in her black curls.

For some reason, Oliver hadn't expected Kimona to be wholly into the festive spookiness of it all, maybe because she always seemed like the most practical one of their quirky bunch. And yet, her costume was the most elaborate of them all.

A large, deep metal pail sat in the middle of the room, with Kimona lying half sunken in the water, her long hair fanned out, reaching to the floor. The caudal fin of the gray-green mermaid tail lay against the side of the pail, fluttering in time with her breathing. A tank top woven of what could be seaweed covered the upper portion of her body.

"Hey," Oliver said, offering them all a small wave in greeting. "I thought you guys were inviting your friends. Where are all the people?"

"They'll be here in a little while," Aurora said. "Nym wanted us to talk to you before everybody arrives."

"All of you?" Oliver said slowly, searching their faces. "Why?"

"I think it's best if he tells you himself." Sky's kind, gentle tone made Oliver's hackles instantly rise. "Or, better yet, show you."

"I don't understand," Oliver said. "Where's Nym?"

As if in answer, something stirred in the shadows in the far corner of the room. Nym unfolded from where he'd been— apparently—crouching on the floor, drawing himself up to his full height, and Oliver took an involuntary step back.

Shaggy brown fur completely covered Nym's towering frame from the tip of a bushy tail to the wolf-like snout. His honey-colored eyes smoldered like embers, bright and terrible and too human in an animal face. He made a low, forbidding sound, and sniffed the air, just like a real wolf would.

"Whoa." Oliver put his hands up, his heart racing from that initial moment of undiluted, primordial panic at confronting an apex predator that had been hardwired into human DNA since the beginning of time. "That's one hell of a costume."

Nym walked—no, stalked—over to him, claws scraping on hardwood floor, and stopped with his muzzle inches from Oliver's face, stooping so they could look into each other's eyes. Hot breath and the smell of wet dog wafted across Oliver's skin, making it crawl with awful premonition.

"It's not a costume."

Oliver turned sharply to where Kimona lounged in her pail. He could've sworn the deep melodical mezzo was the same voice he'd heard singing in his bathroom on his first night at the Lodge.

"You can speak?"

Kimona nodded. "Yes, but only when I'm in my true form. When I walk on land, I pay for it with my voice."

"What do you mean? What true form?"

Water rained down from the greenish tail as she lifted it out of the pail. "Isn't it obvious?"

Oliver glanced around the room, trying to take in everybody's expression. Were they all messing with him? Was this supposed to be a joke, a good-natured prank, or a clever way of bullying?

"I get it," he said, striving to keep his voice light, though hurt and annoyance threatened to bubble up to the surface. He almost wished this was simple bullying because those feelings were much easier to deal with than whatever the other option was. "You're a mermaid, he's a werewolf. Sky's a witch, right?"

Sky nodded silently. Her expression spoke of concern, but he couldn't be sure of anything anymore.

"And what are you supposed to be?"

Aurora took a half step forward from her place next to the hearth. What Oliver had mistaken for a shimmery cape unfolded behind her back, turning into a pair of semi-translucent wings, like those of a giant, weird insect.

"I'm Fae," she said in her deep, raspy voice. "Banished from my realm to wander the human world. It's been a long time since I've had a place I could call home, but now, finally, I do."

Sky reached out and took Aurora's hand, squeezing it in reassurance. "You do, beloved."

"And you?" Oliver jerked his head toward Rafe. Nym remained in his spot, still as a statue, watching him with those intense yellow eyes, but Oliver ignored him for now.

Rafe smiled. His fangs protruded over his lower lip, their points sharp as needles.

"Well, darling, I think you can guess, can't you?" he drawled. "Just don't expect a bad Romanian accent. Oh, and no turning into a bat, I'm afraid. But the rest is pretty accurate."

Oliver put his hands up in a mock gesture of surrender, though his heart flailed in his chest like that of a frightened rabbit. This sick joke deserved nothing better on his part. And this had to be a joke. There was no other possibility because Oliver was an educated, rational adult who didn't—couldn't—accept this paranormal mumbo jumbo as plausible.

"Okay, guys," he said. "You win. That's one elaborate hoax you've pulled on me. You officially scared the nerd. Where's the hidden camera?"

Sky and Aurora exchanged looks, and Kimona tapped her tail against the side of the metal pail, but everybody remained silent. The aggressive music in the background was beginning to chafe on Oliver's overstrained nerves.

"Look, it's not funny anymore," he said angrily, mostly to hide his discomfort, and turned to Nym again. "Who came up with it, anyway? You?"

The werewolf's ears twitched ever so slightly, but he too said nothing.

"It's true, Oliver," Sky insisted. "I know it's hard to take it all in, but it's all true. We didn't want to tell you at first, but I knew from the start we could trust you."

"Trust me?" Oliver gave a laugh that sounded bitter and ugly even to his own ears. "Are you trying to say this was about you trusting *me*? One of you pretended to be mute for weeks just to get me to believe I live in the same house with a witch, a fairy, a vampire, a mermaid, and a werewolf! For what? A—a viral Tik Tok video or something? Is that your idea of a great party?"

"Honestly, Oliver—" Kimona began irritably, but he plowed right on.

"And what about that old guy? Horace, right? Was he in on it, too, or did you get a kick out of fooling him too?"

"Horace Livingstone used to be a tenant here at the Lodge," Sky explained patiently. "In fact, he lived in your apartment."

A trickle of uneasy ran down Oliver's spine, but he refused to acknowledge it. His hurt and exasperation with their continuous insistence on this ridiculous charade was growing with every passing second.

He folded his arms over his chest. "And what is he supposed to be? An Egyptian mummy?"

"He's not a mummy," Rafe said. "He's not anything anymore. Well, I suppose he's something, if you count ghosts."

"Ghosts? Are you fucking— Okay, I'm done listening to this crap."

Oliver's gaze snapped to Nym, and he blinked a few times, willing away the tears that suddenly burned his eyes. The last thing he needed right now was to cry, especially if they were recording this. He'd never be able to live down the humiliation if the image of him breaking down in tears was plastered all over social media, but he needed an answer from Nym. He needed to know just how stupid and gullible he really was.

"This whole dating thing," he said, hoping the tears didn't come through in his voice. "Our friendship, everything that happened…last night. Was that all just a part of the ruse?"

Nym shuddered but remained silent, watching, breathing, like a wary animal assessing a potential threat.

"Why don't you say anything?" Oliver's voice rose despite his best efforts to keep himself calm. "It was your idea, wasn't it? Your surprise. Stop hiding behind that stinky fur and say it to my face, you miserable jerkweed."

Someone (most likely Sky) gasped audibly behind him, but he didn't turn around to check. All his attention was focused on Nym and the way he began to change.

A spasm rippled across his muzzle, and a low, painful growl tore out of his throat. He dropped onto the floor on all fours, his entire body contorting violently, bones sticking out under the brown pelt in awkward angles as the fur visibly dwindled and receded, revealing pale skin spattered with normal, human-looking dark hair.

Oliver stepped back, staring at the transformation happening at his feet. His throat went dry as sand as he watched, dumbstruck, the animal form shifting to the familiar features. Even the sharp smell of musk and deep forest faded to male sweat with a hint of sage. A moment later, all trace of the beastly appearance was gone; all that was left was Nym, crouching stark naked on the floor, his skin shining with perspiration and his shaggy hair plastered to his forehead.

"You believe us now?" Rafe inquired mockingly from his chair, and Sky made a shushing sound at him.

Both Oliver and Nym ignored him. Nym raised his head, meeting Oliver's gaze. His eyes, which a minute ago had burned with wild intensity, had dimmed to their usual amber color. The expression that lurked in their depths was unexpectedly bleak, and his posture was tense as if bracing for Oliver's reaction.

Of course, Oliver could be wrong about that, and the bracing could be due to Nym getting ready to pounce.

"This is a trick." Oliver barely recognized his own voice, it was so choked up. "Please tell me this is a trick, Nym."

Nym shook his head slowly without breaking eye contact. His shoulders sagged, the tension replaced by weary resignation. "I'm sorry, Oliver."

Oliver shook his head, too, as he took a step back. He gripped his useless plastic sword as he automatically cast about for a weapon, anything to defend himself, even if the defense was entirely illusory.

Nym pushed to his feet and stood at full height. Out of the corner of his eye, Oliver saw Sky making an elaborate gesture with her hand while whispering something under her breath. The tips of her fingers took on a soft green glow, and the same glow enveloped Nym's naked body. It coalesced into a flowy, shimmery robe that cascaded over Nym's skin, creating an illusion of modesty.

Oliver staggered back, inching closer to the door, clutching the sword at his hip in a death grip, and looked around, taking in the faces of all the people who he thought were his friends, but who were nothing but a bunch of strangers. An especially dangerous, unpredictable bunch of strangers, now that the real implications of tonight's revelations sank in. Suddenly, it all fit together like pieces of a puzzle—the creepy setting, the oppressive atmosphere of mystery and foreboding, the creatures living on the boundary of shadows and the mundane. Nym had been right in choosing this particular night to unveil his true nature. It was Halloween, the only night for the forces of darkness (or whatever the hell they called themselves) to roam free in the real world.

He'd been afraid of stumbling into an occult clique or a criminal enterprise, then of being ridiculed for his gullibility. Now, he wished for any one of these options to have been true. Anything was better than coming face-to-face with…this.

He drew a deep, shaky breath and took another step backward, to the open door.

"Oliver, don't do this," Nym pleaded quietly. The greenish sheen of his magical gown eerily illuminated his features, giving them an otherworldly appearance. Well, even more otherworldly, considering the circumstances. "Please, let me explain."

"Stay away from me," Oliver warned, even though Nym hadn't made any attempts to close the distance between them. "All of you, stay away, or I swear to God…"

He trailed off because his warning held no power, and he knew it. He couldn't even hold his own against a regular, run-of-the-mill human bully, so what could he possibly do to defend himself against a witch, a vampire, or a freaking werewolf?

There was only one thing he could think of, as cowardly as it was. Oliver turned around and ran.

Chapter Fifteen

"Thank you for letting me stay here tonight," Oliver said for the third time.

Ela lived in a homey two-bedroom townhouse on 37th Street with her boyfriend and her tabby cat, Pawla. Oliver had called her from his car after taking just enough time to throw his laptop, charger, and a change of clothes into an overnight bag before sprinting out of the house, and she'd insisted he come stay with her. Strings of tiny lights in the shape of bats and skulls decorated the stoop, but as most trick-or-treaters were safely asleep at this hour of the night, they'd been turned off.

Her boyfriend Adam was away on a business trip, but that didn't prevent her from offering Oliver the spare bedroom. Pawla, on the other hand, hissed at him as soon as he came in and spent the remainder of the evening glaring at him from her strategic vantage point on top of a vintage armoire. He chalked that up to him smelling of a particularly large dog rather than to any personal grudge the tabby might hold against him, but he could have been wrong about that. After all, he could now boast an extensive experience of misinterpreting other people's (and other creatures') feelings toward himself.

Ela shrugged off his gratitude with graceful nonchalance as she directed him to the guest bedroom and showed him the en suite bathroom.

"Are you sure you don't need to call the police?" she asked.

Her tone was light, but even in his agitated state, he could discern the genuine worry in her question. He hadn't told her exactly what had happened—how could he?—but he'd made it clear enough he'd gotten into some kind of trouble at home.

Hysterical laughter threatened to burst out of him at the thought of lodging a complaint with the police about being harassed by ghosts and monsters on Halloween, but Oliver clamped down on it. He took a deep breath and shook his head instead.

"No. I'm all right, really. I'm sorry you had to leave your party because of me."

Ela, still wearing her Captain Marvel costume, flipped her hair and waved at him dismissively.

"Don't worry about it. I was already leaving anyway. Besides, we're both dressed up, and I have a stash of leftover candy. I can open a bottle of wine, and we can have our own Halloween party right here, if you're up to it. Maybe we can even find a solution to whatever it is that's bothering you. Sometimes it helps to talk things out with someone who can offer a fresh take on the situation."

Oliver rubbed his forehead tiredly. "Thanks. I'd love to talk and explain everything, but right now I just want to get some sleep, if that's okay. I can drive us both to work tomorrow morning."

"Sure." Ela gave him another curious look but thankfully didn't press him any further. "Have a good night, and let me know if you need anything."

Oliver waited until the door clicked shut behind her and then sagged on the bed, clutching his head between his hands. He was dying for a stiff drink, even though he wasn't much of a drinker, but he knew he couldn't hold back the truth about what had happened from Ela if he added alcohol into the mix. Not while he was still reeling, unable to come to terms with what he'd seen and heard.

None of it felt real. As a matter of fact, deep down, Oliver still hoped this would all turn out to be an unfortunate practical joke. At this point, he wouldn't mind making an embarrassing appearance in a viral video or a TV show as long as it meant he hadn't spent the last month living among actual monsters—or that he'd foolishly fallen into bed with one.

Oliver groaned and pulled at his hair. How could he have been so stupid? He'd been putting his life at risk by throwing himself at the mercy of someone he apparently knew nothing about—again. Granted, Nym had never been violent with him the way Jake had been, but then he hadn't told him the truth either. In fact, he'd been deceiving Oliver from the start, so who could tell what else he was hiding? It wasn't as if Oliver possessed an extensive knowledge of werewolves (and where would he have gotten it?), so he couldn't be sure of anything, including Nym's peaceful disposition.

And how peaceful could a seven-foot canine creature re-ally be? Those claws and inch-long teeth weren't made for soul-fully howling at the full moon. Wolves were predators, after all, and logic dictated that a werewolf was a super-predator. A Wolf 2.0 designed to hunt humans, one who had a sprawling urban park on his doorstep that was just secluded enough for people on the fringes of society to disappear there without raising questions.

And the rest of them? All the folks he was starting to think of as his friends: Sky, Aurora, Kimona, even Rafe. They'd all lied to him by common agreement, so they were equally to blame. And if one or more of them were out there sating their bloodlust (Oliver shuddered again, recalling the points of Rafe's fangs), that meant the rest were protecting them. No wonder Nym was so eager to maintain the Lodge—as long as it was operational, it meant he had his own little pack ready to supply him with alibis and maybe even unsuspecting victims.

That particular jump in reasoning had taken him perhaps a bit too far, but at this point there was no stopping the downward spiral of his imagination. Oliver got up and paced the tastefully neutral bedroom, unsuccessfully willing his pulse to return to its normal pace.

He had to do something. What did ordinary people do in books and movies when suddenly confronted with the existence of paranormal forces—aside from being eaten or torn to pieces? They'd all let Oliver go unscathed and without making a serious attempt at stopping him, but he'd left all his stuff at the apartment (which, if he remembered the implications correctly, he'd shared with the incorporeal spirit of the previous tenant, the mournfully poetic Mr. Livingston). It stood to reason he'd return at some point to collect his belongings. Would the Lodge tenants be lying in wait for him when he did? Would they threaten him not to reveal the truth to the authorities?

Oliver sat back down on the bed and took out his phone from his messenger bag. The only person who might believe him (and it was a slim possibility at best) was Pam, but she was most likely still out partying, and he wasn't about to ruin her night with his tales of woe.

He itched to do something, still too upset and wired to sleep. And, realistically, there was only one course of action he could pursue in lieu of calling on law enforcement for help. He flipped through his contacts until he found the number he was looking for, and pressed dial.

He waited impatiently while the phone rang, but for some reason the sound of a suave voice on the other end of the line took him by surprise.

"Yes?" Cox inquired.

"Um... Mr. Cox, hello," Oliver stammered, all of a sudden unsure of his decision. "It's Oliver Foster. From Mr. Thompson's office? I'm sorry I'm calling you so late."

"That's all right," Cox assured him soothingly. Soft music played in the background, accentuated by the clinking of cutlery, indicating he was having a late dinner in a restaurant. "How can I be of help?"

Despite all his shortcomings, Oliver wasn't so naive as to believe Cox's question was in any way sincere, but he didn't really care about the developer's questionable morals. He was on a mission, and Cox was the only ally he could recruit.

Oliver closed his eyes and bit his lip.

"Are you still interested in Lakeside Lodge? Because if you are, I'm willing to provide you with all the information you wanted," he blurted before he could think better of it.

There was a short pause as Cox seemed to absorb this new development.

"I am interested," he said finally. "May I ask what made you change your mind?"

"You know, don't you?" Oliver said, bitterness coloring his words with an ugly tinge. "You know who they are. You know what that place is."

The pause was longer this time.

"I had my suspicions," Cox said easily. "But you wouldn't have believed me if I shared them with you, would you? Besides, you were already beginning to understand there was something deeply wrong with the people in that house, and I hoped you'd learn something on your own to affirm my conjecture and form your own opinion on the matter. It is what it is. All I know for certain is that the place has to be shut down, one way or another."

Cox didn't offer an apology for not giving him a heads-up, but then again, Oliver wasn't expecting one. Like the man said, "it is what it is." In some ways, it made things simpler.

"I agree," Oliver said tersely. "That place has to be shut down. Text me your email, and I'll send you the list."

"Ah," Cox said. "So there *is* a list." When Oliver said nothing, he added: "You're doing the right thing here, you know. That house is not fit for regular people anyway, and the sooner it gets torn down, the better. I'm glad you've finally come to that realization, even though I'm sure it wasn't an easy one."

The absolute last thing Oliver wanted was to explain to Cox his reasons for siding with him. He'd been hurt and humiliated enough without dragging his pain out in the open for a dose of fake pity.

"Whatever. Look, give me an hour, and you'll have your report."

"Wonderful. Thank you, Oliver. And rest assured I'm fully prepared to uphold my end of the bargain. As far as I'm concerned, that housing project is yours to manage."

Oliver had all but forgotten that aspect of their agreement, maybe because from the get-go he'd been skeptical about Cox's promises. The man was altogether too sly to be expected to keep them, and Oliver wasn't doing this for a reward anyway.

"I'll let you know when it's done," he told Cox before disconnecting.

For a minute, he just sat there, staring at the shiny golden tassel that decorated the closet doorknob. Somewhere in the distance, he could hear the sounds of the master bedroom shower running, which meant Ela was preparing to go to sleep.

If only he could do the same—take a shower, change out of his ridiculous costume, and get a good night's sleep before going to work in the morning as if nothing had happened. But there was no use pretending, was there? He had to do what he had to do.

Thankfully, he'd had enough sense to throw his laptop into his bag during his hasty flight. He took it out, powered it up, and settled on top of the taupe woven duvet to compile the list he'd promised Cox.

In the end, it turned out to be quite an extensive report. True to his word and his sense of justice, Oliver hadn't spared a single detail that he thought might be relevant to describe the Lodge's deterioration. He wrote down everything he'd seen and experienced (excluding the metaphysical shenanigans), starting with the leaky pipes, the rotten staircases, the crumbling porch, the unsanitary condition of the garbage cans, and finishing with the landlord's lackadaisical attitude to all those infractions.

It was a cut-and-dry list, and not a single point on it was untrue. And yet, as Oliver stared at the words on his computer screen, he couldn't help feeling that by compiling it he was doing something despicable.

Which, of course, was utterly absurd. He was the wronged party here, he reminded himself sternly. He was the one whose life had been put at risk by sharing his home—and his bed—with someone who could easily rip him to shreds. He was the one whose trust had been broken. Nym knew all about Oliver's failed relationship and why he was sensitive to dishonesty and gaslighting, yet he chose to lie to him anyway, letting Oliver develop feelings that turned out to be entirely ephemeral.

That was what it boiled down to, at the end. Once again, Oliver had become attached to the wrong person, a person who wasn't even real. The man he'd cared about was nothing but a construct of his own imagination and Nym's deceit. So how come losing him hurt so much?

Oliver sighed, his finger hovering over the touch pad. There was nothing to it. He'd promised himself he was done being a victim, and if that meant making some tough choices and doing some uncomfortable things, so be it.

He hit Send and watched the notification of success pop up on the screen. For some reason, it didn't raise his spirits. If anything, he was left feeling even more wretched than before.

Quiet darkness had settled around the townhouse, disturbed only by the occasional passing of a vehicle on the street outside. No howling wind, whispering voices, creaks and groans, and strange noises to disturb his sleep. After spending nearly a month learning to filter them out, Oliver found he was a little unsettled by the numb silence of a completely ordinary house.

He huffed in annoyance at his own inanity, set his glasses on the nightstand, grabbed the change of clothes he'd stuffed in his bag, and headed for the en suite shower. The satisfying pressure of the hot water went a long way to soothing his anxiety and the little aches that still lingered in the aftermath of last night's vigorous lovemaking.

No, *fucking*, he amended bitterly as he toweled off. That was all it ever was, even if it had felt different at the time.

He got under the covers and picked up his phone again. His heart did a flip when he saw the missed call and a voice message notification from Nym's number. His internal debate lasted for less than a second, and he opened the message, his pulse racing again in trepidation.

"Oliver," Nym's voice sounded tinny and pained, though that last bit could be attributed to Oliver's wishful thinking. "Look, I didn't mean to scare you, and I'm sorry. Maybe I should've come up with a different way to tell you. Please, I…" Nym fell silent for a moment, then took a deep breath and continued briskly. "I just wanted to let you know that I would never hurt you, in any shape or form. I hope you can believe that, despite everything. All I want is to talk and have a chance to explain, just the two of us. So…please give me a call." There was another hesitant pause, and Nym added, even more gruffly, "I meant what I said on Saturday night. Every word."

The message ended, leaving Oliver staring at the screen until it went dark. The back of his throat itched and burned, and he clutched his phone, futilely willing the tears away. A sob tore out of him, a harbinger of a break-down, and Oliver clamped his mouth shut, the muffled cries rattling his body. Very carefully, he set the phone down, pressed his face against the pillow, and gave way to the heartache that threatened to suffocate him.

Chapter Sixteen

Oliver didn't call Nym back. Instead, he dedicated the next few days to finding a new place to live with the help of Ela and her boyfriend. Though they had graciously extended the invitation to stay with them for as long as he needed without pressing him to offer a cogent explanation of his situation, he couldn't impose on their hospitality much longer.

If he were completely honest with himself, the main reason he avoided talking to Nym was guilt. The first thing he thought about when he woke up after what felt like merely minutes of fitful sleep were the implications of what he had done by giving Cox the information needed to declare Lakeside Lodge inhabitable. Even if he still didn't believe the sincerity of Nym's message, now he had betrayed him too—in an especially nasty kind of way.

He'd known he was making a mistake even as he was doing it, but yesterday he'd been much too upset and hurt to stop and think things over rationally. He was still upset in the morning, but sleep (even snatches of it on a tear-stained pillow) had calmed him enough to realize he regretted his actions.

Even if he was right, and Nym and his merry band of monsters did pose a threat to unsuspecting humans, there had to be ways to stand up to them that wouldn't leave Oliver feeling so…dirty.

But it was done, and he couldn't take it back, even if he wanted to. So instead, he focused on all the mundane tasks that clamored for his attention—looking up rental ads, putting in more hours at work, refusing to wallow in the backwash of yet another defunct relationship, as brief as it had been.

With Ela's help, he was able to rent a one-bedroom apartment on Mathews Street, which, unsurprisingly, turned out to be a lot more expensive than his previous lodgings. That also meant he had no choice but to go back there to collect his things, or at least as much of them as he could fit in his car. No matter how casual the dress code at Thompson Design was, he couldn't get by on one change of clothes and a *Princess Bride* costume.

The darkened jack-o'-lanterns still sat on the porch steps as he walked up to the entrance late on Thursday night. Aside from the single light above the door, the entire house seemed to be shrouded in shadow, the occupants either asleep or out. Oliver waited for a few minutes, hidden behind the trunk of a towering maple tree and hugging himself against the cold as he watched the house. Nothing stirred either inside or out.

He took a deep breath, berating himself for being silly. All he had to do was go to his apartment, get his stuff, and then text Nym his notice along with the payment. On second thought, it might've been better to drop by during the day when most of the inhabitants would have been out, but Oliver could hardly afford to take another day off at work after that week on sick leave.

He adjusted the strap of his messenger bag, which currently held several trash bags he planned to use for ad-hoc packing, and started off toward the front door. He'd have to make a few trips to his car, but it wasn't raining, so it wouldn't be too difficult to pull off as long as he didn't make any noise.

Just as he expected, no one had bothered to change the locks on his account. He slipped inside and crept quietly along the hall, past the dark and silent parlor, and up the stairs to his apartment.

He briefly considered using the flashlight app on his phone to get around, but perhaps that was taking it a bit too far into the realm of paranoia. He flicked on the side lamp in the living room and took a good look around.

It appeared no one had been to the place in his absence. A few plates and glasses were arranged in the dish rack just as he'd left them, and the plastic sword, which he'd discarded in his haste to make his escape, lay on the floor next to the couch. His bed was unmade, as it had been on Sunday morning, and the bedroom, with its firmly shut windows, had already taken on a musty odor of disuse. Even the barricade on the closet door was still untouched.

Oliver sighed and began to sift through his dresser drawers, dumping all his clothes, shoes, and toiletries into the trash bags. For once, he was grateful he didn't own a lot of possessions and hadn't spent enough time at there to accumulate unnecessary junk. The way things were going, he'd have to leave some of the necessary stuff behind too.

Thankfully, he still had some of the shipping boxes, which he used to repack books and some of his more fragile possessions. By the time he finished piling everything in the hallway, he was seriously considering throwing caution to the wind and simply arranging for a moving company to come and pick everything up tomorrow morning. Surely, no one would dare harass him in broad daylight while accompanied by two or three burly guys with a pickup truck? Or would he be putting innocent people in danger by bringing them over?

No, he was here already. He might as well suck it up and put in some work before he was discovered.

He propped the apartment door open with one of boxes, grabbed a couple of bags, and headed downstairs, doing his best to avoid the extra-creaky steps.

"Oliver," a hollow voice whispered behind him as he passed the parlor, and he nearly dropped the trash bags.

He wheeled around, his heart hammering, but the corridor was empty in both directions, from the front door to the bottom of the staircase.

His first instinct was to bolt out the door, leaving his baggage on the floor, but he managed to restrain himself.

"Oliver," the voice repeated. It sounded exactly like that night in his bedroom, when it had led him to discover the hidden stairway behind his closet, only now, it was coming from the door leading to the memorial room.

Oliver lowered the bags to the floor and approached the door. He hesitated before turning the handle. Was he curious enough to find out what was waiting for him inside? The prudent thing would be to leave right away and never look back, but some part of him still insisted he was brave enough to take a peek inside.

The last time he'd answered the call of that eerie voice, he'd ended up kissing Nym in the dusty attic. Sure, that had eventually resolved itself into a broken heart, but he couldn't deny that whatever had existed between them for that short amount of time had been achingly sweet. He'd really believed—but it was no use wallowing in what could have been.

And yet, he was sorely tempted to see where the voice would lead him to this time. Hell, couldn't be much worse, could it?

With that perversely encouraging thought, Oliver pushed the door open and stepped inside the room. He flipped the electric switch, wincing at the light that flooded his eyes, bouncing off the glass display cases.

The room was empty. It looked exactly as it had when Oliver first saw it, and it reeked of the same sweet scent of decay. Despina Shaw's portrait smiled at him from its pride of place above the hearth, and tiny specs of dust danced before his eyes, like a flock of birds spooked by his approach. The collection of weird artifacts made a lot more sense now, though it didn't make it any less disturbing. Then again, if Oliver wanted to dive into some thorough research on the paranormal after Google had failed him miserably, this would be the perfect place to start.

What—or who—did he expect to see waiting for him here? And why did disappointment prickle at the back of his mind at the realization that no one wasn't?

The room was deathly quiet. Maybe that was why his ears managed to pick up the soft shuffling of footsteps coming down the hall.

On instinct, Oliver flipped the light switch off, plunging the room into darkness, and painstakingly crept away from the door. He crouched behind one of the display cases, holding his breath. Maybe, if he was very quiet, whoever was on the other side of the door would keep on going.

The footsteps stopped right outside the open door, and Oliver mentally cursed himself for leaving the trash bags lying around in the corridor.

"Well, if it isn't our little runaway," Rafe said, sounding deafeningly loud in the anticipatory silence.

Somehow Oliver managed not to bolt. Maybe that was because his blood was already pumping as fast as it would go. He offered no response, silently willing the man to leave.

"I know you're there," Rafe continued. "I can hear you breathing."

Well, that wasn't creepy at all.

"Go away," Oliver said, not bothering to raise his voice since the vampire could boast perfect hearing.

"I promise I mean you no harm," Rafe said. His footsteps echoed inside and stopped beside the fireplace, but he didn't bother to turn on the light. "Want me to pinky swear?"

"Oh, shut up," Oliver muttered.

"I'm serious. Can we talk?"

"There's nothing you can say to me."

"Really?" Rafe sounded mildly amused. "You're not curious at all? I'd imagine you'd have one or two questions. And I was kinda hoping you'd keep an open mind. But hey, suit yourself."

Was he curious? Oliver supposed he was, especially now, after the initial shock and panic had receded. Whether he was curious enough to risk his life by foolishly revealing himself to a vampire was another matter.

Still, he hesitated. He did deserve some explanation, some way to reconcile his new knowledge with the world as he knew it. If Rafe was willing to offer clarifications, he could at least hear him out—at a safe distance.

"Stay where you are," he warned before rising from the floor just enough to peer through the glass. His night vision was close to nonexistent, but he thought he could pick out the outline of Rafe's figure against the lighter shadows.

"As you wish."

"How did you know I was here?" Oliver asked.

"I saw you lurking outside from my window." Rafe chuckled. "Wasn't very difficult to track you down. I wondered whether you'd be back or if we'd seen the last of you at the party. Sky and Aurora were sure you'd come to your senses eventually, but I must admit, I was convinced we'd managed to chase you away for good."

"I'm not back," Oliver retorted, still from in the relative safety of behind the display case. "I just came by to get my things. It's not like I can afford to lose them."

Rafe made a noncommittal sound.

Oliver licked his lips. "Is it all real?" he asked quietly. "Are you really...what I think you are?"

"Yes. It's all real. And the word you're looking for is 'vampire.'"

"Okay. Vampire," Oliver said with a hint of defiance. "You said you wanted to talk, so talk."

"First, let me ask you a question. What is it you're so afraid of?"

"You're kidding me, right?" Oliver said. "You guys are monsters. I mean, actual, honest-to-God monsters. I think fear comes with the territory."

"Yes, we're monsters," Rafe agreed easily. "At least, that's how you regular humans like to define us. But have any of us, the folks living here at Lakeside Lodge, ever given you a reason to fear us? Have we ever hurt you?"

"Well, no," Oliver said after a short pause. "But that doesn't mean you wouldn't have, or that you haven't hurt anybody else. That's what monsters do."

"No," Rafe said. "That's what folktales and scary stories and horror movies tell you we do."

"And in actuality, you're tame as kittens, right?" Oliver said sarcastically.

"Have you ever met a kitten?" Rafe's shadow shook its head. "Anyway, it isn't about tameness. It's about wanting to live our lives in peace and quiet, just as you do. What do you think this place is?"

"A safe house," Oliver said slowly, recalling that long-ago conversation with Nym. "Mrs. Shaw had built it as a safe house."

"Exactly. And it had been a safe house for our kind for well over a century. Vampires, witches, were-creatures, de-mons, warlocks, merpeople, you name it. It has always offered refuge when we were trying to escape persecution or simply blend in and lie low until it was time to move on and try to build our lives elsewhere."

"I thought— "

"I know what you thought. But you got it all wrong. Lakeside Lodge was never meant to pose danger to human-kind. It's meant to shield us from the danger humankind poses to *us*."

Oliver was silent for a long moment, digesting Rafe's

words.

"But you're a vampire," he said finally, still struggling to make proper sense of it all. "Don't you have to drink blood? Isn't that why you work as a nurse, so you can take it from patients without anyone being the wiser?"

"First of all, contrary to common belief, vampires don't have to drink blood every day to survive," Rafe said with the patient undertone of a kindergarten teacher explaining animal sounds to a group of toddlers. "Once a few weeks is more than enough, considering our metabolic rate and nocturnal lifestyle. No, I work at the hospital because I like the job. I get the blood elsewhere."

"Where?" Oliver asked suspiciously. His knees were beginning to ache, but he didn't dare step behind the barrier of the glass case, as flimsy as it might be.

"From willing donors, of course."

"Willing donors? Are you telling me people actually let you bite them?"

"Of course. Though I must admit, they don't know I'm a vampire. As a matter of fact, most of them think *they* are."

"What?"

"You wouldn't believe how many folks out there love to dress up and pretend they're a part of some ancient secret society of vampires, destined to rule the world if they only chant enough incantations at the full moon and drink each other's blood from silver goblets." Rafe sighed dramatically. "None of them are actually vampires, of course. We aren't very sociable creatures."

"What if they want to drink your blood? Wouldn't that turn them into vampires eventually?" Oliver asked, thinking back to every paranormal TV series he'd ever watched.

"That's when that pig blood also comes in handy. The poor saps can't tell the difference."

Oliver exhaled. It all sounded plausible on the face of it, but he had no way of knowing what was true and what was false.

Anyway, it was just words. What tipped the scale was the fact that Rafe hadn't stirred from his place by the fireplace for the entirety of the conversation, though Oliver was pretty certain the vampire could be on him in a blink of an eye.

He rose to his feet, keeping the case between them. His eyes had had time to adjust to the gloom, so he could see Rafe better now, down to the gleam of his watch.

"That's you," he said. "What about Nym?"

"What about him?"

"Well, he's a wolf, right? A werewolf. Are you gonna tell me he doesn't hunt?"

"I doubt our friend Nymphus has time to so much as hunt a squirrel these days. But that's something you should be discussing with him, don't you think?"

He was right, of course, but Oliver's heart clenched at the thought of hashing it out in the open with Nym, so he shook his head.

"I just don't understand. If he's only renting the place to…you guys—" He made a vague gesture in the air. "—why did he advertise the apartment to everybody? Anybody could have answered that. I mean, I did, and I'm just a regular guy. No superpowers or magic or anything."

Rafe sighed and gestured to a couple of spindly chairs arranged around a small half-round side table. It sat beneath a framed lithograph depicting a flock of witches riding broomsticks above the spires of a colonial church. After a moment, Oliver went over and perched on the edge of a chair while Rafe sprawled in the other one with his usual feline grace.

"Again, I probably shouldn't be speaking for Nym here, but... You remember old Horace, right?"

"Horace Livingstone?" Oliver clarified. "The ghost?"

"Yes, that's the one. He used to live in your apartment."

"Jesus." Oliver rubbed his forehead. "And what was he?"

"Just a regular old chap, like yourself. But he'd lived in Lakeside Lodge for the last fifty years, ever since he'd met Brown's aunt and fallen in love with her."

"The aunt who left Nym the house?" Oliver asked, genuinely curious now.

"Yes. She was a werewolf, you see, but apparently love knows no bounds." Rafe's gaze took on a sardonic quality even in the darkness. "Anyway, she passed a few years ago, and Nym took over the management of the building. Old Livingstone had nowhere to go—nor did he want to, after spending his life here with his partner. So he stayed here, in 1B, right until he died about a year ago, and sort of...hung on."

"Great. There's a disgruntled lonely ghost hanging around in my apartment. What does that have to do with me?"

"Well, as I understand it, Brown needed the rent money to cover his upkeep expenses, not to mention the debts he kept raking up on this place. He couldn't find anyone suitable, so he decided to advertise to the general public. We all agreed to keep a low profile for appearance's sake. Besides, we kinda liked you." Rafe raked Oliver over with his eyes, though it lacked real heat. "Sky, for one, became convinced you'd become a part of our little group in no time. What can I say? Apparently, even a witch's precognition gets it wrong from time to time."

Oliver barked a laugh. "I thought I was, you know, part of the group. So I guess I was wrong about that too."

"You weren't wrong about Nym though. Nor was he wrong about you."

"What do you mean?"

"You haven't been here long enough to notice the difference in him," Rafe said. "But we did. We've known each other for a while, ever since he took over the Lodge. That's why we couldn't miss the change in him. From the day you moved in, he's been coming out of his shell, little by little. As someone who's undead, I can see when a man comes alive, in every sense of the word. And Nym has never been more alive than after meeting you."

Oliver bit his lip and looked away to stare at the portrait that dominated the room. Even in the deep gloom, Despina's eyes seemed luminescent, glittering with all-knowing intelligence, her enigmatic half-smile issuing an unspoken dare.

"I don't know what to do." Oliver didn't know who he was confessing to—her or Rafe. "I don't know if I can trust Nym again."

"It sounds like you should be talking about it with him, don't you think? Anyway, I have to be going." Rafe rose from his seat and made to leave, but paused in the doorway. "I may not be an expert on relationships, but I do know you'd be wasting your life if you let fear always dictate your perception of people. You might miss out on some good ones out there."

With that, he was gone, leaving Oliver alone with his ghosts.

Chapter Seventeen

For a while, Oliver just sat in the dark mausoleum, listening to the quiet. He didn't know exactly how much time had passed. When he finally pushed himself to his feet and went back into the hallway, he didn't feel like he was any closer to an epiphany.

But maybe this whole thing wasn't meant to be solved in a flash of inspiration anyway—if indeed he wanted to reach a solution rather than cut all ties and run. Like Rafe had said, if he didn't want fear to guide him for the rest of his life, he needed to conquer it, which meant confronting Nym and hearing his side of the story.

Was that what he wanted?

Oliver paused in the corridor, next to the trash bags waiting for him on the floor, thinking it over—as calmly as he could, setting aside all external considerations. What if he could erase the mental image of a towering creature with a long muzzle and thick fur, and focus only on the man he had grown to care about in the past few weeks? Was the bond between them just as important as the awful secret Nym had been keeping from him? Was it worth the effort of facing his fears head on?

He thought it was. But Oliver had been wrong before. With Jake, he'd been all too happy to pull the wool over his eyes until it was too late. Did he dare take another chance and maybe end up broken again, body and soul?

But Nym wasn't Jake. Yes, maybe he was a monster, but he wasn't *that* kind of monster. Underneath all that fur and fangs and put-upon sullenness, Nym was a sensitive, caring person. He was smart, and funny, and kindhearted, even if his werewolf form was truly terrifying. It was these qualities that had made Oliver fall in love with him.

And he had, hadn't he? He wouldn't be standing here, contemplating his next move, if deep down in his heart he didn't know it to be true.

He wouldn't be in such turmoil if it weren't true.

"Fucking damn it." Oliver rubbed his forehead tiredly, turned around, and started for the stairs.

The smart thing to do would've been texting Ela right now to let her know where he was in case he was making a horrible mistake. But he knew if he stopped now, his courage was bound to falter. So he pressed on, right until he stood in front of the door to 1A.

It was well past 11 p.m., but faint light shone under the door, which meant Nym probably wasn't asleep yet.

Oliver adjusted his glasses, took a deep breath, and knocked on the door before he could wimp out again.

A few tense moments passed until the door swung open. Nym, looking entirely human in a pair of faded jeans and a gray T-shirt, looked down at him with a stony expression.

"Um, hi," Oliver said. With nothing to occupy his hands, he was wringing them, and he willed himself to hold still.

"Hi," Nym said without inflection.

"Look, I... Can we talk?"

Nym regarded him silently for another few seconds but eventually stepped back and gestured for Oliver to come in.

Oliver would be lying if he said he didn't cross the threshold with some trepidation, but now most of it focused on the upcoming conversation.

A single side lamp illuminated Nym's living room. The TV was tuned to one *CSI* or another on mute, and a half-empty bottle of Scotch sat on the coffee table, no tumbler in sight.

Nym retreated to the kitchen counter, which mirrored the one in Oliver's apartment, and leaned back against it, crossing his arms over his chest.

"What did you want to talk about?" he asked in the same flat voice.

He was definitely not making it easy for Oliver. Then again, the rigidity of his posture and the deep shadows under his eyes indicated maybe he, too, was bracing for something deeply unpleasant. In some weird way, noticing it took the edge off Oliver's own apprehension. It they were both nervous about what was coming, that meant no side had the upper hand.

"Can I start by saying I'm sorry?" Oliver said. "I may have...overreacted."

"You're entitled to react any way you want."

"Yeah, but I shouldn't have freaked out like that." Oliver shook his head. "It all came as such a shock. I didn't know what to think."

Nym let out a deep, rumbling sigh.

"I may have chosen a bad way to go about it," he conceded. "It seemed like the appropriate place at the time, with all of us together, on the one night of the year that we can go out in public as who we really are. I thought you might have a clue already, with the talk about the house being haunted, and... Clearly, I was wrong."

"I did pick up on something weird going on, but I never imagined..." Oliver trailed off, reluctant to admit to what he'd been thinking. Perhaps he hadn't been *that* far off the mark, but the truth was so much more complex than his unfounded suspicions. "Anyway, I'm ready to listen now, if you're willing to talk."

"I thought you came over tonight to pack your things and get out," Nym said. "What changed?"

Oliver felt the blush creeping up his cheeks. "Oh. You heard me?"

"You were making so much racket, it would've been hard to miss even without superior senses. I figured it'd be best not to bother you. Frankly, I was sure I wasn't going to see you again," he added with a bit of hesitation. "I was only hoping you were safe wherever you were."

"I was. I am. I stayed with a good friend from work. Ela," Oliver added hastily, in case Nym got the wrong idea. "And honestly? I wasn't sure I was going to come back." He lowered himself on the end of the couch, perching on the edge.

As if Oliver had given a cue, Nym took a chair and sat down, too, leaning his clasped hands on his thighs. Oliver didn't know if it was simply getting ready for a long conversation or if Nym had done it to avoid towering over him while he was sitting, but either way, he was grateful for that small gesture.

How could he ever have been afraid of this man? Nym had gone out of his way to make Oliver feel comfortable and safe in every way that counted, and Oliver had been too put off by the horrible experience of his past to recognize that. He realized now that he'd never given Nym a fair chance when Nym deserved it.

"What changed your mind?" Nym asked quietly.

"Rafe."

"Rafe?"

"Yes. He met me downstairs, and we had a really good talk. He explained some things to me about who you are and what you're about. I admit when I saw you as... as a werewolf and realized it was real, I was petrified. It was like...I don't know, thinking you were living out a rom-com and suddenly found yourself in a horror movie. So, yeah, I jumped to conclusions, about all of you."

"Yeah, that whole 'creatures of the night' thing has been getting us bad press for centuries," Nym said dryly.

Oliver snorted despite himself.

"I can't say I understand everything now," he said. "But I'm hoping you can tell me more. If you want."

"I do, but..." Nym havered again. "I wish you had come to me first. I was hoping you would, after..."

He fell silent, his shoulders slumping slightly.

"Why didn't you tell me before?" Oliver asked softly.

Nym looked up at him, the yellow light reflecting off his weirdly bright eyes.

"It's not something you go around telling people. Our safety lies in secrecy, it always has. Maybe it leads to misunderstanding and superstition, but it's also true that the less people know about us, the less likely they are to acknowledge our existence and try to wipe us out. I didn't want you to know at all at first. I resisted being attracted to you for as long as I could, telling myself it was a bad idea to get attached to an ordinary human again. But the longer you were here and the better I got to know you, the more futile it became."

Nym's jaw moved as if he were clamping down on some raw emotion, even though his voice sounded steady. "You were like a lantern in a dark maze, this inquisitive little light that all of a sudden illuminates a whole new path. And though I knew I shouldn't involve you in any of it, I couldn't bring myself to give you up. I didn't plan on things becoming so serious between us so fast, but they did. And still, I was afraid to tell you. The last time I did, I got my heart broken and had to uproot my whole life. I didn't want to lie to you, but the thought of going through that again…"

Oliver's heart swelled, and on impulse, he reached out and clasped Nym's hand.

"I'm sorry I handled it so badly. I think I felt betrayed more than anything. I knew you were keeping some kind of secret, but this was huge. It was hard to reconcile what I saw at that party with the man I'd gone to bed with."

Nym nodded and covered Oliver's hand with his own. "I think we both fucked up here. We've both been hurt before, and learning to trust someone again, even someone you care about deeply, isn't easy."

His touch was warm, rough, and comforting, a point of anchor for Oliver's turbulent emotions. It was amazing how, after everything was said and done, it all boiled down to the simplicity of that touch.

"Rafe told me this was why you keep Lakeside Lodge open," he said. "As a refuge for your kind. That you only mean to live quietly, without causing harm. Is that true?"

"Yes. There aren't that many of us left in the world." Nym's tone became wistful. "I come from a family of were-wolves, and I've seen our numbers dwindling over the years. So, with my aunt dying, and everything going so wrong in my life, it felt like a calling to offer a safe place for every creature that needed it."

His grip on Oliver's hand tightened, then relaxed. "I want you to know that I've never hurt anyone," he said somberly, gazing into Oliver's eyes. "Not a single human soul, and I would never do so intentionally. Was that what you were worried about?"

"Yes," Oliver said, relieved that Nym seemed to understand him without being incensed. "I've been a victim, and I know how it feels, so... Yes, I was worried."

"I may be different, but I want the exact same things as you. To live, to love, to belong. I thought... I let myself hope I could have that with you."

Nym's words were enough to make Oliver's heart take flight, but his tone was unexpectedly bitter, and that gave Oliver pause.

"You still can," he said slowly. "If you want to."

"Some things happened while you were away," Nym said wearily, letting go of Oliver's hand. "I should've seen it coming, I guess."

Uneasiness stirred at the pit of Oliver's stomach.

"What happened?" he asked, folding his hands back into his lap.

Nym got up from his seat, went over to the counter, and riffled through a pile of mail.

"See for yourself," he said, thrusting a torn envelope toward Oliver.

Oliver took out a crumpled paper with an official-looking letterhead, but the dim lighting and his overall state of agitation made it difficult to concentrate.

"What am I looking at?" he asked.

"A notification for an upcoming home inspection from the Baltimore City Department of Housing," Nym said.

"But… How? When? What can we do?" Oliver studied the text as if its formal wording could provide him with an insight.

"There's nothing we can do." Nym took the letter and threw it back on the counter. "You saw for yourself there's about a dozen of different code violations they can shut me down for. But I appreciate you thought about it that way."

The uneasiness transformed into an awful premonition.

"Why do you think they sent it?" he asked around the sudden dryness in his mouth.

"I can't say I'm surprised," Nym said, sitting down in the chair again. "It was bound to happen sooner or later. I was just hoping I had a little more time to come up with the cash for renovations."

"Can't you take out a loan?"

"I'm already in as much debt as I can get myself into." Nym sounded bleaker by the moment, and Oliver began to suspect the solitary drinking party he'd interrupted wasn't entirely due to Nym feeling bad about Oliver leaving.

"I didn't know that," Oliver said. "I mean, I knew things weren't going that great, obviously, but I had no idea it was that bad."

Nym nodded. "I'd never put an ad for the spare apartment out if it wasn't the last resort for getting a bit of extra income to stay afloat for a few more months. It was a mistake to take on someone who wasn't a paranorm, but I was at a loss for options. Fat good it did in the end. I only managed to make things worse for everyone."

Oliver had seen Nym sad or melancholy before, but never this dejected. It was unsettling in a way he'd never thought possible.

"Don't say that. We'll figure something out; I promise."

"I should've known something was up when that snake called me again last night." Nym tugged at his hair, disheveling it even more.

"What snake?"

"Richard Cox, the developer. He's been trying to buy the Lodge from under me for years. I guess he finally got the leverage he needed to get the Department of Housing on my back." Nym looked up, his eyes flashing in the gloom. "If the building fails the inspection—and it will—I might have no choice but to sell it to him after all, just so we all don't end up sleeping on the street."

Oliver's premonition coalesced into something leaden and foul that threatened to rise like bile from his stomach and suffocate him. It took him a split second to recognize it for what it was—guilt.

He'd almost forgotten about the email he'd sent to Cox, convincing himself it'd make no difference. Apparently, it had.

He couldn't believe Cox would act so quickly and so efficiently. Whether it was Oliver's contribution that had allowed the developer to cut through the mire of municipal bureaucracy or a combination of Cox's own influence with damning information, Oliver was undoubtedly responsible for this turn of events.

His face must have shown his distress because Nym frowned, looking at him.

"What's the matter?" he asked.

"I...I have something to tell you." Oliver's voice came out small and brittle, and he swallowed, wishing he'd asked Nym for a shot of whiskey before opening that damn letter. "Just...promise you'll hear me out, okay?"

"Okay." Nym's frown deepened.

Oliver dug his hands into the edge of the couch seat. Despite his request for Nym to allow him to say his piece, he couldn't force himself to push the words out.

"It's my fault," he said finally, with an effort. "That Cox had been able to arrange this inspection to happen." He stopped again, unable to continue.

"What do you mean? How is this your fault?"

"Sunday night, after the party and that surprise...I was really upset. Maybe I shouldn't have, but I totally went off the rails. All I could think about was that you guys were monsters, and how you could be dangerous to unsuspecting people, cloistered in this house as if it were a hunting lodge. I felt I had to do something, you know? And I realize now I've been deeply, horribly wrong believing all this stuff about you, but at that time, I couldn't think straight. I was so afraid, and it was the only thing I could come up with to protect other people from becoming victims."

Nym's expression changed slowly while Oliver rambled on, becoming more and more shuttered. He'd probably already figured out where this was going, but Oliver knew he had to come clean anyway.

"I met Cox at work," he said in a lame attempt to establish some background to his confession. "He's one of my firm's biggest clients. It turns out he saw me that time he dropped by the Lodge a few weeks ago, and he made me a proposition."

"What kind of a proposition?" Nym asked darkly.

"To report to him any problems I'd witnessed in the building. The wiring, the plumbing, the structural damage, all of it. He hinted that there were enough terrible things going on here to necessitate tearing the place down, no matter for what purpose."

"Really?" Nym all but sneered. "And he expected you to go along with this out of the goodness of your heart?"

"No," Oliver admitted.

He could see by the look in Nym's eyes that he wasn't doing a stellar job of presenting his case, but he had no choice but to try to stumble through it.

"He promised that if I agreed to do this for him, he'd make me the lead architect on his next major housing project. And I'm not going to lie, I did consider it because it was obvious that something was awry here. But then we became friends, and I liked you so much, I just couldn't do it. I couldn't do that to you. But on Sunday, with everything that went down... After I got away and crashed at my friend's house, I called Cox and sent him a list of all the issues I'd seen around the house.

I'm not saying it's an excuse, but I was scared shitless. It was the only thing on my mind at the time—how do I protect people against…"

"Against brutal monsters like me?" Nym finished bitterly.

"It's not what—"

Nym put up his hand, silencing him. "Trust me, it's not the first time I'm hearing it. I'm not blaming you for being afraid, for being misinformed. But I just can't believe you'd do something like that, knowing what that vile man was after. That you would jeopardize the safety of my tenants, rob them of a place to live, take away my heritage because you were upset? You just don't do that to a friend, least of all to someone you claim to have feelings for. How could you?"

Nym didn't raise his voice, but his tone was sharp enough to cut, and every word lodged itself in Oliver's heart like a dagger.

"I'm sorry," he tried again through the burn of nascent tears. "I really am. I regretted doing it immediately afterward, but there was no taking at back at that point. Please, Nym. I know I screwed up, but I'll do anything I can to fix it; I promise."

"Fix it?" Nym repeated. "You can't fix this. You've broken it beyond repair."

He stood up abruptly and crossed the living room toward the door.

"You came here to pack," he said, avoiding Oliver's stunned gaze. "Maybe you had the right idea. You should go now."

"What? Nym, come on. Don't do this. We can figure it out together. Maybe we can run a campaign, raise some money, hire a lawyer. Just because there's an inspection doesn't mean it's all over. We can fight this. We can do something."

Nym looked at him then, yellow eyes simmering with repressed anger.

"Oh, I think you've done enough, Oliver. I just hope it got you everything you wanted."

Chapter Eighteen

It was well after midnight when Oliver finished his last round of bringing his stuff out to the car. It started to drizzle, and the biting wind blowing from the lake was getting under his jacket and chilling his bones, but he was so numb he barely noticed it.

Maybe it was for the best, because it also meant he was too numb to cry. He didn't know if Nym had bothered to watch him go in and out of his apartment with trash bags full of his belongings, but a small part of him was glad he hadn't been sobbing while doing it.

An even larger part didn't give a damn if he had.

In any case, the point was moot. He locked the car and stood for a full minute in the rain, considering his next move with a hollow detachment. Finally, he stuffed the keys in his pocket and walked back to the Lodge.

He told himself it was only to take one last look at the apartment to make sure he hadn't forgotten anything, but deep down in his heart, he needed to say goodbye for the last time, even if there was no one to hear him except wandering spirits.

Traces of his habitation still clung to the space—the arrangement of furniture, the cheap but cheerful area rugs, the assortment of takeout menus on the fridge. And yet, the apartment felt colder and emptier than the day he first walked in. It seemed even old Horace was disappointed enough to snub him.

Oliver made a perfunctory round of the kitchen and living room, though even if he had left some of his things lying around, he probably wouldn't have noticed. He had cleared out the bedroom, making sure not to pack any of the linens that came with the apartment, and covered the bed with a white sheet. Now it reminded him of a tombstone, blank and somehow mocking.

He sat down heavily on the edge of the bed, not caring if he was crumpling the neatly laid sheet, and lowered his head into his hands.

It was silly to act so heartbroken. Mere hours ago, he was ready to cut all ties with Nym and Lakeside Lodge, to leave and never return in genuine fear for his life, and now, he was ready to break down because Nym had thrown him out. But so much had changed over the course of these hours. He'd opened his eyes and his heart, let himself feel and hope—only for those hopes to be dashed by his own prejudice and impulsiveness. His own lack of trust didn't justify such a betrayal, and Nym was right to be repulsed by Oliver's behavior. But the knowledge did absolutely nothing to dull the pain that wove a tight net around Oliver's heart, a tangle of sticky cobwebs that squeezed and squeezed until Oliver couldn't breathe.

A sob tore out of him, the sound desperate and pitiful as if his heart had truly burst under the pressure of his guilt and remorse. It was quickly followed by another, and Oliver gave up on trying to keep them all in. It was impossible; his body was too small and fragile to contain so much pain without giving it an outlet, however brief and futile. He tore off his glasses and cried, hot tears streaming across flushed cheeks.

He didn't know how long he sat there, wallowing in his anguish. The weeping left him drained and tired, and the thought of driving back to his new place through the night streets filled him with an even deeper weariness.

"Oliver," a spectral voice called out to him just as he started to get up, the whisper reverberating through the empty room like a shout.

"Oh, shut up," Oliver muttered, wiping his eyes. "It's all over anyway."

As if in answer, the closet door swung open with an ominous creak.

"Oliver." The voice grew stronger, losing some of its ethereal quality. Now it sounded more and more like a woman, someone used to being in command. "Seek inside."

"Seek inside?" Oliver repeated, rising from the bed and looking warily to the sides. "What does that mean? Who's there?"

No one answered. Whoever the voice belonged to, they were not making an appearance.

"This is ridiculous." Oliver put his glasses on and eyed the closet door, which still stood open, as if in invitation.

Would it be wise to answer the call again? So far nothing and no one in the house had been out to hurt him, despite his fears and trepidations, but what if this time was different? He had wronged Nym and, by extension, all the inhabitants of the Lodge, whether live or dead. Maybe he'd finally pissed off the unknown spirit enough for it to take drastic action.

But if so, why instruct him to seek something? Surely, a malevolent presence could arrange a fatal accident without going to all the trouble, especially in a house already prone to malfunctions. And, in all honesty, he did owe it to all of them after what he'd done.

He grabbed his phone and slowly walked to the closet. It stood empty, so it was easy to see that no one was lying in wait inside. He had no trouble locating the correct knot, and he pressed it once, pushing the back panel to reveal the opening to the secret passage.

He paused on the small landing, phone in hand, illuminating the stairs that ran up and down from where he was standing. Last time he chose to go up, which resulted in his kissing Nym in the attic. There wasn't much hope of him kissing anybody tonight, so that was probably the wrong way to go. He might as well try going down this time.

Oliver gripped his phone firmly as the bluish light picked out the stairs leading down. The next landing was the ground floor, opening into what he assumed to be a hidden space behind the parlor wall. He must have missed a secret door there while he was busy hanging Halloween decorations, but then again, he hadn't been exactly looking for one. The stairway continued downward, until it ended on concrete floor.

Oliver stopped and raised his phone, following the wall until he found a light switch. As he'd assumed, the passage led into the basement, which spanned the entirety of the underside of the house, supported by square concrete pillars. Unlike the attic, however, the cavernous space was mostly empty aside from a large, antiquated furnace that labored noisily in a corner. Shelving units lined the walls, storing half-used buckets of paint, scraps of tile, and rolls of what appeared to be vintage wallpaper, all arranged neatly but covered with a thick layer of dust.

If Oliver had still been worried about coming onto a scene from *The Basement*, the view before him would've quelled all fears. So far, the basement was by far the most ordinary and most boring part of the house.

What could the spirit possibly want him to seek here? And what did "inside" mean? And who did that disembodied voice belong to, anyway? In a house that seemed to be packed with ghosts, it was difficult to tell, but if Oliver had to guess, he'd say it was the late Despina Shaw's attempt at once again calling the shots on a property she still considered her own, though he'd be hard-pressed to prove the supposition.

If it was Despina, what could she possibly want from him? When he'd answered her call before, it had set him on the path of a budding relationship with Nym. The second time, her voice had led him to have a conversation with Rafe so he could gain a better understanding of the situation. All things considered, it was safe to presume she had his best interests at heart— provided they coincided with her own.

Could she be trying to help him discover a solution to his problem? Well, to be accurate—*Nym's* problem, caused in no small part by Oliver. He had told Nym he'd do anything to mend his mistake, and he'd meant it. What if he actually had a chance to make good on his promise?

Despite the prominent smell of mold and the damp chill that even the furnace couldn't entirely dispel, Oliver's heart lifted. He made a round of the space, examining the walls and flooring, looking for any clues or evidence of another hidden passageway, but found nothing but cracks in the concrete. The basement seemed to have been redone sometime in the last couple of decades, its stark utility erasing every trace of the original plan.

Oliver paused in the middle of the space, looking around in indecision. The longer he stood there, the more he became convinced he was missing something important, despite the mundane surroundings. He couldn't say where this certainty was coming from, but he was inclined to believe his hunches.

He walked around the room again, paying closer attention to the layout. Sure enough, now that the idea had taken root in his mind, it was easy to notice the discrepancy in the proportions of the room. Ostensibly, the open-plan basement should have measured up to the size of the ground floor, but if Oliver's impression was correct, a few square feet of space was missing on the south side.

A shelving unit stood against the south wall, laden with the same surplus of maintenance and construction items. Thankfully, it wasn't bolted either to the wall or the floor, but it took Oliver more than ten minutes to unload it enough so he could push it out of the way. The metal made a shrill screech as he dragged it across the floor, and he winced at the noise.

He dusted his hands on his jeans and cast a critical eye over the exposed surface of the wall as he waited for his labored breathing to return to normal. As far as he could tell, it was old plaster over bricks, stained with years of damp and dust. But the position of the wall definitely didn't align with the outer contour of the house by quite a significant margin. Whoever renovated the basement must have closed off a portion of it, for whatever reason.

Oliver's heart started to beat faster. Was this what the spirit meant by "seek inside"? Was there a hidden compartment behind that wall, just as there was a secret passage behind his closet?

He crouched and knocked on the wall, going left to right. It was hard to be completely sure, but he thought the echo sounded hollow. Could this be it?

Oliver straightened and looked around. The only way to find out for sure was to open up the wall, but would he really do that? What if he was making a mistake and would only end up causing unnecessary damage? Then again, it would pale in comparison to the damage he'd already wrought. After that, making a hole in a wall didn't feel like such a big deal.

He sighed and cast about for something he could use. He had to take the chance even at the price of appearing deranged to his former landlord and neighbors. If he was wrong, he'd explain everything to Nym tomorrow and offer to pay for wrecking his basement.

The only thing that came close to a demolition tool was a large hammer he had taken off the shelves along with the rest of the junk. He weighed it in his hand, took a deep, steadying breath, and swung it at the wall with all his might.

Dirty plaster rained down, and he coughed. Handyman he was not, but it was too late to stop now. He pulled his T-shirt over his mouth and continued to hammer at the wall. He really didn't want anyone, least of all Nym, coming down to investigate the noise, but there was no way to keep it down. Maybe whoever heard the thumping would blame it on Horace Livingstone cantankerously rearranging the furniture in his apartment following Oliver's departure.

It was a slow process. He'd been right about the bricks, and it took a lot of effort to chip at them. After a few minutes of hard swings, his shoulder began to ache and his wrist twinged unpleasantly, but he kept going. Finally, he managed to dislodge a couple of bricks and push them inside, revealing a gaping blackness beyond.

Oliver paused, breathing hard. He fumbled for his phone and shone it inside, but the darkness was too deep to be penetrated by a single beam. He couldn't discern anything within, yet the discovery renewed both his strength and his determination. He'd been right; there was *something* behind the wall, and he was about to find out what it was. Picking up the hammer once more, Oliver did his best to put in a little more effort.

He stopped only when he'd made a hole big enough for him to squeeze through. It was a good thing he couldn't boast of a towering frame because he was already shaking with exhaustion, drenched in sweat, and covered in dirty white dust that had gotten in his eyes and throat. He left the hammer lying on the floor and stepped into the opening, cursing under his breath when his jacket caught on the jagged edges. With one foot inside, he took out his phone once more and raised it above his head, illuminating whatever lay on the other side.

He'd been right in his calculations. The enclosed space was at least six feet wide, spanning this entire side of the basement. Oliver didn't know what exactly he hoped to see— maybe a treasure chest filled with gold and jewels, or a cache of priceless art, or a bookshelf stacked with first editions of Shakespeare, all signed by the author. Whatever he'd imagined, it wasn't a pile of old furniture.

Oliver moved the beam of his flashlight over the detritus, picking out a disassembled metal bedframe, a set of dining chairs stacked on top of each other, and an antique filing cabinet. He'd hoped to find something other than discarded garbage, but not so much as a glint of gilt winked back at him. He felt like an intrepid archaeologist who'd bravely weathered the deadly traps of an ancient tomb only to discover the golden statue he'd been seeking had already been replaced with a bag of sand.

He wiggled his way further inside, looked around, and came face-to-face with a ghost.

Oliver's heart seemed to stop, and the scream that he'd intended to let loose inexplicably lodged itself in his throat, choking him. He swallowed hard, taking in the frightening apparition—powder-white face, short coppery hair standing on end, wide eyes behind smeared glasses.

He was staring at a mirror.

"Fuck my life," he muttered when he felt he could once again suck air into his lungs. He glanced warily at the tarnished full-length mirror propped against the wall behind a rickety chair, his heart still pumping with residual fear, then turned his attention to the rest of the space.

There was barely any room to stand, much less walk around to inspect the compartment, but he attempted to do it anyway, determined not to let anything escape his notice. Maybe there was a jewelry box tucked into one of the skewed drawers of a peeling lacquered clothes press, or a portable safe hidden in one of the boxes in the corner. Despite evidence to the contrary, Oliver refused to admit defeat so easily. So he searched every nook and cranny he could reach, bumping into sharp corners and bits of furniture sticking out, hissing and swearing with irritation more than pain. But there was nothing. Not a single golden coin lying on the floor, not a meager silver spoon lingering in a drawer. The most significant discovery was a door that had once most likely opened through some passage into the garden as a possible escape route, but it was nailed shut.

Oliver turned toward the makeshift exit and promptly bumped his knee on the filing cabinet. Tears welled in his eyes, and he kicked the poor piece of furniture in frustration. He could do absolutely nothing right!

The sound of his kick against the metal side of the cabinet boomed in the tight space, but not as hollowly as he expected. Unlike the clothes press and the boxes, the filing cabinet wasn't empty.

Frowning, he crouched in front of it and pulled out one of the drawers, revealing neat rows of files. The brown paper covers were old and faded, powdery to the touch as if about to crumble in Oliver's hands. He propped his phone on top of the cabinet to get a little more light, pulled out a file at random, and opened it on the first page.

It was hard to make out what he was looking at, the shadows around him too solid and the light of the phone too glaring to read by comfortably, but he made out an official-looking letterhead on a note addressed to Mrs. Shaw. As he continued to study it, his heart began to beat faster.

He was looking at the copy of the original building permit for Lakeside Lodge from the City of Baltimore, dated 1901.

He quickly skimmed the letter and flipped through the rest of the papers, careful not to get dirt all over them. Property deeds, tax records from the first half of the twentieth century, it was all there. But it was the next folder that held the real jackpot.

In it, Oliver found detailed correspondence between Mrs. Shaw with the office of one Acton Kemble, who'd apparently been the lead architect that designed the house. The name was instantly familiar to anyone who had even a cursory interest in the history of nineteenth and twentieth century American architecture. Famous for his varied and often whimsical styles, Kemble had produced building designs that had since been considered important landmarks all over Washington DC, Maryland, and Pennsylvania—some of which had gone on to become a part of the local cultural heritage.

It was like discovering the pretty landscape that had hung for decades in your grandmother's living room was, in fact, an original Monet. Oliver berated himself for failing to recognize the fanciful style for what it was, for not picking up on the clues. But considering how (perhaps deliberately) obscure this property was, it wasn't at all surprising.

He had to take a minute to compose himself as he let the implications sink in and then continued with his perusal, willing the excited trembling in his hands to subside.

Surely enough, another file held a stack of blueprints, faded to indistinct gray but still legible. Oliver itched to lay them out on the floor and go over every inch of them to see what other secrets he'd missed, but there wasn't nearly enough room to spread them all out, and he didn't dare do anything that might damage them.

As he leafed through the papers, a sepia-toned photograph fell out of the folder. Oliver picked up the discolored picture. It depicted a regal-looking woman in a lacy Edwardian-style dress, wearing a wide-brimmed hat and holding a parasol, standing on the steps leading to Lakeside Lodge. She smiled the same sardonic smile as in her portrait in the memorial room, and even with the out-of-focus background, the house appeared new and stately and just as eccentric as it did now.

Oliver turned the photograph over. The once-black ink had turned brownish with time, but it was still legible and written in a strong, elegant hand:

> *"To O. Do the right thing and take good care of my boy, darling. Blessed be. D."*

Oliver's heart swelled. He'd hoped to find a treasure trove of some kind, and this was it. All the missing paperwork on the house, all the documentation needed to register it as a historical landmark. It was all here, patiently waiting for years to be discovered by someone desperate enough to actually go looking.

"Thank you," he whispered into the gloom, having no doubt Despina could hear him.

There were a lot more folders, all most likely filled with equally important records. He gathered as many as he could carry, grabbed his phone, and crawled back through the broken wall into the basement.

The room was just as silent as when he'd left it, but right away Oliver got the distinct impression he wasn't alone. He paused by the breach, straining to hear whatever it was that had made his skin prickle, and then he saw it.

A pair of burning yellow eyes watching him from behind the shelves.

Chapter Nineteen

The rational part of his brain told Oliver he should be afraid, but strangely, this time he wasn't. So instead of screaming, or fainting, or running for his life, he waited patiently with a stack of folders in his arms as the werewolf slowly emerged from behind the shelving unit Oliver had pushed out of the way earlier.

There was no doubt it was a hair-raising sight, especially now that Oliver could appreciate that it was the real deal rather than an ultra-realistic Halloween costume. Standing at well over seven feet even with a pronounced stoop to his shoulders, the monster lifted its head and sniffed the air, baring a row of sharp teeth and punctuating the action with a low growl. Its hind legs, with a long tail swishing between them, resembled a wolf's, while its arms were more humanlike, despite the formidable claws. Thick, dark-brown fur covered its entire body, with surprisingly endearing tufts on the points of the perked ears.

Oliver remained standing where he was even when the werewolf came so close that he could feel its hot breath on his face.

Perhaps Nym was deliberately trying to scare him off, but Oliver knew with absolute certainty he had nothing to be afraid of here—even if an angry werewolf was confronting him while trapped alone in a dingy basement. Instead, all the adrenaline coursing in his blood, coupled with Nym's physical proximity, had a very different effect on him, causing a sharp spike of arousal.

Oliver blushed and lowered the folders to hide the embarrassing tent in his jeans, though it was probably pointless since Nym could smell his reaction. It was so strong Oliver fancied he would smell it himself if he tried hard enough.

The werewolf paused, a look of confusion flickering in his eyes as he raked Oliver over with his gaze. Oliver couldn't blame him for being bewildered; he was equally flummoxed by the startling turn of events.

He cleared his throat to get his thoughts back on the right track, and Nym's eyes snapped back to his face.

"You can stop. I'm not afraid of you anymore, and I'm not running away this time," Oliver clarified. "And I'm sorry I made such much noise and woke you up. Oh, and for digging through your wall. But you have to see what I found. Despina told me where to look, and she was right. We can save Lakeside Lodge!"

He realized he was blabbering in his excitement without making much sense, but he had to convince Nym not to throw him out again before he could hear him out.

The werewolf snarled, but the sound was more resigned than agitated. He stepped back and dropped to all fours, convulsing as the transformation took hold.

Oliver hastily averted his eyes as Nym pushed himself upright again and walked behind the shelf, where he'd left his clothes. He emerged a minute later, barefoot and in nothing but a pair of sweatpants and a long-sleeved T-shirt.

"What are you talking about?" he asked, not bothering to keep the annoyance out of his voice.

"Okay, just please don't get mad again," Oliver said pleadingly. "I think I have the solution to all our problems. Well, your problems that I've caused."

Nym's jaw tightened. He crossed his arms over his chest, but at least he seemed willing to listen, which was a good sign. So Oliver took a deep breath and launched into a lengthy account of everything that had happened since he left Nym's apartment a few hours earlier, starting with him hearing a beckoning voice in his bedroom and finishing with his astounding discovery of all of Lakeside Lodge records.

That last bit certainly got Nym's attention. He stopped frowning and accepted a folder Oliver handed him, then flipped through the papers inside.

"I don't understand," he said finally. "Why would anybody want to seal off all the important paperwork—literally?"

Oliver shrugged. "I was thinking about it myself, but we might never know for sure. You said yourself your family wasn't interested in the property. Maybe your aunt hid all the documents here for safekeeping, not knowing what would become of the house and whose hands it might end up in, and by the time you took over the inheritance, it was all forgotten. In any case, whoever did it made the right decision because it's all here, organized and intact."

Nym raised his eyes from the folder and studied Oliver with a thoughtful expression.

"And you think it'll be enough to put the house on a historical registry?" he asked.

"I know so." Oliver couldn't hold back a proud smile. "A house built by Kemble himself? No one would dare demolish it, even if it were crumbling around you. And we can prove it. Like I said, it's all here—the deed, proof of ownership, the original plans, signed letters, photographs, the first guest book with all the signatures, even tax deductions from Despina's various local charities. All you have to do is get it all authenticated and notarized and then file a petition with the city, along with a proposal for conservation. With so much evidence of historical significance, it'll be a breeze. Cox won't be able to touch it once you get the approval."

Nym continued to look at him, still holding the papers. If the cold seeping from the concrete floor into his bare feet bothered him, he didn't show it.

"Why are you doing this? All of it," he added, gesturing to the heap of masonry next to the wall and the gaping hole in the middle. "Trying to help, looking for a solution. Why would you want to?"

Oliver held his gaze steadily.

"I want to help because I owe it to you after making such a mess of things. I fucked up, and it's not enough to simply say I'm sorry. It doesn't mean anything unless I do everything I can to fix it. So…I did. With your great-great-grandaunt's help, so I guess I'm lucky she kinda likes me."

In the face of Nym's prolonged silence, he continued, "I can do more than just knocking down the walls in your basement. I've done nothing but fill out forms and file for permits with the city since I began working for Thompson Designs. Granted, I've never submitted an application for a historical property, but I know how the process works. I'll be glad to do it for you, if you let me. I realize you might not trust me after—"

"It's not that," Nym said. "I do believe you when you say you want to make amends. And, frankly, I'd be grateful for any kind of help navigating the paperwork and the legal matters. It may come as a shock to you, but I'm not very good at handling bureaucracy." He gave Oliver a crooked smile.

Relief flooded Oliver, so strong his knees almost buckled. Nym had agreed to accept his help, and that meant there was still a chance, however small, that eventually he'd be willing to forgive Oliver and maybe even be his friend again. It was funny how until now, Oliver hadn't realized just how much the idea of losing Nym hurt, and how much he wanted him back in his life, even if their budding romance would never blossom. He'd gladly forgo the possibility of kissing Nym ever again if it meant never seeing the scathing disappointment in his eyes.

Well, maybe not gladly, but he'd take whatever Nym was prepared to offer.

"Is that the only reason?" Nym asked. "Because you owe me?"

Oliver bit his lip. "Of course that's not the only reason. But the other thing doesn't matter anymore, does it?"

There was a long pause, heavy with everything that remained unspoken.

"No, I suppose it doesn't," Nym said at last. He looked down at the folder in his hands and sighed. "Why don't you sit down for a bit. I'll get the rest of it."

★

It was only the beginning of November, but the temperatures had dropped significantly, and the pronounced nip in the air served as a warning that the winter was near. Visions of black cats and bats and pumpkin spice had given way to the arrival of turkey dinners and the good cheer of the upcoming holiday season.

Without the swaths of fake spider webs, bloody curtains, and leering jack-o'-lanterns, the facade of Lakeside Lodge looked subdued but not sleepy, despite the late hour. Oliver doubted if the house ever really slept. Even with all the windows darkened and only the overhead porch light pooling on the steps, the silence had an expectant quality.

Oliver shifted from foot to foot, pushing his hands deeper in the pockets of his parka, and looked up at Nym. The other man leaned on a porch post with his arms crossed over the front of his scuffed leather jacket. He hadn't moved or said anything in over ten minutes, but somehow, Oliver could sense a streak of nervousness under the poised exterior.

"Are you sure he's going to come?" Oliver asked, watching his breath materialize into white vapor in the chilly air. "He could handle it all through his lawyers and save himself the trouble."

"Cox has been dying to get a leg up on me for a long time," Nym said. "After the message I left him, he must be convinced I'm finally gonna roll over and let him take the house from me. Trust me, he's gonna be here for this."

Oliver hummed in agreement and eyed the building again. He itched to ask Nym whether someone had already rented his old apartment but thought better of it. It wasn't his business anymore anyway. He was here to have Nym's back, and that was it.

It was weird being here again, standing so close to Nym. Oliver had stayed in the Lodge for less than a month and only spent one night in the man's bed, but, absurdly, it felt like coming home again. Or it would have, if he were in any way welcome.

"Here he comes," Nym said in a low voice, jolting Oliver out of his unhappy reverie.

Oliver drew himself up to his full height and watched Cox walk up the path to the house, his camel wool coat buttoned up against the biting wind.

"A welcoming committee? I'm honored," he remarked as he climbed up to the porch.

"Don't be," Nym gritted.

"Now, there's no need for that kind of attitude," Cox said soothingly. "I really *am* glad you called. It's about time you had some sense, instead of choosing to be obstinate."

"It's not a matter of choice, is it? I know what you're trying to do. Having the Department of Housing condemn the premises so you can swipe it out from under me for cheap? I knew you were a weasel, Cox, but I didn't think you'd stoop that low."

Cox shrugged. "And who's fault is that? Had you been reasonable from the beginning, I wouldn't have had to resort to such tactics. In any case, if you want to be successful, you must be willing to play dirty. That's just the way the world works. Whining about it won't help, it'll only serve to make your check that much smaller. And as for this juvenile name-calling," he added with a sneer, "let me remind you that I can think of worse things to call you than a weasel."

Nym stiffened at the implied threat, although it was pretty much an empty one. Exposing Nym as a werewolf without hard evidence would damage Cox's reputation before his.

"Now, if you're done posturing, I suggest we go inside and talk business," Cox continued when Nym said nothing. "I'm willing to make you a new offer before they slap the official precondemnation notice on your front door. It might not be as generous as my previous proposals, but it'll certainly be better than bearing the cost of demolition."

He made a move for the door, but this time it was Oliver who put out his hand, stopping Cox in his tracks.

"Not so fast, if you please, Mr. Cox."

Annoyance flashed across Cox's face before he regained his astringent smile.

"I wasn't expecting to see you here, Oliver," he said. "If you wanted to discuss our arrangement, you should've simply called."

"I'm afraid I have to break off our arrangement," Oliver said. His heart thumped wildly with a mix of nervousness and excited anticipation, but he hoped his voice sounded calm.

Cox raised an eyebrow, his smug expression slipping by just a fraction. "Is that so?"

"Yes," Oliver said more firmly. "Nym?"

Nym detached himself from the post and produced a folded piece of paper from the inner pocket of his jacket. He handed it to Cox, who took it warily.

"What is it?" Without waiting for an answer, he unfolded the letter and began reading, his expression altering as he did so.

"It's an application to the Baltimore Commission for Historical and Architectural Preservation for the designation of Lakeside Lodge as a historic city landmark," Oliver said, though the contents were pretty self-explanatory.

"A city landmark?" Cox sneered. He retained the appearance of composure, but tiny cracks of doubt now ran through it. "You can't possibly fool anyone into believing this dump has enough cultural significance to be classified as a landmark."

"Oh, I don't know. I'd say a house designed by Acton Kemble might fit the criteria. And that's without taking into account the founder's local community outreach. I'm no expert, but I'm confident the Commission will grant us the approval."

That gave Cox pause. The cracks deepened and pulled apart, like fissures in a faulty foundation, and he rounded up on Oliver.

"Us? You mean you're siding with Brown on this? Let me tell you right now, you're making a big mistake here, Oliver."

His voice was low, but it held a clear undertone of malice. Nym must have sensed it, too, because he moved to stand closer to Oliver as if offering his protection even though Oliver knew Cox would never go for him.

No, if the man wanted to take a swing at Oliver, he'd do it differently. Oliver had no illusions that Cox could do some serious damage to his career if he wanted to. He'd known it when he filled out the application and contacted the CHAP, when he insisted on being here by Nym's side. Doing the right thing always came with a price, and this time, he was willing to pay it.

Cox's gaze swung back to Nym.

"You can't prove any of it. I've done my research on this place, and Acton Kemble's name never came up. You're either bluffing or trying to jack up my price."

"We're not bluffing," Nym said firmly. "But you can think so if you want. To be honest, I don't much care."

"Even if you were to buy the property now, any building permit you'd want to file for your project would be suspended pending the CHAP review process of our historic landmark application," Oliver interjected. "So even if our application ends up being rejected—and I have a feeling it won't—and you do manage to strong-arm Mr. Brown into selling, you might lose months, even years, sitting on a worthless piece of property. What were you saying earlier about the demolition costs?"

Cox drew himself up, every pretense of equanimity and good-natured exasperation gone from his face, and thrust the letter back to Nym.

"Fine," he gritted out. "You won, freak. But I promise you and your little fuck buddy here are going to regret it."

Nym took a step forward, exposing his suddenly sharp teeth as his features rippled and contorted. He didn't fully transform, but it was enough to make Cox recoil. Throwing them both a last dirty look, the developer turned and briskly walked away. The low-hanging branches of the maples that lined the path swayed violently in the cold breeze from the lake, drawing muttered curses from Cox as they snagged on his expensive coat and lashed at his head.

Nym followed him with his eyes until Cox was out of sight and then turned to Oliver, frowning, his face back to its normal semblance.

"What did he mean? Can he really cause you problems at work?"

"He can try," Oliver said lightly, though he wasn't feeling at all confident.

"Maybe you taking a stand against him with me wasn't such a good idea."

"No, it was," Oliver said firmly. "I'm glad I stood up for myself. And for you."

"Okay," Nym said, though he didn't look convinced. "Anyway, thank you for everything. I wouldn't have known where to begin this whole process."

"It's not over yet," Oliver said. "The approval will take a while, and there's no guarantee Cox won't try to put spokes in our wheels out of spite. I'll help you handle it all for as long as you need me."

Nym dipped his head in acknowledgment. "I appreciate it."

For a moment, neither of them said anything, simply gazing into each other's eyes as the wind shook the trees around them, showering them with shriveled brown leaves.

Oliver felt he had to say something, seize the opportunity to mend this horrible rift between them. But his courage, which had risen to the challenge mere minutes ago, utterly deserted him now. It was as if he were Schrodinger's cat, trapped in the box of an impossible dilemma. So long as neither of them said anything, their relationship could be thought of both as having a chance to survive this ordeal and as being broken without repair. Only by hashing it out would they know for sure; but the possibility of facing a resounding, final goodbye terrified Oliver more than he thought it would.

Nym was the first to look away and cleared his throat while tucking the letter back into his jacket pocket.

"So, how's your new apartment?" he asked, his tone neutral.

"It's okay, I guess." Oliver shrugged. "Kinda boring without all the ghosts to keep me company though."

Nym's lips tugged in an uncertain smile, but it was gone in the next instant.

"Well, I guess I'll see you, then," he said.

"See you," Oliver pushed out.

There was another short pause, and then Nym turned and walked to the front door.

Oliver's throat closed as he watched it close behind him with a soft thud that seemed to resonate in his soul.

Chapter Twenty

The weather reflected in the tall windows that encircled the offices of Thompson Designs matched Oliver's mood perfectly.

Rain drummed against the glass in an incessant staccato, and heavy clouds drifted across a slate-colored sky. According to Oliver's colleagues, snow wasn't very far behind, but he couldn't bring himself to be excited about the prospect of a real-life white Christmas.

"Are you okay?"

Oliver started guiltily and looked up at Ela, who came over and leaned against his desk.

"Sure. Why wouldn't I be?"

Ela shook her head. "You tell me. You've been moping for weeks now." She leaned in closer and dropped her voice. "Is it because of that former landlord of yours you've been telling me about?"

Oliver flushed and adjusted his glasses. He hadn't told Ela the whole truth about what had happened between him and Nym, of course, but he did let slip that they'd been on the verge of a new relationship before it all went south (the reason for which he also hadn't shared). He'd told Pam pretty much the same, although she'd been far more insistent than Ela at trying to get him to spill the beans.

"I haven't been moping," he said defensively. "I just have a lot on my mind, that's all."

"Right." She didn't look convinced, and he was sure she would offer either sympathy or advice, but then he noticed a movement by the entrance out of the corner of his eye, and all thought of continuing the conversation evaporated.

He watched with bated breath as Cox crossed the open space, making a beeline to Thompson's office. He didn't stop to chat with anyone or deign to answer greetings and swept past a distressed-looking Owen, who made a feeble attempt of inquiring whether he had an appointment. The office door banged shut behind him, and Oliver winced.

"Wow, he looks pissed," Ela remarked. "I wonder what's gotten into him."

"I might have something to do with it," Oliver confessed. He glanced at the office door, but it remained closed, and no sound came from it.

Ela frowned. "You? What did you do?"

Oliver made a humming sound, at a loss at how to explain it. At the same moment, Thompson opened the door and yelled: "Daniel! Get in here right now!"

"Here we go," Oliver muttered. He slid off the chair and made his way to Thompson's office under the curious stares of his coworkers, all of whom stopped whatever they were doing to see how the scene would unfold.

In some ways, it was a relief. He'd been waiting for the other shoe to drop for weeks, and when Cox had failed to either contact him or show up at the firm, he'd let himself believe the developer had forgotten all about him. But, of course, he should've known better. Men like Cox didn't appreciate being thwarted, especially when their position allowed them to exact revenge. At least now he wouldn't have to live with the apprehensive anticipation.

Oliver went inside, surprised to discover that Ela had trailed after him despite not being summoned. Cox stood by the far window, pretending to examine the 3D model of Thompson's Tower of Light, which was now on permanent display in the office. He didn't turn his head when Oliver entered, but Oliver could see from his faint reflection that he was paying close attention.

"What is this nonsense Mr. Cox is telling me about you messing up his project and blocking an acquisition of a property he was interested in?" Thompson demanded without preamble, not waiting for the door to close behind Oliver and Ela. He was red in the face, his eyes glinting with displeasure. "I don't know what would possess you to do something like that, but I expect you to apologize to Mr. Cox immediately! And if you want to keep your job, you're going to sort this whole thing out!"

"With all due respect, sir, this has absolutely no bearing on my work here," Oliver said firmly. "I was merely helping a friend file an application with the Department of Housing. If Mr. Cox chooses to take offense with that, it's really not my problem."

"Not your problem?" Thompson repeated incredulously. "When one of my biggest clients threatens to take his business elsewhere because of one of my employees' impertinent behavior, it becomes that employee's problem! I demand that you apologize to Mr. Cox right away, Daniel!"

Only a few weeks ago, Thompson's shrill command and forceful attitude would've been enough to make Oliver's resolve shrivel up like a raisin. But if those weeks had taught him anything, it was that he could handle a lot more than he believed he could. He was done with letting other people intimidate or manipulate him.

"No," he said, raising his chin defiantly, though his heart beat wildly in his throat. "And by the way, my name is Oliver."

He heard Ela shuffling uncomfortably behind him while Thompson turned another shade of red.

"I don't care if your name is Prince William," he thundered. "I knew hiring some inexperienced upstart from Florida was a mistake. You've been trouble since day one. Not showing up for work, making all of us look bad in front of our clients with your stupid ideas, and now sabotaging the firm for God knows what purpose! You're an absolutely useless, spoiled little brat, and you've done nothing but bring your whole team down the entire time you've been here—which, let me assure you, is well and truly over!"

"I must disagree with you there, Mr. Thompson," Ela interjected before Oliver could offer a response. "I've been mentoring Oliver for over two months now, and I can attest to the fact that he's intelligent, professional, and hard-working. I don't know what happened between him and Mr. Cox, but Oliver has been a great asset to the team when working on the Potomac Street housing project, and has done some great work which I'm sure Mr. Cox could appreciate. To fire him over something that doesn't have any connection to the workplace would be both unfair and unethical."

"I see this is becoming a team meeting issue," Cox said dryly. "I'll leave you folks to sort it out among yourselves, but

I meant what I said, Colin. If you want to get my next assignment, get that little shit out of here."

Oliver scowled at him, but Cox was already out the door, slamming it loudly behind him.

Thompson wheeled round on Ela. "Look what you've done!" He pointed at the shut door. "Who asked you to butt in? If you're so eager to defend your little buddy, maybe you should go looking for another job right along with him."

There was a brief moment of stunned silence.

"Ela, don't," Oliver said quietly. "It's not worth it."

"He's right for once," Thompson said with a disdainful look at Oliver. "He's certainly not worth it."

"You know what," Ela said, her tone as hard as Oliver had ever heard it. "You're the one who's right. Maybe I *should* be looking for another job."

"Ela—" Oliver began while Thompson bristled, but she steamrolled right over him.

"I've been with this firm for over five years and not once have I or any of my team members felt appreciated. I'm sick and tired of your arrogance, condescension, and snobbery. I'm a highly qualified professional, and I deserve better than to be treated this way. So guess what? You want to fire Oliver and me because your client got his feathers ruffled and he can't handle it like a mature adult? Go ahead because I quit anyway. Take your Tower of Light and shove it where the light doesn't shine."

With that, she turned on her heel and strode out of the office. With one last look at Thompson, who had now reached the shade of a boiled lobster, Oliver hurried after her. Behind him, Thompson shouted for Owen, no doubt to inform him that both Oliver and Ela were no longer employed at the firm, effective immediately.

"My God, what have you done?" Oliver said when they reached Ela's desk. "I never meant for you to lose your job over me!"

Ela let out a long, weary sigh.

"I did what I should've done a long time ago. This whole mess with Cox and the way he was harping on you just made everything come to a head, but it's not really a spur-of-the-moment decision. It's been brewing for a long time. Besides," she smiled wryly, "it felt so good to finally tell that asshole off."

Oliver snorted and looked around. People all over the office were pretending very hard they weren't watching them, but with Thompson still fuming loudly, no one dared to approach them with inquires, whether curious or sympathetic.

"I'm glad you think so," he said, "but I'm still sorry I put you in this situation. Now we're both unemployed without references."

It was a terrifying prospect, but he found it wasn't as debilitating as he imagined it would be. Sure, it would be a huge challenge to face, especially with such abruptness, but he knew, deep down, he could rise to it—he and Ela both.

Instead of sitting down and wrapping her hands around her head in despair, Ela leaned against the desk and gave Oliver an appraising look.

"What if said I know someone who wouldn't care for your references?" she said.

Oliver looked at her in confusion. "What do you mean?"

"I'm going to start my own architectural firm." Deep determination colored her words. Perhaps she was right about this being a long-brewing decision. "I know things will be rough at first, and the pay won't be as good as with Thompson Designs, but I'll need someone talented and ambitious to be my partner if I want to build a successful business. So are you with me?"

A slow smile spread on Oliver's face as he reached out to shake Ela's hand.

"There's no one else I'd rather be with."

With snow piled on the gable and the dormer windows and colorful string lights wrapped around the porch posts, at first glance, Lakeside Lodge looked cheerful.

Upon closer inspection, however, it became clear the attempt at embracing the holiday spirit was half-hearted at best. The lights were the only concession to the season, and only half the bulbs were working. No wreath hung on the front door, and no snowflake decals were stuck on the windows. The contrast with the lavish Halloween decorations was stark and obvious, as if the inhabitants of the building either didn't care about Christmas or didn't care for it.

It didn't seem as though any work had been done on the exterior of the house either. The posts leaned at odd angles, and paint peeled from the window trims. Considering the latest bout of bad weather, Oliver supposed he couldn't blame Nym for postponing any work that required being outside for more than a few minutes at a time.

Oliver climbed the stairs and used the brass knocker. It was early Saturday morning, so the house was quiet and dark. On second thought, perhaps he should've called before dropping by, but he was nervous about coming here as it was. Talking to Nym on the phone was bound to make him even more apprehensive.

He listened to the echo of the knock dying down in the hallway inside. Maybe Nym wasn't home. Oliver didn't know if the possibility made him feel better or worse.

He was debating whether to knock again or just pick up the phone, when the door was flung open, revealing Nym in his usual jeans and flannel shirt. At the sight of Oliver, his surly expression brightened, but only for an instant before shuttering again.

"Hey," he said in a guarded tone. "I wasn't expecting to see you."

"Yeah, sorry. If you're busy, I can return another time," Oliver said, suddenly aware he might be intruding on a post-date morning.

"I'm not busy." Nym opened the door wider and stepped back, gesturing for Oliver to come in.

Oliver followed him into the parlor, which was empty and freezing. He sat in one of the armchairs as he watched Nym switching on the lamps and going over to light the fireplace.

"So," Oliver said, aiming for nonchalance while watching Nym move about the room. "Have you got a new tenant already?"

Nym looked at him over his shoulder from where he crouched by the fireplace and shook his head. "Not yet. I decided to wait till I can find a paranorm like the rest of us to rent the apartment."

"Right. That makes sense."

Nym took a chair across from Oliver and folded his hands in his lap. If Oliver didn't know better, he'd say Nym was nervous too.

"Do you want something to drink?" Nym glanced at the window that bore faint traces of frost. "Tea, maybe?"

"Thanks, I'm fine."

There was another awkward pause.

"How have you been doing?" Nym asked. "I haven't heard from you for a while."

Did Nym actually want to hear from him, or was Oliver reading something into nothing?

"I'm pretty good," he said. "My friend Ela and I are scheduled to open our own design office after the holidays. We found this awesome place on Keswick Rd., right by Wyman Park. Some of our former colleagues might consider joining us too."

"That's terrific," Nym said in a much warmer tone. "I'm glad you're making this happen."

Oliver shrugged. "Striking out on our own may not work out, especially in this economy. But at least we tried, right?"

"You'll make it work," Nym said with absolute certainty. "You're passionate about the things you believe in, and you're a go-getter. I don't have a doubt in my mind you and your friend will do great."

Oliver flushed at the praise. He'd been afraid Nym would give him the cold shoulder, but it seemed that once again his fears concerning the man were unfounded.

"Speaking of go-getters, I have something for you," he said. "You're going to get the official letter in the mail soon, but I thought you might want to see this as soon as possible, so I printed out the email notification for you."

He took out a piece of paper from his pocket and handed it to Nym. Watching the other man's eyes light up as he read it, every bump and hurdle he'd had to clear to get to this point suddenly seemed worth it.

A slow smile spread on Nym's bearded face, and he raised his eyes to Oliver.

"I can't believe it."

"Yep." Oliver grinned back at him. "Lakeside Lodge is now officially a Baltimore City Landmark. It means you'd have to file for permits every time you want to change things around here, but the upside is that nobody can touch it, no matter how rundown it is. And if we get the approval for a tax credit for historic restoration, it won't stay rundown for long."

Nym's fingers tightened on the paper. "Thank you for doing all this. I…I don't know what to say."

"You don't have to say anything. I'm happy to do it." Oliver looked around, taking in the peeling wallpaper, the uneven floor, the threadbare rug next to the fireplace. "It may sound strange, but this place grew on me. I'd like to see it restored to all its former glory."

"Me too. Provided we don't get rid of the ghosts."

"I don't think we could even if we tried." Oliver smiled. "Not that I'd want to. To tell you the truth, I kinda miss hanging out with old Horace. With all of you guys."

"All of us?" Nym asked with a peculiar inflection, watching him.

"Well. Some more than others," Oliver said, striving for lightness and failing miserably.

Nym looked at the paper he was holding and then carefully put it down on the coffee table.

"You could've called or forwarded the notice to my email," he said. "You didn't have to come all the way down here."

"No," Oliver agreed. "I didn't. But I wanted to because…well, because I have something else to say to you."

Nym inclined his head ever so slightly, indicating he was listening.

Oliver swallowed and adjusted his glasses. "I know I've disappointed you, and I wouldn't blame you if you never forgave me or trusted me again. But I have to let you know how much our time together meant to me. You've been a great friend, but it wasn't just that. I was attracted to you, yes, but somewhere along the way I've fallen in love with you without noticing. You know how you don't realize how good something is until it's gone? Well, that's the way it's been for me. I didn't know I'd lost my heart until it was in pieces."

He took another steadying breath, feeling self-conscious under Nym's unwavering gaze. But no matter how vulnerable he was making himself in front of the other man, he had to let it all out in the open. The truth will set you free, wasn't that what they said?

The truth also hurt; but maybe, just maybe, hope could be born out of that pain.

"I didn't want to say anything until this whole situation with the historical status of the Lodge was resolved, so you wouldn't feel as if I was using it for some kind of leverage. But now that it's done… Do you think…there's any chance for us to start over?"

The silence was so complete it was as if the entire house held its breath, waiting for Nym's answer.

"For the record, I don't think you'd use your help with the CHAP application as leverage," Nym said after what seemed like an eternity compressed into a few dozen seconds. "You're not that kind of person."

"Thanks."

"As for the other thing…" Nym hesitated for another moment. "Are you sure that's what you want? To be with someone like me?"

"Someone like you?" Oliver repeated. "Someone kind, sensitive, and considerate, who will have my back no matter what? Someone funny and intelligent who appreciates me? Someone strong and ferocious who wouldn't dream to lay a hand on me, or anyone else? Yes, you bet I want to be with someone like that."

Nym's jaw worked, his eyes going dark with emotion.

"If you really mean that—"

"I do."

"—then, yes. I've been hoping, waiting for you to show up because I feel the same, and I had the same reservations about pressuring you. I think we can try to start over. Or better yet, pick up where we left off."

Just as with their first kiss in the attic in what felt like a lifetime ago, Oliver didn't know which one of them moved first, but in the next moment, they were standing in each other's arms, kissing as if the other person was the sole source of oxygen in the room.

"I'm sorry," Oliver pushed out when they finally surfaced, gasping for air. "God, I'm so sorry—"

"Shh. Don't. I'm sorry too. But if we start apologizing to each other for all our collective blunders, we'll be here all night," Nym said with gruffness that contrasted with the tinge of moisture in his eyes. "I have a much better idea of how we can make up for lost time, and talking is not it."

Oliver gasped as Nym scooped him into his arms, parka coat and all. He wrapped his arms around Nym's neck, holding on like a drowning man to a lifeline.

"I missed you," Nym breathed and nuzzled Oliver's neck. "So much."

"I missed you too." Oliver bit his lip, trying to hold back both tears and a moan of pleasure. "I promise to never overreact to anything you have to tell or show me ever again."

"And I promise, no more secrets," Nym growled.

"Good." Oliver smiled and buried his face in the crook of Nym's shoulder, his heart so full he was afraid it'd burst if he made the wrong move. "Because I plan to be here long enough to learn all of them."

Epilogue

"Wow, the patio looks great!" Sky exclaimed and swirled on the neatly arranged geometric concrete tiles, her long skirt swooshing around her.

Rafe walked past her to the far side of the patio, where it ended in a brand-new deck overlooking the garden. Strings of fairy lights and moonflower vines hung from the ornate pergola above a seating arrangement of low outdoor sofas and side tables, bright against the rapidly gathering dusk. Several trays held glasses filled with sparkling rosé and an assortment of artfully cut fruit.

"Nice." Rafe whistled appreciatively. "Very romantic."

He turned and winked at Nym, who went red in the face but didn't take his arm from around Oliver's shoulders.

Oliver grinned and shoved his hands into the pockets of his jeans. "I thought you might like it. It wasn't part of the original renovation plan, but it's such a great spot, so Nym and I decided to do something with it anyway."

"Amy was upset by all the noise, especially when they were pouring the foundations," Aurora said from where she was standing next to the trashcan, now tucked neatly in a niche by the side of the building. Behind her, Kimona nodded. "But I believe she'll grow used to the new setup."

A loud plaintive grumble sounded from inside the trashcan as if in agreement.

"Sorry for the inconvenience, Amy," Oliver said. "I'm afraid we're not quite done with the racket yet. There's still a lot of work to be done on the house interior, replacing the insulation and the electric wiring. How about I throw out a few steaks tomorrow to make it up to you?"

The grumble transformed into a contented grunt, and everybody laughed.

"There's another surprise in the garden," Nym said. "Let's grab a drink and go down and take a look."

They all filed down from the deck into the back garden after taking a wine glass from the tray. Only birdsong and the hum of bumblebees penetrated the peaceful sleepiness of the wild patch of greenery, secluded under the shade of the old chestnut oaks. The late spring air, fragrant with the smell of flowers and fresh leaves, mingled with the scent of cut grass and overturned earth.

"There's a hole in the ground," Rafe pointed out, though the freshly dug and marked rectangular pit in the middle of the lawn was readily apparent. "Are we here to bury a body? And if so, is the poor chap still fresh?"

Sky giggled and Aurora rolled her eyes. "Yeah, like you'd drink *that*."

"No dead bodies, fresh or otherwise," Oliver said firmly. "Don't you see what it is?"

"Oh my god, you're going to add a pool!" Sky gasped, understanding dawning in her blue eyes. "That's so awesome, Nym!"

"I hope you'll like it," Nym said, turning to Kimona.

She smiled uncertainly and whipped out her phone.

Really? For me?

Nym nodded. "You all deserve it, guys. For putting up with me and this old place. But now, I can finally turn this house into what I always dreamed it could be, for all of us. And I couldn't have done it without Oliver." He turned and raised his glass. "To Oliver!"

Oliver blushed and raised his own glass. "To Lakeside Lodge!"

Rafe whooped, and everybody cheered before downing their drinks. As they drifted across the garden and the deck to examine the layout of the future pool and lounge on the sofas, Nym moved closer to Oliver, and by some unspoken agreement, they walked unhurriedly to the shadow of a tall maple, its low-hanging branches shielding them from prying eyes and the excited chatter of the others.

"You didn't have to toast me," Oliver said. "You did all the hard work."

"I meant it though. None of it would have been possible without you." Nym gestured back to the house, taking in the scaffolding that currently surrounded the turret and the construction dumpster half blocking the pathway. "And I have something for you."

Oliver's heart did a little flip. This wouldn't be the first time he and Nym had exchanged gifts of varying degrees of meaningfulness during the months they'd been dating, but for some reason this felt different. Perhaps it was the somber expression in Nym's eyes or the touch of tension in his posture.

"What is it?"

Nym took Oliver's glass and set it down along with his own on a nearby tree stump. He produced something shiny out of the pocket of his denim jacket and handed it to Oliver as if he were passing on something precious.

Oliver examined the object in his palm. It was a simple key with the number 1A engraved on it, hanging off a silver key chain adorned with a wolf's head charm. He looked up at Nym, stunned.

"Does this mean what I think it means?" he asked softly, afraid to believe it.

"Yes. I'm asking you to move in with me, Oliver." Nym's gaze searched his eyes. "I want us to be together, always. If you'll have me."

Oliver closed his palm over the key, clutching it. "I want it too. I love you, Nymphus."

Nym grinned, and his shoulders sagged a little in relief. "I love you too. Even when you use that name."

"Then you'll have to show me how much," Oliver murmured and drew Nym down for a kiss.

The red maples and the chestnut oaks rustled gently all around them, the crickets taking up the night song while the birds settled in their nests.

Leaning into each other, Nym and Oliver made their way back toward the little circle of friends as the faint echo of a woman's laugh followed them.

Acknowledgements

A special thank you to the wonderful team at NineStar Press, and especially to Raevyn and to my editor, Elizabetta, for their continuous good work and support.

About Isabelle Adler

A voracious reader from the age of five, Isabelle Adler has always dreamed of one day putting her own stories into writing. She loves traveling, art, and science, and finds inspiration in all of these. Her favorite genres include sci-fi, fantasy, and historical adventure. She also firmly believes in the unlimited powers of imagination and caffeine.

Email
info@isabelleadler.com

Website
www.isabelleadler.com

Twitter
@Isabelle_Adler

Other NineStar books by this author

Staying Afloat Series
Adrift
Ashore
Afloat

The Castaway Prince Series
The Castaway Prince
The Exile Prince
The Homecoming Prince

Fae-Touched Series
A Touch of Magic

Standalone Books
Frost
Irises in the Snow
The Wolf and the Sparrow
In the Winter Woods

Also from NineStar **Press**

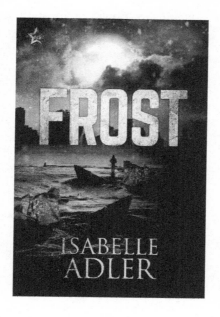

Frost

The end of the world as they knew it had come and gone, and the remnants of mankind struggle to survive in a barren landscape. Twenty-three-year-old Finn sets out on a desperate mission to scavenge for the much-needed medicine to help his sister. He knows better than to trust anyone, but when a total stranger saves him from a vicious gang, the unexpected act of kindness rekindles Finn's lost faith in humanity.

The tentative friendship with his rescuer, Spencer, gradually turns into something more, and for the first time in years, Finn lets himself yearn for joy and hope in the dead of nuclear winter—right until Spencer goes missing.

They say love is the greatest power of all, but it seems it would take nothing short of a miracle to overcome the dangers that threaten to destroy Finn's only chance for happiness and the lives of his loved ones.

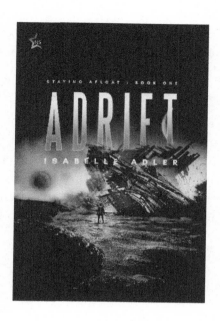

Adrift

Some jobs are just too good to be true.

Captain Matt Spears learns this the hard way after a mysterious employer hires his ship to hunt down an ancient alien artifact but insists on providing his own pilot. Ryce Faine is handsome and smart, but Matt has rarely met anyone more obnoxious. With tensions running high, it isn't until they are attacked by the hostile Alraki that Matt grudgingly begins to respect Ryce's superior skills, respect that transforms into a tentative attraction.

Little did he know that their biggest challenge would be reaching their destination, an abandoned alien base located on a distant moon amid a dense asteroid field. But when Matt learns that Ryce isn't completely who he says he is and the artifact is more than he bargained for, he is faced with a difficult choice. One that might change the balance of forces in the known galaxy.

Matt doesn't take well to moral dilemmas; he prefers the easy way out. But that might not be possible anymore, when his past comes back to haunt him at the worst possible moment. When faced with a notorious pirate carrying a personal grudge, the fragile connection Matt has formed with Ryce might be the only thing that he can count on to save them both.

A Touch of Magic

After returning to the straight and narrow, Cary Westfield hopes to rebuild his life as a stage magician. Only thing is, the success of his new show is entirely dependent on a strange medallion inherited from his late grandfather—an amulet that holds a rare and inexplicable power to captivate the wearer's audience.

Ty prides himself on his ability to obtain any item of magical significance—for the right price. When a mysterious client hires him to steal a magical amulet from a neophyte illusionist, he's sure it will be a quick and easy job, earning him a nice chunk of cash.

As it turns out, nothing is sure when greed and powerful magic are at play. When a mob boss with far-reaching aspirations beats Ty to the snatch, Cary and Ty form an unlikely partnership to get the amulet back. The unexpected spark of attraction between them is a welcome perk, but each man has his own plan for the prize.

All bets are off, however, when it is revealed the magical amulet holds a darker secret than either of them had bargained for.

The Castaway Prine

Ostracized by his family for his sexual identity, Prince Stephan is forced to flee his homeland before his older brother ascends the throne.

Stephan has been drawn to feminine things for as long as he can remember, so when the dire need for secrecy arises, he seizes the chance to don the perfect disguise. With the help of his loyal servant, Stephan picks his way through hostile territory, hiding his identity by posing as a woman. His only hope for asylum lies with the man who had been his friend and lover three years ago. But when that man also happens to be the crown prince of a rival country, things are a bit more complicated.

With war looming on the horizon, the danger of discovery grows by the moment. With all odds stacked against him, will Stephan find a safe place where he can be his true self, or is he doomed to remain a castaway?

Connect with NineStar Press

www.ninestarpress.com

www.facebook.com/ninestarpress

www.facebook.com/groups/NineStarNiche

www.twitter.com/ninestarpress

www.instagram.com/ninestarpress

Made in United States
Orlando, FL
11 May 2022

17770022R00178